Have you never known Love?

Have you denied Love?

Abused Love?

Lost your magic as a result?

The Magecraft Treatment Center can help.

Come to Sedona, the land of vortices
and unexplainable powers.
Let our witches and wizards help heal
your heart—and your magical powers—
through classes in Invocation,
Levitation, Transmogrification and more!

Apply for your chance at admission today!

ABOUT THE AUTHORS

With twenty-six novels under her belt, *USA TODAY* bestselling author **Julie Leto** has established a reputation for writing ultra-sexy, edgy stories in both the romance and romantic-suspense genres. A 2005 RITA® Award nominee, Julie is about to launch a new series of single-title romances starring sexy, Gypsy-cursed brothers, to be released in 2008. She lives in her hometown of Tampa with her husband, daughter and a very spoiled dachshund. For more information, check out Julie's site at www.julieleto.com or her blog at www.plotmonkeys.com.

A Waldenbooks bestselling author, past RITA® Award nominee and *Romantic Times BOOKreviews* Reviewers Choice nominee, **Rhonda Nelson** writes hot romantic comedy. With nineteen published books to her credit and many more coming down the pike, she's thrilled with her career and enjoys dreaming up her characters and manipulating the worlds they live in. In addition to a writing career, she has a husband, two adorable kids, a black Lab and a beautiful bichon frise who dogs her every step. She and her family make their chaotic but happy home in a small town in northern Alabama. She loves to hear from her readers, so be sure to check her out at www.readRhondaNelson.com.

Award-winning author **Mia Zachary's** first completed contemporary manuscript placed second in Harlequin Books' 2000 Summer Blaze contest. She's written four Harlequin Blaze novels since then, including the bestseller *Afternoon Delight*. Mia is thrilled with the chance to stretch her creative wings in different genres for 2007. In addition to "Spirit Dance," her first romantic mystery *Another Side of Midnight* comes out in October. Mia lives in Maryland with her husband of seventeen years and their beautiful little boy. Visit Mia online at www.miazachary.com for excerpts, reviews, articles and more!

WITCHY BUSINESS

Julie Leto

Rhonda Nelson

Mia Zachary

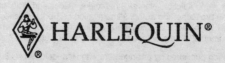

HARLEQUIN®

TORONTO • NEW YORK • LONDON
AMSTERDAM • PARIS • SYDNEY • HAMBURG
STOCKHOLM • ATHENS • TOKYO • MILAN • MADRID
PRAGUE • WARSAW • BUDAPEST • AUCKLAND

ISBN-13: 978-0-373-83716-8
ISBN-10:   0-373-83716-X

WITCHY BUSINESS

Copyright © 2007 by Harlequin Books S.A.

The publisher acknowledges the copyright holders
of the individual works as follows:

UNDER HIS SPELL
Copyright © 2007 by Julie Leto Klapka

DISENCHANTED?
Copyright © 2007 by Rhonda Nelson

SPIRIT DANCE
Copyright © 2007 by Mika Boblitz

CONTENTS

UNDER HIS SPELL

Julie Leto

* * *

For Rhonda, Mia and Stacy...
great time working together, ladies!

And of course, to Samantha Stephens,
her much-more-fun cousin, Serena, Mildred
Hubble, Elphaba and Galinda, Buffy Summers,
Willow Rosenburg, Prue, Piper, Phoebe and
Paige Halliwell, Hermione Granger, Ginny Weasley,
Minerva McGonagall, Morgan La Fey, and all
the other witches, both fictional and not,
to whom I present this homage.

And as always, to the amazing writers in
TARA, who wielded their red pens at chapter one
with magical results.

Dear Reader,

I've always had a huge fascination with magic. When *Charmed* came on the air, and before that, *Buffy the Vampire Slayer,* I was in supernatural heaven. This new generation of storytelling not only enchanted me, but also featured strong, courageous, sensual women who could kick some serious demon/vampire butt.

You have no idea how thrilled I was when I got the chance to create my own magic-wielding, kick-butt character, Regina St. Lyon, for this anthology. And who else to pair her with but a super-sexy, over-the-top-dangerous witch-hunter like Brock Aegis? I wrote this novella quickly and on a wave of excitement that was nearly magical in and of itself. I hope you enjoy the results!

And if you are curious about Regina's sister, Lilith, be sure to check out my full-length Harlequin Blaze novel, *Stripped,* which was released last month. For more information about me and my upcoming books, please visit my Web site at www.julieleto.com or stop by and say hello at www.plotmonkeys.com.

Happy reading,

Julie

CHAPTER ONE

FILLING HER LUNGS with the smoldering night air, Regina St. Lyon closed her eyes tightly and chanted. After one verse, she tripped over the words. She cursed, struggling to remember the phrases in the right order, to speak the forbidden language of her Wiccan ancestors with the right inflections. She took another deep breath and nearly choked on the mixed scents of charred herbs, burnt grass, singed skin and blood. The blood of her beloved.

"Regina, don't do this," Brock demanded. He'd dropped to his knees, pain evident in each syllable he uttered. His face, once so devastatingly handsome, now was simply devastated.

Regina's palm still simmered from the magical burst of energy she'd used to defend herself. He'd betrayed her. And if she didn't recite the forbidden curse now to banish him to the middle realm, he'd destroy her entire race.

She squeezed her eyelids tighter, blocking out the sight of the man she'd once loved, holding back the rush of tears threatening to burst through. She hadn't asked to be chosen as Guardian of Witches, but the responsibilities had been bred into her from birth. She hadn't asked for her mother to die, forcing the Council to coronate Regina as Guardian when she was only sixteen. She certainly hadn't asked for Brock Aegis to sneak into her life ten years later, posing as a male witch seeking help from the Magecraft Treatment Center so he could seduce her and then to turn on her like the Hunter he was. She hadn't asked for this heartbreak, but now, as always, she had to stand strong.

She had to destroy him before he destroyed her.

She chanted again and again until the intonations spilled off her lips like the rush of a swift river. She opened her eyes, calm as she surrounded herself with the power of her ancestors. Her mother. Her grandmother. Her great-grandmother and great-great aunt— all women of the St. Lyon line charged with the protection of the witching world, from the non-magical mundanes who followed the tenets of Wicca to the magical sacreds who, like her, possessed powers at odds with the laws of physics and nature.

As the magic stirred, Brock tried to stand. The ground around him shook. Cracked. Still, he straightened and balanced his body, squared his shoulders and locked his eyes on her, his mouth dropping open when he realized what she had done.

She'd opened the portal to the middle realm.

"Regina," he said, his voice dropping in volume, but not in intensity. She didn't want to stare into his wide, black eyes, but she could not look away. Until he was gone, she'd forever be under his spell—trapped by the grand illusion of love and devotion that had nearly cost her life.

"You give me no choice, Brock. You hunted me. You caught me. But now your prey has broken free."

He opened his mouth to speak again, but the vibration of the ground around him cut him short. The crust of the Earth split in a spiderweb of cracks around him. The Hunter had become the quarry about to be swallowed by the source of all witching power.

Brock gave her a nod. Had he accepted his fate? Around him, rocks burst into the air and columns of red-hot steam spiraled into the sky.

Regina locked her knees, bracing herself for his descent, but her legs shook so violently, she had to grab on to the nearest tree. When a root shot out of the ground and, like a snake, slithered toward Brock, she swallowed a scream.

She wanted to stop this. She wanted to save him from a fate that rivaled death in cruelty. But despite the tears clouding her vision, Regina knew she'd acted as Guardian in the fullest sense—sacrificing her own heart in the process. The heart he'd tricked, lied to and broken.

The dirt-encrusted roots slid across the ground from four directions. With his eyes trained on her, Brock held out his arms to the monstrous vines. They twined around him, binding his wrists, ankles, midsection and neck. He didn't protest, didn't curse, didn't speak a single word even when the roots yanked him down through the broken ground and into the tempest below.

Regina fell to the ground at the same second he disappeared. As the clearing reformed, erasing all evidence of the battle, Regina allowed herself to weep for her humiliation and for her loss. By the time she'd calmed, the clearing where she'd led Brock had returned to normal. Crickets and frogs sang in the distance. Wind rustled softly through the verdant leaves.

Except for the sound of her ragged breathing, no one who stumbled into this park on the grounds of the Center and the Registry would ever know the violence that had erupted here—all at her hand.

"Regina."

She shot to her feet, her muscles protesting, searching for the source of the sound.

"Regina."

"Brock?" she responded.

She glanced at the ground at the center of the clearing where she'd formed the ancient circle and banished her lover to the underworld. Not even a blade of grass looked out of place.

"Regina, wake up."

His voice sounded hollow, as if far away. Stumbling, she made her way to the core of the clearing and pawed at the ground. It was solid. He was trapped. She'd used the forbidden curse. No magic, not even the powerful spells handed down from her ancestors, could undo his doom.

"Regina, please. You have to remember. There isn't much time."

Suddenly a choking sensation gripped her. She clawed at her throat, trying to relieve the invisible pressure strangling the breath out of her. Her hands made contact with the platinum chain she wore around her neck and the metal burned.

And then, broke away.

She gasped for air. Her eyes snapped open, jolting her out of her nightmare and into the cold reality of her room. The full moon just outside her uncovered window threw blue streaks across her bed. Drenched with sweat, her sheets coiled around her body, tangling with the silk boxers and T-shirt she'd worn to sleep. Beside her, incense smoldered, injecting the air with the lingering perfume of lavender and sandalwood, meant to calm her. The herbs had failed miserably. Her heart was still trying to pound its way through her ribs. Her lungs, fed by ragged breaths, ached inside her chest.

She dragged her hand to her neck and this time, registered the absence of her talisman.

"Looking for this?"

Brock Aegis emerged from the shadows, boots first, the leather dirty and torn. His jeans, ripped at the seams, hung loosely, as if his muscles had atrophied or his body weight had simply melted off his normally powerful frame. His shirt still held the stains of his injuries from their battle three months ago. Dried blood mingled with the smoky streaks of scorch marks.

She remembered.

All of it. Every detail. Every emotion.

With a thought, she sparked the lamp beside her bed. The glow instantly reflected off the amulet he dangled between his grimy fingers. The alexandrite, nearly the size of her palm, shined purplish red in the incandescent light. Brock had not only returned from the middle realm where she'd banished him, he'd stolen the talisman she'd enchanted to block the memories of him from her mind—memories wrenched from the darkest recesses of her soul. Memories that kept her from performing as Guardian.

"Give it back," she demanded.

"So you can forget about me again? Forget what you did to me?"

"You gave me no choice." She wrestled to remove the tangled sheets from her body. When she succeeded, she slid off the bed and faced him. She jutted her chin forward even as her betrayed heart screamed for her to crumble into a mottled mess on the floor. "You came to Sedona to kill me. Or did you expect I'd let you murder me simply because you'd tricked your way into my bed?"

He dropped his hand, the talisman dangling uselessly at his side. She had no idea how, but Brock had returned. Now, she would need her painful memories to protect the Registry. To protect her people. To protect her heart.

"I intended to destroy you, yes," he explained, his voice raspy. "But I never meant to...I never meant to love you."

"Spare me, Brock! How can I accept the word of a Hunter? You were born and raised with one motive, just as I was. But while I was trained to protect my people, you were trained to destroy us. I cannot change who I am any more than you."

"I have changed."

Regina's bitter laugh rent the suddenly stifling aromatic air. "You are a Hunter. How many witches did you kill before you found me, Brock? How many?"

He took a step forward, but Regina stopped him by raising her palm. As the Guardian, she possessed a rare and terrible power—the ability to harness energy and concentrate it into a ball of electric pain that she could hurl at will. The energy bursts had given her the upper hand in her battle with Brock three months ago. Why did she hesitate now?

"Regina, there isn't time for me to explain, but I've come back to save you."

"Save me from what? I survived you. What could possibly be worse?"

Brock threw Regina's talisman on the bed, his shoulders taut and his eyes dark. A shiver rippled from the hairs on the surface of her skin to deep inside her belly.

"Old Movert," he replied.

Regina's chest tightened under the weight of this enemy's name.

"Old Movert is a myth. He doesn't exist."

Brock chuckled, but his laugh contained not a hint of mirth or happiness. "You're wrong. Old Movert is very, very real. You'll know that for yourself soon, when he comes here to kill you."

CHAPTER TWO

HATE COURSED THROUGH Brock's bloodstream. White-hot. Toxic. Not hatred for Regina. As she claimed, she'd acted exactly as he'd forced her to—exactly as he would have if their roles had been reversed. His hatred focused entirely on himself. On who and what he was. On what he'd done to her. On the creature that had sent him on this vile quest to destroy the Guardian of all witches.

The woman he loved.

"How…how did you escape from the middle realm?"

Brock allowed a jolt of pride to stretch into his shoulders. In the whole of his lifetime, he'd accomplished nothing as significant as cheating certain death. "I bargained my way out. Tomorrow is the Feast of Fools. On Feast Eve, the masters of the middle realm allow one of the banished to return to the living realm to undo their past sins."

She swallowed deeply. The subtle undulation of her throat held him in thrall. "Why you?"

He stepped forward. Her palm sparked. He stopped. The abject yearning to feel her close consumed him, but he wasn't stupid. She'd spared his life once, sending him to the middle realm rather than killing him outright. He could not count on her mercy again.

"*I* wasn't chosen for mercy—you were. The masters of the middle realm decided that your life was worth saving. For all the creatures you and your line have sent to the middle realm, Old Movert sent legions more. As long as I am in your service, I have leave from the middle realm to vanquish the threat against you. If I betray you again, I descend into the lower realm forever. If I succeed, I am released from my bond to the underworld."

Her eyes widened and her jaw dropped open. "You mean if you kill your master, you go free? After what you tried to do to all of witchdom? Who are these masters of the middle realm? Reprobates and killers, no doubt. Other Hunters intent on destroying witches everywhere. The banished pardoning the banished? How dare they!"

Brock gave her a slight bow, pain shot up his back and the agony felt like heaven. At least he was alive. At least he was breathing sweet, Regina-scented air and not the putrid stink of the underworld. "Those are the terms of my release."

"Then prepare to return," she said, her voice quaking only slightly. "I have no need of you. I reject you as my servant. I reject you completely."

Their language had drifted into the old cadence. Witch versus Hunter. Good versus Evil. The battle that had raged for a millennia between those bestowed with mystic powers—the sacred witches—and the Hunters, destined to murder what they envied and feared. Brock had never heard the story from the opposing perspective until Regina had banished him to the middle realm. There, his torment had included a reading of the history—a true accounting, not words twisted by his father, a Hunter himself. Not lies taught to the race of Hunters by Old Movert himself.

Brock took another step forward, stopping again when he spied sparks twirling in her outstretched palm. The stench of his own burnt flesh still lingered in his nostrils.

"Reject me, but do not reject my help or you will die. I'm your only hope."

"I'd be a fool to trust you. You tried to kill me. You tried to steal the records at the Registry so you could murder all the witches in North America. Do you expect me to forget what you attempted to do?" she challenged.

"No," he said, his chest tight as he owned up to his crimes. "You were wrong when you trusted me before. When you believed I was a male witch in search of sanctuary and peace. When you saved me and took me into your bed."

He watched her lips tremble and every wound he'd experienced in the middle realm seemed to rip open and bleed anew. He'd betrayed her on a level deeper than he'd ever thought possible. Until Regina, he'd never known love. And just when she'd taught him the depth of trust and intimacy, she'd discovered his ruse and banished him.

He'd deserved her wrath. But that was the past. He had one way and one way only to perform the contrition he needed to save his soul. He had to keep her alive now that Old Movert had finally raised his army. The legendary Hunter King was on the brink of an attack and only Brock could keep Regina out of harm's way.

"I won't listen to your lies," Regina hissed.

"Fine," he agreed. "Don't. Consult the Oracle. Ask her if my claim is true. Call together your finest psychics. Ask them if they feel the tear in the balance between good and evil. Old Movert was enraged when I failed to destroy you. He wants the North American Registry. He wants the magic of the world's most powerful witches for himself. In my absence, he has gathered troops of Hunters. Rumor has it he's making pacts with warlocks and demons. Their one and only charge is to find the Registry rolls and destroy you."

Regina tilted her head back and laughed. As he watched the curve of her neck dazzle beneath the warm lamplight, he realized why she'd been chosen Guardian. Her beauty and confidence were unsurpassed, even in the face of imminent death.

"Tell your master that he is too late." Her smile was small, but potent. "Before I cast the charm to protect myself from the memories of your treachery, I removed the ancient records from the Registry. They are safe and guarded by spells he'll never breach. They are scattered to the four corners of the continent and my protection squads have been put on high alert. You can send your Hunters, but we will fight. You will not use our census against us."

Brock nodded, pleased. He'd hoped she'd take the necessary steps to protect her people. Except for Regina, the witches staying at the Magecraft Treatment Center within the Registry were likely safe. Most of the witches here were damaged, troubled, unable to harness the powers bestowed on them by their birth. They meant nothing to the Hunter cause.

And Old Movert would likely not attack witches in such great numbers without the promise of a huge payoff. Like all Hunters, his one-time master did not wish to awake the suspicions of the mundane police. Sometimes, battles could not be avoided, but massacres could complicate and prolong wars. Hunters were not immortal. They could suffer the death penalty like any other mundane.

"Then my only charge now is to protect you," he decided. "Movert will kill you for no other reason than to make a dramatic show of his return."

Her eyes narrowed, sparkling with lilac flame and igniting every nerve ending in his body. But the needs she triggered would never be assuaged. He'd broken her trust at the foundation. The most he could hope for was that she'd allow him to save her life.

She spoke a spell quickly, before his dulled brain could react. His muscles instantly froze.

Slowly she closed in on him. Her scent, intensified by the sweat still glistening on her skin, taunted him. She circled, assessing, planning, questioning. She didn't have the power to probe his mind, but she had others at her disposal who did.

In an act of pure torture, she slid her open palm up his arm. He swallowed a wince when the pressure aggravated the injuries beneath his sleeve.

"I'll check your claims, Aegis. And when I verify your lies, I'll send you to the lower realm myself." She stood directly in front of him, the malice in her gaze clear and unmistakable. "You play the abeyance act well, but I know the truth. Your servitude to me would be only a game, another chance to seduce me. I won't succumb this time, Hunter. You've hardened me so that I'd shatter before I let you touch me again. Do you understand?"

She shimmered out of the room. He understood all too well. She would resist him. And for that, she'd pay with her life.

REGINA MATERIALIZED outside her aunt's room, collapsing against the wall as a full wave of vibrations racked her body. She shivered as if plunged into ice-cold water and no matter how she wrapped her arms around herself, she could not find warmth.

She was only mildly aware of Marion throwing open her door.

"Regina! Good goddess, what's happened?"

Despite her advanced age, Marion dropped to her knees beside Regina and rubbed her arms vigorously. When Regina didn't stop shaking, Marion leaned back, touched the amber charm she wore around her neck, spoke a calming spell, then transferred the warm energy from the stone into Regina's flesh. She repeated the procedure three times before Regina could finally breathe.

"Come inside," Marion ordered, helping her niece to her feet.

The instant the door closed and Marion, as usual, sealed the exit with a powerful protection spell—a leftover habit from an old war—Regina released the emotions trapped inside her. She wailed and wept until she couldn't cry anymore. When she came out of her grief, she heard Marion muttering words of comfort, her lined face etched with worry.

"I'm sorry," Regina managed.

"For what? Your talisman is gone. You remembered him, didn't you?"

"Worse. He's returned."

CHAPTER THREE

OVER A CENTURY of living had taught Marion to control her reactions to disturbing news. She allowed surprise to show on her face, of course. But she kept her intense fear in check. Brock's return could mean only one thing.

"How is that possible?" she asked.

Regina shook her head, her cascade of dark hair sticking to the tear streaks marring her fair skin. "He said the Feast of Fools."

The Feast of Fools? Now there was a celebration Marion hadn't observed in a while. Made Mardi Gras look like a church social. In typical stodginess, the living realm had abandoned the full holiday centuries ago. But she imagined the prisoners of the middle realm held on to the tradition with desperate claws. The Feast was a time of wild abandon, a time when good became evil and evil cleaned up its act—a time when light and dark fought, merged and observed temporary cease-fires. A time, clearly, when the banished found a way to break free of even the most powerful curses.

"He bargained for his release, then," she concluded.

Regina's eyes widened. "It's true?"

Marion shrugged. In her lifetime, she'd amassed a

great deal of information here and there about their history, from books or from experience or from eavesdropping on her sister, the Guardian before Regina, while she memorized her lessons. Marion had become quite adept at keeping her true intelligence to herself unless someone she cared about truly needed her information. With the St. Lyon blood running through her veins, Marion knew that smart women weren't allowed to exist in peace. Talented witches in her line were bound to eternal service, no matter the price, no matter the sacrifice. Look at Regina. By demonstrating her talents before she was wise enough to keep them hidden, she'd been tapped at sixteen to be the next Guardian. Though Marion had been the next in line, her mediocre magic ensured that she was overlooked.

Just as she'd always planned.

"Truth is a relative term, my dear. I've heard rumors of the tradition in the middle realm, where the inhabitants still retain some power. But it's my understanding that few, if any, creatures are ever able to convince the masters of the worth of their release. Mainly the Eve celebration is a chance for the masters to toss the applicants into the lower realm and cull their cursed herd."

Regina blinked a half-dozen times. "I don't understand."

Marion rose and wandered to her bookshelf. She was fairly certain she owned a text that outlined the traditions of the middle realm, written by a warlock who'd managed to break free over a century ago. She smoothed her callused fingers over the spines, but couldn't quite find the book she wanted. "If my memory serves, and goddess knows it rarely does, if the petition for respite fails, the petitioner is sent to the lower realm forever. Nasty stuff, that."

The information hit Regina hard. Her naturally fair skin paled and her breath caught audibly. Poor girl. She'd risked so much to create the spell that had allowed her to forget all about her doomed relationship with Brock Aegis. If the Hunter had indeed returned, he'd done so at great peril—not only to her, but to himself as well.

Selfish bastard.

"He says Old Movert has returned."

Marion shivered. Just like a man to make up such an outrageous story. "That's not possible."

Regina shot up and grabbed Marion's hands, her grip desperate. "Why not? Old Movert was the most powerful witch Hunter in history. Legend claims his father was a warlock, which gave him the ability to steal a witch's magic and use it against her."

"Most of the first Hunters were descendants of warlocks. That's why they were so dangerous back in the day. Warlocks mean only to steal our magic. Hunters use the magic to kill. Over time, many Hunters lost the ability to absorb magic, which only enraged them more. Now, they kill for sport and zealotry. Movert and his ilk, thankfully, are long gone. The coven of Creed destroyed Old Movert hundreds of years ago. If he was going to come back, he would have done so long before now."

"No one ever saw any proof," Regina insisted, her eyes bright with the terrifying possibilities. Marion allowed her aged bones to settle into her overstuffed couch. The event had occurred before her time, but the stories were legend. Old Movert had been the cruelest, most evil, most determined Hunter in centuries. If he'd truly returned, the living realm was in big trouble.

"Do you believe Brock?" Marion asked.

Regina shook her head forlornly. "How can I? He's lied to me about so much. But I told him the Registry records were no longer here. That he couldn't use our census against us. He seemed…relieved."

Marion pinched her lips together, not liking the confused and pained look on Regina's face. Young or not, Regina was their Guardian. She'd put their entire community at risk in her affair with Brock Aegis, though in her defense, every witch who'd met him had fallen instantly in lust. Virile, handsome and mysterious, he'd set aflame quite a few libidos in Sedona, including Marion's, though he'd had eyes, hands and lips for Regina alone. Their scorching glances and heated exchanges had rivaled the sun, even the ultrahot ball of fire beating down on Arizona. Marion could only imagine how incendiary her niece's once nonexistent love life had become once Brock showed up. For the first time since becoming Guardian as a teenager, Regina had seemed happy. Unburdened, even for just a few hours every day, from the responsibilities of not only cataloging the names and locations of every witch in North America, but arranging for ceremonies, presiding over special occasions and, last if not least, assessing the conditions of witches who needed the healing and educational services of the Magecraft Treatment Center.

Then Regina had discovered Brock's true purpose. She'd been devastated to the core, but she'd mustered the strength to not only focus on her duty, but also to conjure the mighty magic she needed to defeat him. Regina alone had fought and banished the man she'd loved.

"Then you don't trust him?" Marion concluded.

Regina's amethyst eyes widened. "Of course not! Even if what he says is true, I have no reason to believe he wants to help me."

"Then banish him again."

Regina glanced down at her hands, turned palm up. "If I do so, he won't go back to the middle realm. He'll die."

Marion stood as straight as her slightly arthritic shoulders would allow. "Yes, he will."

Regina ran her hands through her hair, groaning in wretched frustration. "I killed him once and it nearly tore me to shreds. I don't know that I can do it again."

Poor child. Marion massaged Regina's shoulder. While Marion's powers were greatly underestimated, even at her strongest, she couldn't solve this problem for Regina. She could, however, offer suggestions.

"Maybe you won't have to kill him again," she suggested. "First, we need to verify his claims."

Regina nodded eagerly. "Can you go to the Oracle?"

Marion took her niece's hand and patted the smooth flesh gently. "Of course. She and I are old friends. You know, if you could convince that sister of yours to change her mind…"

Regina shook her head violently. "No. Never. I'd never ask her to make that sacrifice."

Marion sighed. Though a spinster, Marion had had her share of lovers over her long lifetime. She'd always been discreet and she'd never found a man fully worthy of her love, much less worthy of sacrificing her destiny. But Regina's sister, Lilith, tapped to become the next Oracle, had refused the opportunity in order to chase warlocks with her mundane lover, a former Chicago police detective. And then Regina had nearly sacrificed her life, and her position as Guardian, because of her desire for the duplicitous Brock Aegis. St. Lyon women might be known for their unmatchable skills as witches, but when it came to men, they could be horribly unlucky.

"Then I'll go to the Oracle and pray she has the strength left to locate Old Movert. Should you alert the other Guardians?"

Each continent had one high witch assigned to the protection of all the witches, mundane or sacred, on their soil. Together, they comprised the Council, who along with several advisors, ruled over their kind. Regina was by far the youngest, and often the most suspect because of her inexperience. In an attempt to keep her niece from losing face, Marion had hidden her debacle of a relationship with Brock Aegis. But they'd have to confess if the safety of other witches came into question.

"Not yet," Regina decided. "Go to the Oracle and find out if what Brock says is true. Maybe I can turn the tables—use him to destroy Old Movert before anyone else has to know he resurfaced."

Marion nodded, agreeing with the choice despite the sheen of perspiration forming along the back of her neck. The plan had merit, but the best of intentions often went awry, especially when love and lust were part of the equation.

"Where is he?"

"Frozen in my room," Regina replied. "He's not going anywhere until I say so."

Marion handed her a crocheted blanket, then made sure she was tucked in comfortably. Even Guardians needed pampering now and again. "Then why don't you stick around here and gather your wits. He can wait. And you're going to need to be top of your game to defeat him a second time. You do realize that, yes?"

Regina's eyes grew cold and despite the chill that Marion experienced watching the transformation, she knew the hardness was necessary.

"Oh, yes. I realize it more than you'll ever know."

CHAPTER FOUR

BROCK'S NECK ACHED. His thighs throbbed. He hadn't eaten in…months. He should have anticipated Regina's use of the containment spell, but even if he had seen it coming, he couldn't have blocked it. Well, he *could* have. Countercurses had been his nursery rhymes. Instead of football or lacrosse, the ancient art of *silambam* had strengthened his muscles and sharpened his reflexes. But if he'd fought back when Regina had cast her spell, she'd never trust him. And if he couldn't regain her confidence, she would die.

And it would be his fault.

Minutes passed. Hours. Slowly the air in Regina's room changed. The lavender and sandalwood scents permeating the space surrendered to something more acrid and sharp. The smell of evil. The smell of death.

"How convenient," a malevolent voice hissed from the shadows to Brock's left. "The traitor trapped by the witch, both now ripe for me to pluck and devour without breaking a sweat."

Brock couldn't turn his head, but he didn't need to. Old Movert had found him. He'd found Regina…because Brock had led him right to her.

A cold puff of wind blew over Brock's mouth,

allowing him to speak. "Only a coward would attack a man who cannot defend himself."

The ancient Hunter's laugh overflowed with malice. "Only a fool would let such an opportunity pass."

A wave of heat flashed across Brock's back. Even if he could have retaliated, he wouldn't have. The sensation was not to inflict pain, but to provide a subtle threat. As if a madman like Movert needed subtlety.

"My minions in the middle realm report that you were very convincing in your plea to the masters on behalf of your witch," the aged Hunter taunted. "They claim you renounced me."

Brock chose his words carefully. He didn't much care if Old Movert destroyed him, but he couldn't leave Regina unprotected. Not after all he'd done to her in the name of a false history taught to him by the demonic Hunter King.

"I'm back, aren't I?" Brock replied.

Old Movert neared. He remained out of Brock's sight, but the stench increased as well as the temperature around him. "You aren't trying to convince me this was all part of some greater plan, are you? I am many undesirable things, Aegis, but an idiot is not one of them."

Unfortunately the Hunter King was right.

"I did what I had to," Brock added. "The middle realm isn't exactly Fiji."

Old Movert chuckled and this time, genuine humor lightened his ominous tone. "No, I suppose it is not. But you do understand that your failure with the Guardian witch before your banishment cost me much time in my quest. I want the records."

Brock took a deep breath. He'd sure as hell never

imagined breaking such devastating news to his evil leader while entrapped in a containment spell. "She's dispersed the records. They are no longer here."

Silence pressed down on the room. Brock wordlessly cursed the containment spell that left him so vulnerable.

"A worthy opponent," Old Movert finally said. "I'd expect no less from a St. Lyon witch. But I'll not have her minor precautions alter my ultimate plan. Once she is gone, I'll rebuild the Registry records so that I can hunt down every last witch on this continent. At last, the perennial battle between Hunters and witches will cease."

Old Movert flashed in front of Brock, his movements a blur. Once he stilled, he pressed his peeled and bent nose against Brock's, his breath coiling into Brock's nostrils so that Brock thought he might gag. His former master wore an oval talisman in his left eye socket. An eternally red scar slashed down his face, tearing the pocked skin in two, one side as evil and obsessed as the other. His neck bore slash marks of the countless times witches had tried to rip out his throat. His right hand, reportedly carved from the ivory of Ganesha's stolen tusk, had splintered and had but four fingers. In Brock's absence, Old Movert had battled. And though he may have won, he showed the signs of potential defeat.

Internally Brock smiled. He could beat him. If only Regina would believe in him. If only she would set him free.

Old Movert spit in his face, the saliva hot and acidic, singeing his skin. "You dare betray me, even with your thoughts?"

"You are not a Seer, Old Movert, nor have you murdered the Oracle and stolen her power. You have no idea what I am thinking."

"Except that you want to kill me," he murmured.

"An easy supposition. The entire brotherhood of Hunters hate you beyond measure, nearly as much as most hate witches. They follow you only out of fear."

The laugh spewing from Movert's twisted lips shook the glass on the windows. "So true, so true. But you were ever loyal to me, Brock Aegis. I expect no less from you now, even if you strayed in your lust for the Guardian witch. The time has come for you to redeem yourself. The triumvirate of the middle realm saw fit to give you a second chance. I will do the same. Once Regina St. Lyon is dead, her powers will give you the means to fight banishment to the lower realm. You'll be free. Not only from death, but from me. Kill the witch and you will be free of your oath to the Hunters, free to live as a mortal and find this love you seem to value so desperately. I'll have what I want—the witch's life—and you'll have your freedom. We both win. You have until the next descent of night to bring the witch's lifeless body to me."

In a swirl of smoky robes, Movert faded from view. Yet Brock could still sense his presence heavy in the room. The Hunter's ominous chuckle shook the paintings on the wall, confirming that he had not left completely.

"But first, I will help you, my once-loyal follower," Movert said and in the same instant, Brock dropped to the ground, free from Regina's spell.

And yet, he thought before he passed out, he was still utterly enslaved.

REGINA WAITED for Marion to return, but when the sun sneaked into the room with slivers of pink and orange, she had no choice but to return to the tower. Despite her exhaustion, both physical and emotional, she couldn't avoid Brock forever. She had to at least keep him with her long enough to figure out if what he was saying was true, or if he'd once again ensnared her with a web of lies.

After he'd served his purpose, she'd return him to the middle realm. She had no choice. She couldn't free a Hunter who would surely turn around and kill—if not her, then another witch under her protection.

She murmured the counterspell to unseal her room, but the knob wouldn't give. She repeated the spell, and again, the lock remained frozen. Attributing her failure to fatigue, she took a deep breath, closed her eyes and placed both hands on the doorknob before chanting, aloud, the incantation to release the lock. Only then did she hear a gentle click.

When she pushed the door open, she saw Brock lying motionless on the floor.

Her first instinct was to rush to him, but she quelled the gut reaction and slid slowly inside instead, locking the door behind her. Her room was isolated high in what looked like a decorative tower but what was really a highly fortified stronghold against dark magic. But Regina did not wish to yet again unleash the danger of Brock's presence on the witches staying at the Registry. Her first order of business, once she revived him, was to get him off the property.

"Get up," she ordered, wondering exactly how he'd broken free of her containment spell. He'd barged into her room with no warning, stealing her amulet and flooding her mind with memories of him that she'd magically banished from her brain. She must have been sloppy in her spell work, or else his weakened state was just a ruse, hiding the masterful Hunter skills he'd yet to truly renounce.

But he didn't move.

Regina narrowed her gaze. "I will not fall for your tricks, Brock. Not this time. Get up now!"

She raised her hand, palm out, but the energy burst she summoned simply fizzled in her hand. Sparks tickled her flesh, then sputtered and died. She tried again, to no avail.

Regina gasped. Had she lost her powers—just when she needed them the most?

CHAPTER FIVE

"WHAT THE—?"

With a groan, Brock stirred. Instinctively Regina yanked her hand behind her, her mind swirling. She couldn't remember the last time she'd been unable to form an energy burst on command. Since taking over as Guardian, her magic had never failed her. Never.

When Brock didn't move again, she turned around, her back to him and held her palm out, cupping her hand slightly to encourage the collection of high-voltage electricity. Wordlessly she spoke the magical charm that formed the burst. She managed an impotent sparkle and then, nothing. She spoke the words aloud, forcefully, which did nothing more than cause Brock to grunt and roll a few feet to his left in a feeble attempt to protect himself. He needn't bother. She couldn't form a burst.

"What's happening?"

Immediately struck by a wash of vulnerability, Regina dashed to her nightstand and rifled through the haphazard collection of books and cards and scarves and spare change until she found her wand. She shouldn't treat the magical object with such irreverence, but she hadn't needed to use a wand to focus her magic for over a decade. Most days, she used it to hold her long hair in place once she swirled it into a lazy coil.

When she turned, Brock was trying to pull himself into a sitting position, but wasn't succeeding. With a curse, she shoved the wand into the waistband of her silk boxer shorts and crouched at his side.

Before she could make a snarky remark about the aftereffects of her containment spell, Brock forced his gaze on hers, his eyes grim.

"Movert was here."

"That's impossible," she countered.

Brock shook his head, his breathing labored. Her chest stung with regret. She shouldn't have left him in the containment spell for so long, not in his weakened state.

Damn! Why should she care? He'd tried to kill her! Destroy her people. Why did her heart urge her to wrap her arms around him and help him to his feet?

She scooted a few inches away, but the distance did nothing to assuage her burning desire to offer him solace.

"Not impossible," Brock insisted. "Search the room. You'll know."

His words came out in choppy pants, but his suggestion was a good one. Retrieving her wand, Regina went to the center of the room. She balanced her feet evenly with her shoulders, cupped the wand gently in one palm and then curled her other hand underneath, buoying the magic. She spoke with a spell that would reveal the presence of evil. She rotated, slowly, as she chanted. Took her three tries, but then an eruption of ice-cold air flew against her, penetrating her clothes and shocking her skin. Shivers racked her body and her joints ached when she pulled her arms in and tried to hug away the cold.

"Something evil," she managed to say through chattering teeth.

"I told you. Old Movert was here. He released me from your spell. He ordered me to kill you."

Defying her reaction to the evil presence, she swung on Brock, wand high. "Maybe the something evil is you!"

He'd managed to drag one knee beneath him. With a grunt, he yanked the other into place, then grabbed her armoire and pulled himself to a standing position. His face, drenched in sweat from the exertion, yet white as marble, reflected his emotions. Fear for her. Fear for himself. Fear for them all.

"I'm nothing compared to Old Movert, and you know it. He's given me until tomorrow night to bring him your dead body. If I kill you, he'll release me from my blood bond."

Regina refused to let his words add to the intense cold already assaulting her body. Old Movert was a legend. A bogeyman. A frightening monster whose infamy had been used to frighten little witch children into staying within their parents' sight. He may have, at one time, been the leader of Brock's Hunter race, but that was hundreds of years ago. Before the coven of Creed damned him to the lower realm.

"If he wants me so badly, why doesn't he kill me himself? If he was here, why didn't he wait until I returned? I would have walked right into his hands."

Brock tried to move forward. Regina readied her wand, though she doubted she'd be able to conjure more than a puff of smoke. As her blood pumped, melting the icy aftermath of the evil presence, she realized how weak she really was. Not as weak as Brock, but her wounds were not physical. They were metaphysical. Her powers were deserting her when she needed them most.

"I don't know why he didn't kill you himself."

A crack drew both of their attention to the doorway. The magical lock Regina had placed on the door fizzled and Marion stepped gingerly into the room.

"He didn't kill you himself because the act of killing a Guardian would send him directly to the lower realm," Marion informed. "Permanently."

Pinching the pearl button at the top of her pale cashmere sweater, Marion shut the door gently, then gave Brock an assessing glance before turning to Regina.

"Sweetheart, you really should have locked that door."

Regina glanced at her wand. "I did."

Marion raised an eyebrow. "Oh," she said, clucking her tongue. "I was afraid of this."

"What are you talking about?"

Marion shuffled over to Regina and leaned in to whisper so Brock couldn't hear. "Not in front of the Hunter, dear."

Regina waved her wand to freeze Brock in place, but nothing happened. He looked just as weak and about to topple over as before. Marion spied her ineffective spell and cast one of her own, quickly, before Brock noticed.

"What's happening to me?" Regina asked.

Marion pursed her lips, the wrinkles around her pink lips deepening with worry. "You're losing your powers."

"Why?"

"You've denied love," Marion replied.

"What?" she asked, incredulous, though she was well aware of Marion's meaning. In their world, there were three ways for a witch to lose her powers, all related to love, the most powerful emotion in a witch's arsenal. If a witch abused love, never knew love or denied love, she risked imploding the very core from which she drew her magic. Regina couldn't imagine, after all she'd been through, after how she'd been betrayed, that she'd lost her abilities because of Brock and their doomed affair.

"I…I denied love? I was betrayed!"

Marion patted her frizzy blond hair, giving Brock a disdainful glance over her shoulder, as if she were contemplating doing something nasty to him while he was frozen in place.

"Yes, love, you were betrayed in the most horrible way. But you still love him."

Regina's knees buckled, but she managed to brace herself. "I don't."

Marion's expression was pure sympathy. She took Regina by the shoulders and helped her to the bed, propping her up on the pillows.

"You do, Regina. You cast your forgetting spell before you had time to heal from his betrayal. The moment he removed the amulet, that love came rushing back. You've denied your true feelings for him and you're paying the price now with the weakening of your powers."

Regina squeezed her eyes shut. This couldn't be happening. The goddess could not be so cruel as to strip her of her powers in the face of such great danger.

"What about Old Movert? What did the Oracle say?"

Marion sighed sadly. "I wish I could tell you Brock Aegis was lying," she said, her voice brimming with poison as she spoke his name. "But he was not. Old Movert has indeed resurfaced. The Oracle didn't know how, but she does know why."

"He wants to kill me."

"No, he wants Brock to kill you. The cold-blooded murder of a Guardian witch is an instantaneous death sentence. By having Brock Aegis kill you, Movert rids himself of not only the most powerful witch on this continent who has chosen no successor, but also a Hunter who has betrayed him and all he stands for."

Regina shook her head, trying to process what her aunt was saying. "Brock didn't betray the Hunters. He tried to kill me. If I hadn't reacted as quickly as I did, I'd be dead."

"Seems to me," Marion said softly, "if he'd really tried to kill you, he would have succeeded. Brock Aegis is no novice Hunter. He wouldn't have attacked unless he was sure of the kill."

Regina shoved back against the pillows, knocking her head against the oak headboard and hardly registering the pain. "What do you mean? You know he tried! You hate him as much as I do."

"I hate what he is and what he tried to do to us, what he did to your heart. Otherwise, I don't care a whit about him one way or another."

Regina shook her head, trying to stop the swimming sensation in her brain. "And yet you think I'm losing my powers because I deny that I love him? How can I love a man whose mission in life is to destroy me?"

Marion shrugged with a nonchalance that belied the seriousness of their discussion. If Regina lost her powers, she couldn't protect anyone, much less herself. The Registry, the Magecraft Center and all the witches in their care would be vulnerable to a race of predators who would stop at nothing to destroy them all.

"You loved him before you knew what he was, sweetheart," Marion explained, her voice soothing but firm. "Your brain may have turned off your love for him, but your heart hasn't had time to catch up. After a while, you might heal enough to retain your powers, but perhaps you cast the spell too soon. This couldn't come at a worse time. You need your powers to protect yourself against Old Movert. If he can't get Brock to kill you, he'll simply find someone else."

The weight of all Marion said crashed on Regina hard. She fought the dueling needs to scream, cry and curse until her tongue turned blue. She glanced at Brock, still pale and weakened and frozen, and wondered how a man who had seduced her with such raging passion could have betrayed her so completely. But more than that, she wondered if Marion was right. Did she still love him? Was her denial of that love putting her life and the lives of all the witches at the Registry at risk?

"What do I do? I can't fight Old Movert or anyone else without my powers."

Marion nodded. "No, you can't. So for the time being, you need to leave. Any protection spells you cast will begin to break down, if they haven't already. I can reset them, but since you've dispersed the Records, the Registry shouldn't be a target long as you are gone. In the meantime, you need to work out what you feel for this…man, and hopefully, your powers will return."

"And I just leave him here?"

"Oh, no," Marion said, scandalized by the suggestion. "If you want your powers back, you're going to
have to take him with you and keep him close. As
close as you can stand."

CHAPTER SIX

WITH A GASP, Brock awoke to the smell of smoke. Not acrid and sulfuric like the putrid atmosphere in the middle realm, but sweet and spiced, floating on warm air tainted by magic. Tainted? No, enhanced. He had to learn to let go of his prejudices. His hatred for witches had brought him nothing but misery and servitude his entire life. The one instant of peace he'd experienced had been in Regina's bed. There was a lesson in that. Too bad it took his banishment to the upper region of hell for him to figure that out.

But he wasn't in hell anymore. No, he was in the living realm. With Regina. On the cusp of a second chance. Breathing in deeply, and despite his sandpaper-dry mouth, he managed to mutter her name.

"Yes, I'm here," she replied.

Despite the lack of kindness in her voice, Brock forced his eyes open.

"Where are we?"

Regina dipped a cloth into a carved pewter bowl and then cautiously dabbed the cool, wet material against his cheek and forehead. "Someplace safe. Temporarily, at least. You need to regain your strength. I can't fight Old Movert and protect your sorry ass at the same time."

"Why would you want to?"

She snorted and Brock didn't press, unwilling to delve deeper into her sudden change of attitude until he'd assessed his situation further. He moved to sit up and his muscles protested, though the pain was bearable. "What did you do to me this time?"

She arched her brow over her sparkling lavender eyes. "A weak freezing spell. Made travel easier. Aunt Marion also thought it might be wise to give you a healing draft before we left. She packed food, too. So unless you're planning on cramping my style, eat up."

Fighting a smile behind a wince, Brock tried to clear the fog from his head without upending the bowl Regina had shoved beside him. In her own way, she was being kind to him. He should be grateful. Instead suspicion ruled. Once a Hunter, always a Hunter.

One sniff told him the broth was laced with herbs that weren't included for flavor alone, though one sip revealed tastes that made the inside of his mouth dance. His stomach growled loudly. Luckily, besides herbs, the broth had thick chunks of meat and vegetables, which he wolfed down quickly, before Regina changed her mind about feeding him. She tore him half a loaf of multigrain bread, then picked on the other half as she watched him warily.

Once he drained his bowl, Regina wordlessly refilled it from a crock she kept near an open fire. Only then did he notice they were tucked deep in a cave, sharp stalactites above them and the humid air of a hidden water source nearby. Smart move. Stone of the earth blocked magical exploration much more effectively than standard building materials. Even Movert himself had chosen a cave as a base of operations, though his lair was far from Arizona. But at least her choice of hiding places might have bought them at least a few more hours of life while Movert attempted to track their location.

Brock waited to comment on her defensive choices after he'd sopped up the last of the stew with his bread. Regina had barely made a dent in her half of the loaf.

"You going to eat that?" he asked.

With a roll of her eyes, she handed him the baguette. "You seem to have regained your appetite."

"I never lost it," he pointed out between mouthfuls. "Since my return, I've had more important things to do than sate my hunger. The middle realm is not exactly a day spa, but then, you know that, I'm sure."

The dancing shadows of the fire deepened her scowl. "I'd hope not. How insulting would it be to think that the reward for attempting to murder me was a massage, a facial and a California Cobb salad for lunch."

He snickered. Her humor depended largely on sarcasm which, luckily, he appreciated. "Anything to drink?"

She reached across and handed him a flask. He unscrewed the top and took a sniff before bringing the liquid to his mouth. "This isn't poisoned, is it?" he asked before drinking.

"Shamefully, no. But it is enchanted with a potion that will accelerate your healing."

He took a huge swig. "You do realize you could be fortifying the man who will soon kill you on the orders of his master."

Her lip curled derisively. "If I thought you were a threat, I'd have tossed you out of the tower window and gone back to sleep."

"You also could have cursed me directly to the lower realm."

"Trust me," she said, her voice sharp with deadly seriousness, "if I could have, I would have."

He took a long draft of the spiced wine and tried to blow off the pain from her sharp retort. "Why didn't you?"

She held out her hands. "I can't."

Brock tilted his neck back and enjoyed the full-bodied flow of the wine against the back of his throat. When he looked at her again, she still had her hands out, her stare locked with his. He blinked, suddenly realizing that Regina was not holding out her hands in mock surrender.

She was trying to create an energy burst. With no successful results.

Brock jumped to his feet. For once, the fast, instinctive move didn't cause dizziness.

"What happened to you?" Dread, coupled with a need to jet forward and take her defenseless hands in his, sliced through his veins. To defeat Old Movert, Regina had to be at the top of her game. The Hunter Master was old, but over the centuries of his lifetime, he'd amassed huge stores of magical knowledge and skill. Old Movert had learned from his warlock father how to kill witches and steal their magical powers at the same time, though since he wasn't a warlock himself, he had to rely on enchanted items to hold the magic, whereas a warlock could absorb the power into his own body. Brock had been taught the ways, though he'd never used the skill.

But while most warlocks only retained stolen powers for a short spell, Old Movert had learned how to integrate the supernatural into his mundane existence. He'd become as powerful as any witch, demon or warlock. He'd become precisely what he'd strived to hunt into extinction, but no one in his circle was brave enough—or stupid enough—to point out the irony.

Regina took the flask from Brock and after wiping the spout, took a swig herself. "My powers are gone."

"Completely?"

She shrugged, as if the event meant nothing to her, when Brock knew that, Old Movert notwithstanding, Regina valued her magical abilities above all else.

"When did this happen?"

"When you showed up and swiped my amulet."

"I gave it back," he protested.

"When?" She shook her head. "Doesn't matter. You broke the memory spell I'd cast over myself, which apparently, caused an emotional overload that short-circuited my powers. I'm defenseless, thanks to you."

Brock sat back down, his stomach churning from this unanticipated turn of events.

"That's why we left the Registry," he guessed.

"My protection spells were failing, as evidenced by your claim, at least, that Old Movert materialized in my room. Marion reset the spells as best she could, but we thought it best to draw any evil away from the Registry altogether."

"What about your protection squads?"

Regina frowned. He wasn't supposed to know about her witch's secret army. Few in number but highly effective, the protection squads operated amid secrecy that rivaled even the witches they protected. The Brock Aegis who had shared her bed as a lover would never have known about the protection squads. The Hunter attempting to infiltrate the upper echelons of the witch hierarchy in order to destroy her would.

"My best protection squad is on alert, but investigating a Hunter attack of one of our largest covens in Newfoundland," Regina said, her tone emotionless. "Besides I need to assess the situation further before I draw my best protectors out of hiding and into this fight. Tell me everything you know about Old Movert. Leave nothing out." The blade of a knife flashed in the firelight. The handle sparkled just as brilliantly.

Luckily Marion had been able to retrieve the weapon from the archives on short notice. The athame, unlike most, was not ceremonial. This one had been forged for fighting. For killing.

"The Creed athame?"

She grinned. "What better weapon to wield than the one that vanquished Movert the first time?"

Brock shook his head. "The coven did not vanquish him. They merely wounded him, sent him into hiding."

"I'll do better."

"Without your powers?"

"The coven of Creed were mundanes."

"Were they? Legend has it they were the medicine women of seven Native American tribes who banded together to fight a shared evil."

"You know your witch history," she sniped.

"Just like you know your Hunter history, I'm sure."

She acknowledged his guess with a curt nod. "The women were all descendants of high witches, but drew their power from mundane magic. They banded together across language barriers and tribal mistrust and created this athame." She slid the weapon into her palm, caressing the gleaming metal with her fingers. "The stones and ivory handle came from this land, stolen first by Movert and his followers from the Incas, Aztecs and Mayans and then by the coven to fight him. Every sharp angle and decoration came from this continent. It's this magic that Movert wants. No matter what witch powers he protects himself with, this is the magic that can kill him."

"But not before he kills you. Without your powers, you can't fight him. He isn't a mundane Hunter. He's survived all these centuries through the magic he's stolen. The coven weakened him, forced him underground, but over time, he's amassed an army and more magic than you possess alone. His father was—"

"A warlock. Yes, as you said, I know my Hunter history."

And yet, she seemed to cast off his concern with a wave of her hand. Regina St. Lyon possessed great confidence in her abilities, in the magic that had been handed down to her ancestors from the goddess herself, or so the legend claimed, but Brock knew her. Intimately. He knew that underneath the cool bravado existed a woman who'd been thrust into the hierarchy of witchdom when she was still a child, who had taken on the responsibilities of a mother she loved, a mother murdered before she'd had the chance to properly hand over her mantle to her elder daughter.

"He'll steal your magic," he warned.

Regina snickered. "He can't steal what I don't have. He'd already begun to collect magical relics prior to his encounter with the coven of Creed. But he has to have a weakness or else he wouldn't need you. Did you know that killing me, a Guardian, would result in your being banished to the lower realm?"

Brock glanced down at the empty flask in his hands. He screwed the top on and tossed the pewter container into the pile of supplies near the fire. "Movert assured me that he could call me back."

"And you believed him?"

"Why wouldn't I?"

"Oh, because he's never conjured anyone else from the lower realm before?"

"He claims he has. He had centuries of lore to back up his declarations. Look, Regina, you had a childhood where Movert was the stuff of your night terrors, an old symbol of evil like Jack the Ripper or Adolf Hitler. But to me, he was a legend. He's been a presence in my life since my birth. My father's family has been his caretakers since they were explorers of the New World and found his battered body in the plains of what was then unexplored country. I've had hundreds of years of my family's legacy, seeing him as a hero, pounded into me. Witches, to my people, are evil abominations that must be obliterated or else they'll take over the world and enslave all mundanes."

"Like we've tried and succeeded at that…when?"

Brock shook his head violently. "You can't introduce logic into this argument, Regina. We're talking blind obedience and zealotry. That's all I've had around me since the moment I was born."

"And you expect me to believe you have renounced all that after only three months in the middle realm?"

"Have you been to the middle realm? Trust me when I assure you that you'd renounce your own mother if it meant the agony abating just for a split second."

She flew to her feet. "So you're turned to my side only to get out of hell?"

He matched her stance, their noses only inches apart. "I turned to your side the minute I fell in love with you, my sworn enemy."

Her jaw tightened. Her left eye twitched. Though he didn't break eye contact long enough to look down, he could sense her fists clenching. Powers or not, Regina had been trained in hand-to-hand combat. With his strength only newly refreshed, she could likely knock him on his ass with one or two moves.

Instead she took a step back. "Well, falling in love with you has cost me my powers and if hating you is the only way for me to get them back, then prepare yourself. Sending you to the middle realm will be nothing compared to what you're going to go through next."

CHAPTER SEVEN

THE INSIDES OF HER palms chafed from the impotency of her threat, but Brock looked wounded all the same. Either he was acting, as he had been with her before, or her venom stung. Powers or not, she'd find a way to conquer him again.

She had to. Her life depended on it.

Only he wasn't really her problem. Not like before. Killing him wouldn't necessarily douse the love still burning deep within her heart. Her mother was dead, but Regina's love for her remained strong as ever. What Regina wanted—what she needed—was to hate him. Then and only then would her powers return.

Over and over during the preparations for retreat to the hidden cave, she'd reminded herself of how he'd betrayed her—how he'd drawn a stake from beneath the pillow on her bed and had attempted to jab the weapon into her chest. When Hunters couldn't burn a witch at the stake, they impaled them. But he'd been too slow—or she too quick. In seconds, the stake had flown from his hand, he'd been trapped by a freezing spell and she'd forced him, magically, to reveal the full breadth of his plan to kill her on behalf of the Hunter King.

She hadn't known then that he'd meant Old Movert.

She'd only known that the man she'd come to trust with her innermost secrets had tried to tear her from this life with a silver stake and no regrets.

In her mind, she'd replayed their final confrontation, the one she'd worked so hard to forget, until the scene felt like a clip from an overly dramatic film rather than a moment from her own life. But no matter how she allowed the betrayal to rend her heart in two over and over and over, her powers remained at a distance. Taunting her. Just out of reach.

She could still remember how he'd once spoken with her, how he'd touched her, how he'd listened. She could still remember every laugh they'd shared, every meal, every lazy moment in the sun. Until she could squelch those images, her residual love for him would remain.

Perhaps if she worked through the betrayal entirely—from start to finish—if she heard his reasons, she could buoy her hatred with his evil motives and twisted loyalties to the killer, Old Movert. She hadn't had time three months ago to find out why he'd stooped so low in his seduction. Now she did.

"Sit down," she ordered.

He crossed his arms, squaring his shoulders so that she knew the herbs and potions Marion had added to their food and drink were working. "We've no time to chitchat, Regina. If you don't have your powers, we need to train and plan. Some of your spells create results no matter who utters them. We need to brush up on those. Movert will have stolen magic at his disposal, but his minions, for the most part, will not. They'll attack conventionally and we'll meet them hand to hand. Your fortress here will keep us hidden temporarily, but Movert *will* find us. He cannot rid this continent of all witches until you are dead. Luckily his army, while loyal, will not wait long now that the gauntlet has been thrown. They'll want results quickly, which may force him to act before he's entirely prepared."

Regina smoothed her tongue across her teeth, thinking. His plan was logical. Focused. Practical. But she hadn't brought him with her to this retreat as her partner. He was simply a means to an end.

"You're not in charge," she reminded him coolly.

He arched a brow over deep dark eyes, the sardonic strength in his expression causing a disloyal flutter deep in her belly.

"I'm only trying to—"

"Help? You want to help? Find the water Marion packed, wet your whistle and start talking. I have questions that need answering. Now."

She could practically see the smoke fuming from his nostrils as if from a ready-to-charge bull. If she emasculated him with her demands, so be it, though she seriously doubted she could decrease his level of his manliness simply by barking a few orders. Brock oozed testosterone the way a demon oozed acidic puss.

Brock retrieved two water bottles, handed her one and then sat on a smooth rock not far from the fire. She slipped the creed athame into the sheath she'd attached to her belt and tried to absorb some of the magic buzzing from the blade. Forged with ancient magical blood born of two spiritual lines—the Native Americans and the Wiccans—the weapon might be her only chance for survival.

Once she purged Brock Aegis from her heart.

"Tell me how Movert recruited you," she ordered.

"The Aegis line has been forever linked to Movert."

"Everyone in the whole family?"

"The men," he said quickly. "Some did the Hunter's bidding with the blessings of their wives, others acted in secret. According to history, Movert was the first Hunter to cross onto this continent as part of a Spanish expedition. He was shocked to confront Native Americans and learn some of them followed the principles of witchcraft. He vowed to destroy them, but they banded together and got him first. My ancestor was a part of Movert's expedition and discovered him as he lay dying. He swore fealty to the injured Hunter and vowed to care for him until he healed. Movert taught my ancestor how to find witches and steal their magic, which is how Movert has remained alive all these hundreds of years. And since then, every generation of Aegis men has given him one of their male offspring to train and command."

"Can you steal magic, too?" she asked.

"I've never tried. It's a lost art and one Movert guards jealously."

"And why did your ancestor take up Movert's cause so quickly? Why did your family hate witches?"

He snorted. "What God-fearing people didn't all those centuries ago? My family didn't create the prejudices against your people, but Movert fed the hatred and fear with tales of mundane slavery and witch torture and cruelty. He used fear. He had it easy in the primitive times."

"Clearly even the twenty-first century has had no effect on your outlook," she snarked.

Brock had the decency to look down at his hands.

"The hatred I unleashed on you and your race has been bred into me since birth. I am not making excuses, just explaining," he insisted.

She paced in front of him and gave him a nod. She'd been bred to understand witchcraft as something special, yet normal for the women in her line. The fear and loathing she felt toward the evil of their race, warlocks in particular, would be nearly impossible for her to ignore. Especially since one had murdered her mother, thrusting her into the position of Guardian long before she had been ready.

But she was ready now. Just as in the past, she had no choice.

"And you renounce those prejudices now?" she asked.

Brock closed his eyes tightly and when he opened them, she was struck by the honesty in the dark depths. "Yes."

"Why?"

"Because I love you," he whispered.

Without the power to conjure an energy burst, she used her palm to slap him instead. He barely flinched, though a deep red imprint of her hand sizzled on his cheek.

"Don't say that again," she commanded.

"Why not?" he countered. "It is the truth!"

"You tried to kill me!"

"I failed," he insisted, his tone proud, "or did you not notice?"

Regina stepped back, putting the fire between them as quickly as possible.

"That's what Marion said," she admitted. "That you'd failed on purpose."

"Your aunt is wiser than she lets on."

"Then why didn't you just tell me of Movert's orders? Why didn't you confess who you were before pulling that stake on me?"

Brock stood and stalked toward her with so much force, she nearly stumbled out of his way. He grabbed her arms to keep her from falling and without her powers, without her ability to reach her weapon, she could do nothing but scream in protest.

"Let go of me!"

"No," he countered. "Not until you hear me."

"Admit that you are lying. Tell me you're trying to seduce me again to gain your master's favor."

Her voice cracked with the sound of desperation, but she didn't care. She didn't want to hear that he loved her, that he'd risked everything in order to save her.

"I can't," he insisted. "I can't lie to you anymore."

Yanking her forward, Brock smashed his lips against hers. She closed her eyes so tightly, they teared, but she refused to respond to the desperate press of his mouth. No matter how his taste seeped onto her tongue. No matter how his scent assailed her, flooding her with heady need.

After a moment, he let her go.

She swiped the back of her hand across her mouth and unsheathed the athame. "Don't do that again."

His chest heaved and his fists clenched. She wasn't sure if he was preparing to fight or about to attempt another sensual assault. After tense moments, he cursed and took a step backward, wisely assessing that the better tactic would be to keep his lips to himself.

"I didn't tell you about Movert's orders because I feared he'd learn of my double-cross and send someone else to destroy you. I'd hoped," he said, his tone dripping with bitterness, "that by allowing you to best me, his prized Hunter, the last descendant of the Aegis line, he'd consider you too powerful to attack without a detailed plan, giving me time to rally the Hunter corps against him."

She rolled her eyes. "You were plotting a revolution from the middle realm?"

He shook his head. "I had no idea you'd banish me there, but I'd hoped you, at the very least, wouldn't kill me, giving me a chance to stop this madness."

"The only madness was my falling in love with you," she claimed.

"No," Brock asserted. "If you hadn't fallen in love with me, I wouldn't have been able to break free of Movert's clutches. Until you loved me, revolution was the furthest thing from my mind. Your love made me decide that you deserved to live and to ensure that, I was willing to die."

"Are you still?" she asked.

In another time and place, the hurt that flashed through his eyes might have broken her heart.

But not today.

CHAPTER EIGHT

BROCK WATCHED HER FACE, conscious of every change in her expression from shock to disbelief to disgust. But before she could spit at him or curse him or smack him again, he held up his hands.

"I know what you're thinking," he said.

"That you're a lying son of a bitch who's trying to manipulate me into forgiving him for trying to impale me with a silver stake?"

He couldn't suppress a quirk of a grin. "Well, that about sums it up."

She opened her mouth, but popped her lips shut as his agreement registered. Moments later, she claimed, "I don't buy your explanation."

"You don't have to," he said with a shrug. "What happened is the past and we can't change history. Knowing my reasons and my plan will not make you hate me, sorry. I know that's what you're trying to do. The only thing that can destroy the love you feel for me is knowing I tried to kill you. This you already know. So how's that whole hate thing working for you?"

Enraged, Regina stalked off toward what he assumed from the slight breeze stirring the fire was the entrance to the cave. Good. Her absence gave him a moment to think. He dropped back on top of the rock and stretched. He could feel his muscles reknitting, his energy surging. Whatever Marion had put into their food and drink was powerful stuff. Now, what else had she sent along?

In the packs of supplies, Brock found two cases of weapons: Chinese stars; knives of various sizes, though all were honed to paper-thin sharpness; several loaded automatic pistols; a compact flamethrower. Regina wasn't messing around. Good for her.

She also still loved him, which gave Brock a more powerful rush than any spell or potion ever could.

She still loved him.

After all he'd done.

His heart surged even as his brain cursed. That love, tainted by his betrayal, was blocking her from accessing the powers they'd need to defeat Movert and free Brock of his blood bond. How could he entice her to drop her need to hate him, to embrace the love, to embrace him and all they could be together?

Strategy for romance flew out of his mind the minute he heard her scream. Grabbing a handful of knives, he flew toward her voice. At the cave entrance, he saw her, flanked on either side by Hunters wielding crossbows. She had her wand at the ready. Several arrows lay at her feet, but a gash across her forearm proved that while she was wily with her spell work, she was, for the moment, outgunned.

"Guardian!"

He shouted to her by her title, and then tossed a knife in her direction. The blade spun, the handle slamming into the palm of her hand on the rotation. In the split second when his Hunter brethren expected him to finish off their quarry, Regina spun, kicked out with her leg, knocking one Hunter to the ground while she sliced the other across the base of his neck.

He crumbled to the ground just as Brock leaped over his body and caught the second Hunter by the scruff. He disarmed him, flinging his crossbow out of reach.

"Your name," Brock ordered.

The Hunter choked out a moniker Brock didn't recognize.

"How did you find us?"

The Hunter didn't respond quickly enough, so Brock applied pressure to the side of his neck until he screamed in pain. The man was not wearing a protective amulet, one of the many Movert had created for his legions. He was either in disguise, undercover, or not associated with Movert's war at all.

"This is our territory," the Hunter replied.

Brock's mind raced and he guessed that Regina's safe haven of a cave must have been an old, established witch's hiding place—perhaps one she didn't realize had long been plotted on Hunter maps. Rogue hunters often trolled near these areas in hopes they'd stumble onto prey and perhaps, tonight, they'd just gotten lucky.

Or else Old Movert had found them.

"Who do you serve?"

The Hunter's eyes widened and his lip curled in disgust. "I serve me and I'll have that witch's heart on my mantelpiece." He narrowed his gaze at Brock, then spat at Regina, who'd started murmuring a spell, rotating her wand in small circles.

Brock flung the Hunter against the hard stone wall.

In a flash, Regina uttered the final word of the incantation and the Hunter disappeared in a flash of blue smoke. She did the same to the body on the ground, though she had to repeat the incantation twice.

She swallowed hard, looking down at the wand, seeing it for the fragile stick of wood it was. "I can't defeat Movert this way. It's too slow. Children play with wands, not Guardians."

Brock tossed his remaining knives to the ground, knowing he couldn't approach her armed. He stepped into her personal space, mindful this time of moving too quickly and scaring her away.

"Then take back your powers," he said.

When her eyes met his, the liquid lavender swimming in her irises stopped his heart. "How can I?"

He swallowed thickly. "Love me."

She shook her head. "You tried to kill me."

"I tried to save you. Even tonight, I could have let these Hunters kill you. They were rogue. Movert would never have known it wasn't me and my blood oath to him would have been fulfilled. Believe me. I love you. I've put my life on the line for you and I'll willingly die for you—that much I've proved. But you can save yourself by giving in to what you know is true. Surrender to what your heart desires and everything you cherish will be yours again."

She was shaking. He could see the conflict raging in her as she shook her head, trying to deny her heart.

He took a chance and smoothed his palms over her arms, careful not to grip her too tightly. "You're hurt."

She snorted. "'Tis but a scratch."

His snicker lightened the moment, reminding him of the night they'd cuddled in her tower bed naked, munching on popcorn and watching Monty Python movies until dawn.

"Let go of your pride, Regina. You can love me and then let me go if that's what you need to do, but only surrendering to your feelings will gain you what you need to survive. You can't act as Guardian without your powers. And for the record, I won't betray you again."

In a flash of movement, Regina grabbed Brock by the collar of his shirt. For a split second, he hoped she'd kiss him, but instead, she dragged him back deeper into the cave, to where the fire smoldered and the atmosphere heated with smoke and spark. She released him, stalked over to the cache of supplies and dug into a duffel bag until she found an assortment of herbs. Choosing carefully, she created a bouquet of greenery, then tossed the collection into the fire, whipped out her wand and spoke an ancient incantation around the suddenly fragrant flames.

"I thought your powers…" he started, but stopped when she shushed him harshly, then grinned.

"Like you said before, I know spells that work no matter who utters them. So I guess I still have a few tricks up my sleeve."

Brock returned her smile. Regina was nothing if not resourceful.

"Grab that poultice," she said, flicking her wand toward a fragrant cloth that had tumbled out of the herb bag.

He complied.

She continued to wave her wand and chant, an incantation he hadn't heard before. When she reached the third repetition, she switched her wand to her other hand and held out her injury. "Wrap my wound."

She resumed her chanting. The fire burgeoned and the aromas crackling from within the embers started to affect his vision. He blinked, but applied the medicated cloth to her arm until the wound was covered and the gauzy material was knotted in place.

"Good," she said, not opening her eyes, barely taking a break between reiterating the spell. "Now take off your clothes."

Brock backed up, surprised, but the tiny grin teasing her lips told him she knew exactly what she was doing. In the past, getting naked with Regina had never been a bad thing, so once again, he obeyed.

By the time his jeans had dropped to the ground, he noticed a swirling shower of sparks encircling them, casting a rainbow of flashing colors in a circle around them, bringing to mind images of psychedelic acid trips or movie special effects. He thought about how this blatant display of magic should appall or disgust him as he'd been taught all his life, and yet, the beauty of the twinkling lights and the intimacy of the tight space and warm atmosphere seriously turned him on. His sex hardened, lengthened. His heartbeat accelerated and the concentrated heat in the cave caused a sheen of sweat to coat his exposed skin.

Regina put down the wand.

"We're safe," she said, unbuttoning the blouse she wore with delicious slowness. "Safe within this circle to do whatever our hearts desire."

Brock understood, but despite the drugging effect of the magic, he clung to the knowledge that a pretty protection spell might not be enough to hide them from Movert's forces if the Hunters they'd fought at the cave entrance hadn't been rogue as he'd surmised. Still, the rotating sparks were hypnotic and little by little, he could feel his concerns melting away.

"Movert," he managed to say.

She shook her head as the material of her blouse fluttered to the ground, leaving her lacy flesh-toned bra exposed to the light. "Even if he walked into this cave right now, the magic would show him nothing but bare stone walls." She reached behind her and unhooked her lingerie, allowing the straps to caress her shoulders and arms as they slid to the ground. "Make love to me, Brock. Reawaken my love for you so that my powers will return."

He wanted to ask, "And then what?" but he squelched the question by dipping his gaze to her breasts. Round, full and tipped with hard, dark nipples, they begged for his touch, his tongue. He strode toward her and dropped to his knees in front of her, splaying his hands over her hips.

"This can't be real," he muttered.

She maneuvered her hands between his, undid the top button and zipper of her jeans, then speared her hands into his hair, tugging him close so that he could inhale the scent of her arousal. "As real as magic."

He had her naked in no time and though he longed to thrust his mouth into her sex and lap up the juices he sensed stirring within her, the magical miasma inspired him to take his time. Instead he stood and caressed her cheeks lightly, pressing his body close to hers so that their curves melded together.

"Tell me what you want," he said.

Her eyes closed tightly for a moment and when they reopened, they flashed with a mixture of regret and anticipation. "That's the whole trouble, isn't it? You know what I want. Like no man ever has before."

Pride surged through him. No matter his previous motives, Brock had made it his mission to learn everything about this woman. Never had he imagined that his manipulations would give him a chance to prove his love. He dipped his head and kissed her, not too hard as he had before, and not so soft that she didn't know he intended to fulfill her demand to the letter.

CHAPTER NINE

WILLFULLY and completely, Regina surrendered to the wave of sensation. Brock's hands slid over her shoulders, down her arms, across her backside. His fingers teased along the center of her buttocks, acknowledging but not yet fulfilling the needs thrumming in the erogenous zones hidden there. His mouth's assault on hers, demanding yet gentle, forced her to meet and match his need to taste and arouse, while he lead her into the insanity of sexual pleasure.

Magical sparks danced beside them. The air filled with the utter essence of magic to add a million sensations to those already coursing through her. Even though she'd relied on spell work and herbs and borrowed enchantments to conjure the mist, she reveled in the cocoon of privacy she'd created. Wielding power made her powerful. Making love to Brock made her invincible.

He wrapped his arms tightly around her waist and lifted her lightly to feast on her breasts. He knew precisely when to suckle, when to nip, when to lave. His tongue on her sensitive nipples drew her into a spire of longing that she'd only escape through orgasm. The pressure between her legs built to a delicious pain, which he freed entirely when he dropped to his knees, curved her over his lap and pressed a single fingertip inside her.

Instantly the sparks flying around them burst into flames, like tiny fireworks that regenerated even as they burned. She'd worked the magic while in the throes of lust, inevitably tying the enchantment to her own sexual excitement. As she spiraled downward to the edge of reason, Brock kicked the sleeping bag closer and laid her across the nylon cushion. He leveled his body over hers, kissing just above her eyelids, across her cheeks, on her nose and chin. Pleasure washed her from the inside out. He was suckling her neck when she experienced a moment of clarity and realized he'd give her a thousand solo orgasms if she let him, all to prove a love she wasn't sure she believed in.

As much as she appreciated his generosity, she had some serious reciprocation on her mind. Bracing her hands on his chest, his skin slick beneath hers, she broke mouth-to-skin contact.

"What are you doing?" she asked.

He arched a brow. The answer was, after all, fairly obvious.

"Making love to you. Am I not doing it right so that you have to ask?"

Was he nuts? "You're doing a fine job, thanks," she replied, unable to contain the burble of laughter in her voice.

He wriggled his eyebrows. "No, thank you," he said, chuckling before burying his head into the crook of her neck and plying his amazing mouth to her sensitized skin.

She closed her eyes and wrapped her arms around

him, momentarily enjoying the reawakening of her senses after the fall of climax and the return of the playful banter they'd once mastered. This is how he'd ensnared her so tightly all those months ago—by acting as the perfect lover. Giving. Funny. Unafraid of intimacy on any level. Falling in love with him had been so easy—could it possibly be true that he'd been as unable to resist the pull as well?

While her mind swirled, he teased her mercilessly with his mouth, particularly when he rediscovered the spot just beneath her earlobe that drove her wild with wanting. Slowly she stroked his back, loving the feel of his muscles beneath her fingertips.

When he winced, she sat up.

"What's wrong?"

"Nothing," he said, attempting to lure her back down. "You just hit a…sore spot."

She curved around him and gasped at what she saw. Slices of flesh puckered and scarred, as if from a whip freshly applied.

"Good goddess," she said.

He turned away from her exploration. "It's healing."

She grasped his shoulder and held him still, drawing a gentle fingertip along the side of his injury, careful not to aggravate the wound. "This is from the middle realm? From my sending you there?"

"I deserved it," Brock said.

She shook her head. No, he hadn't. Not if she believed the story he'd told her about faking the murder attempt in order to throw Movert off her trail. And the claim was beginning to sound very credible. "I did this to you."

"Movert did this to me, Regina. My family who

sold me into his servitude before I had a mind of my own did this to me. One thing you experience in the middle realm is a great deal of clarity about the nature and causes of the crimes that sent you there. I don't blame you. I love you. Why can't you believe me?"

Unable to form words in reply, Regina grabbed his neck and pulled him into an insistent kiss. She did believe him. Banishing him to the middle realm three months ago had been her only option at the time. She'd had no choice but to act to protect her people, but now, she couldn't betray her heart. She loved the man. No matter his crime, she couldn't destroy him. And she wouldn't allow Movert to hurt him, either.

The rest of their lovemaking came fast and furiously. Every kiss made her more hungry; every sensation made her feel more deprived. Even when he tugged her on top of him, rolling onto his injured back, she plied her body against his, impatiently needing to feel him around her, beneath her, inside her. The flavors of his skin on her tongue heightened her need until she could no longer wait. She eased her sex onto his, her body thrumming with keen vibrations the moment the tip of his penis touched the edge of her clit. The magical swirl around them instantly brightened, swelling so that the glow nearly blinded her. She braced her hands on his chest, but Brock wove his fingers with hers, connecting their bodies with a sweet intimacy that rivaled the melding of their sex.

Clutching her hands in his, Brock braced her hips, guiding the rhythm that soon exploded into a cacophony of sensations. He filled her so thickly, so completely, she couldn't help but want him harder, deeper. Leaning slightly forward, his cock curved into her with perfect thrust and she climaxed again.

He joined her moments later, his hands gripping hers tightly as sensations more colorful than the fireworks flying in a dizzying spin around them burst through her body. When he screamed out her name and pumped into her one final time, the magical sparks exploded, raining tiny embers onto their hot and sweaty bodies, then settling back into a gentle twirl of glistening color that would protect them, temporarily, from the threats of Old Movert and the conflict between Hunters and witches that had existed since the dawn of time.

CHAPTER TEN

COLD, REGINA REACHED for her comforter, blindly feeling around for the plush, satin and velvet trimmed bedcovering that matched the curtains in her tower room. She found nothing except the alternately rough and scarred, then smooth and warm, skin of a naked man. Skin she knew. Skin that caused her flesh to buzz with heat in response to contact. Brock's skin, simmering with the decidedly male scent that belonged to him and him alone.

They weren't in her room, she remembered. They were sleeping on the stone-cold floor of a cave, tangled together on top of a sleeping bag. And he was hogging their thin flannel blanket. She threw her arm over her eyes to block out the light turning the insides of her eyelids a bright, painful red. The blanket didn't matter. She needed a cold, harsh dose of reality.

What the hell had she been thinking?

She'd been thinking that making love to Brock would earn her back her powers, that surrendering to the desire spiking between them would be for the greater good.

She'd been thinking that his story sounded genuine and that his regret had been too real to be faked.

Good goddess, she'd either had the best makeup sex

in the history of witchdom or she'd once again been played for a fool.

"So which is it?" she muttered.

"I was just about to ask you the very same question."

Regina's eyes flashed open at the sound of a voice that was not Brock's. She scampered backward, out of range, her feet slipping on the sleeping bag. Dust kicked up around her and though she climbed over a form she believed to be Brock, she couldn't be sure. He wasn't moving.

A cackle of a laugh sent shivers up her spine a hundred degrees chillier than the air in the now fireless cave. Ignoring the fact that she was naked and unarmed, Regina dove behind a rock and waited. Through the swirls of ash and dust, a man emerged.

With gray hair that dragged to his waist and clothes that reminded her of the classic great white Hunter in his outback vest, khaki pants and jaunty hat, Old Movert appeared nothing like she'd expected. She had no idea why she'd conjured an image of dark robes and slim face with razor-sharp cheekbones and a mouthful of canine teeth, but this Hunter King bore no resemblance to the monster in her childhood nightmares. He was terrifying in his own way, however, beginning with the colorful array of pins, amulets, charms, *jujus* and fetishes displayed around his neck and on his chest—all prizes from witches he'd killed, no doubt— and ending with his scarred face and the oval-shaped talisman he wore in his eye socket, the stone glistening with an inner fire all its own.

In her mind, Regina cast a freezing spell.

Old Movert continued toward her.

Behind the rock, she turned her hands palms up and tried to conjure an energy burst. Not so much as a tingle flashed against her skin.

"What did you do to Brock?"

Her question gave him pause, but the amusement in his one cold blue eye told her his hesitation was only temporary.

"The traitor is right where you left him, witch. Sated and drunk on your wicked juices."

"Why can't he move?" she asked, trying again for even a small spark in her hand, this time muttering the spell under her breath. Where was her wand? The athame from the coven of Creed?

Tucked into the sleeping bag. Out of her reach.

Movert belched, his tone bored, as if eliminating her was nothing more than an annoying chore. "He'll awaken soon enough."

"To find me dead?"

The Hunter King's grin cut his face in half, emphasizing the slant of his soulless eye and the scars along the base of his chin. "You are the temptress, aren't you? No, no. You'll live for the time being. I have use for you, or didn't you realize? If I hadn't found you myself, thanks to my scouts, which you so rudely dispatched, I would have started picking off your followers one by one until you were forced out of hiding. How merciful that my Hunters revealed your hiding place before all the dirty witches in your Registry had to die."

"You have no intention of sparing them," she argued.

He chuckled. "No, but with you out of the way and your protection squads busy with crews I sent out specifically to Canada to leave you unprotected, I can now take my time killing each and every one and milking them of their feeble powers."

"You still won't have the witch census."

"I won't need it," he snapped. "With you out of the way and no Guardian in the wings to take your place, I will hunt your kind into extinction and use your beloved Registry as my headquarters."

Unable to conjure her magic and unwilling to cower in the face of her greatest enemy, Regina stood. Movert winced at her nudity and for a split second, glanced away.

"Cover yourself," he ordered.

She quirked a grin and shifted her stance, her fist cocked on her hip. "Ah, you're a true old school Hunter, aren't you, old man? Your hatred of my kind spawns from your—" she glanced boldly at his crotch "—inadequacies."

His sneer emphasized the gold tips on his blackened teeth. "I don't even remember why I hate witches anymore, to be honest. For over five hundred years, witches have been my prey, my enemy, my motivation to live by whatever means necessary."

"You've only lived to five centuries because you feed off our magic," she countered.

He caressed the prizes sewn into his war vest. "Amazing how that works. Most Hunters simply kill and move on. I'd thank my warlock father for teaching me to extract magic from filthy witches, but he, such a corruption to the natural world, was my first kill."

Regina had long known that warlocks and Hunters had no respect for life, but to hear the Creed spoken of so offhandedly turned her stomach. "And you call me filthy?"

He licked his lips, his tongue nearly as blackened by age and disease as his teeth. Regina fought her instinct to gag, knowing any reaction might show weakness. Now, without her powers, she had to show nothing but indefatigable strength.

Which was why she didn't so much as flick her gaze in Brock's direction. She had no idea what Movert knew about their night together, but she did know that if Brock was still allied to his old master, he wouldn't still be motionless on the floor. He'd be standing at Old Movert's side, proud of his second, even more cunning seduction of the Guardian witch.

Movert bent low to retrieve her discarded clothes. She nearly sprang forward, but heard movement behind him. He shook the dust and dirt from her blouse and jeans, chuckling as he held them out to her.

"I haven't lived five centuries by approaching witches without reinforcements," he said.

She snatched the clothes from him, if for no other reason than she couldn't stand the thought of him tainting the material with his touch. "Why don't you just kill me?"

"Why don't you attack?" he shot back. "That's an interesting question, don't you think? One I've been grappling with since I announced my arrival in your little love nest here. I must assume that you do not attack because you cannot. Perhaps my apprentice provided assistance in your capture even as he betrayed me," he said, his gnarled hand sweeping toward Brock on the floor.

His gesture gave her a chance to look at Brock without consequence. His chest moved, but the motion was not fluid and calming as it had been last night against her back. A small pouch, tied with a feather-ended strap of leather, lay on his chest. A *juju*—powerful magic that had rendered him unconscious.

She slid her gaze back on her enemy. "I will attack when I am attacked, rest assured of that, Hunter."

Her cocky attitude clearly unnerved him. He stabbed the ground with the cane she now realized he clutched in his other hand and had kept tight to his side to hide his infirmity. Maybe he wasn't so scary after all.

"Get dressed!" he ordered. "Your witch's wiles mean nothing to me or to my followers."

She glanced at his crotch again. "How come that doesn't surprise me?"

With a flick, he touched a charm draped around his neck, then from his fingertips, aimed a charge of electric heat at her shoulder, sending her flying backward. Pain stabbed through her flesh and hellfire sliced through her nerve endings. She clamped her mouth shut to contain a scream, but a whimper escaped, causing Movert to laugh heartily.

"You'll not insult my manhood again, witch. Get dressed or I'll strike your lover in the heart with that same excruciating power."

Regina dressed quickly, ignoring the agony of her injury, jabbing her legs into the jeans and pulling on the blouse as fast as she could with only one useful arm. Her eyes watered, but she remained defiant. If Movert had wanted her dead, he would have killed her by now. Same went for Brock. Maybe the Hunter King was willing to let one of the lackeys hiding behind him to do the deed, but for the moment, he wanted both of them alive. She had to use that knowledge to her advantage.

She stalked toward Movert, her shoulders drooped, her eyes focused on the boots lying two feet from Brock and the sleeping bag. The Hunter kept his hand on the charm that had given him the ability to strike, ready to send another jolt into her if she deviated from her path. Prepared this time, she reached down, grabbed the boots and swung the heels hard in Movert's direction, allowing the rotation of movement to throw her across Brock's body. As she sailed over him, she knocked the fetish off his chest.

She landed in a roll, but flattened herself to the ground. Movert threw a bolt above her, giving her another second to grab a fist-size rock and beam it at his head. His temple spurted with blood. In a mad dash, she rushed Movert and grabbed the pin set in his eye socket, hoping she'd correctly identified the magical properties. She shoved him to the ground in time to see his Hunter forces advancing.

Brock had begun to sit up when she tackled him to the ground and yelled, "Hang on!"

One ancient phrase later and they fell into a vortex of darkness. Regina concentrated, focusing her mind entirely on her mother's ancestral home. Seconds later, they materialized in the middle of the parlor. Regina threw the talisman to the ground, grabbed a nearby marble statue and crushed the charm with one powerful slam.

"Where are we?" Brock asked, groggily.

Regina collapsed, the wound on her shoulder on fire, her lungs yanking in air and nearly choking her. They were safe. But for how long? Movert wouldn't be able to track them through the charm she'd stolen—but how hard would it be for him to find the house where she was born?

Brock crawled over to her, wincing when he saw her injury. "What happened? I thought I heard Movert."

She reached up with her uninjured hand and cupped Brock's face, reading the shock and worry in his dark gaze. Goddess, she wanted to trust him. Had he been part of this ambush? Had he alerted his master to their location or had he simply been a victim of Movert's murderous plot?

"You did hear him. He gave me a little gift," she said, glancing at her shoulder, which was bleeding through her blouse.

Brock ripped her blouse off carefully, but the action still jolted her. She bit down hard on her lower lip and arched her back as the pain sapped her strength.

"Tell me what happened," Brock insisted.

She shook her head, trying to break the fog of agony seeping into her brain. "In the kitchen, under the sink, there's a healing kit. Bring it here and I'll fill you in."

Brock started to move, then leaned down and kissed her gently. "Do I want to know how close you came to dying?"

She forced a smile through her agony. "That's the best part. I don't think I came that close at all."

CHAPTER ELEVEN

"So you think he knows what happened to my powers?" Regina asked, lapping up the last of the tasty broth Brock had whipped up and laced with a magical painkiller he'd found in the emergency kit under the sink. A really good magical painkiller. None of this fresh or dried herb crap. He'd used concentrated magic that had stewed in the cupboard, sealed and protected by enchanted glass, for who knew how long. His knowledge of her kind came in handy, that was for sure. She not only couldn't feel the pain in her shoulder, but she was pretty sure she wouldn't so much as wince if someone tried to slice her head off with fishing wire.

At the slightly slurred quality of her voice, Brock took away the last of the soup. "He may not have before, but he does now. So, is this 'denying love' thing common knowledge?"

She stuck her tongue out at him. Childish, yes. But effective. She still couldn't believe she'd told him everything. A woman needed secrets, right? What was wrong with her?

"You didn't know," she sniped.

"I haven't lived five hundred years with little else to do but study the lore and history of my hated enemy," he countered.

Regina moved her arm, glancing at the clean white bandage Brock had applied. She saw no blood break through the gauze, so she moved again, stretching until he stopped her by laying his hand just above the wound.

"It's healing, not healed. Take it easy. Try to wrap your mind around our current dilemma."

She had to think. Oh, yeah. Movert.

"I suppose he could know," she surmised. "The curse that zaps a witch's power if she never knows love, denies love or betrays love isn't applicable to every romantic situation or else every witch on the dating scene would lose her powers a dozen times or more. But there is always a risk. It has to do with fate and destiny," she explained, snickering at the faraway sound of her voice. "You know, the big stuff."

"You mean like us?"

Brock moved in with no warning, but unlike her dealings with his boss—or former boss, she still hadn't completely decided—she made no defensive move. His kiss was soft, but full of promise. His tongue teased the edges of her lips, grazed her teeth, then sparred with hers in a contest for control. Somewhere in the back of her brain, she knew they didn't have time for seduction. She'd spirited them away, yes, but only to her ancestral home. Sooner or later, Movert would figure out their location and attack.

The thought must have occurred to Brock as well because with regret swimming in the dark depths of his eyes, he pulled away. Only when he took her fingers in his and pulled them away from his chest did she notice how she'd burrowed into his shirt so tightly.

"So he knows I'm powerless. What do we do next?" she asked.

He arched a brow. "We figure out why you still don't have your powers."

She shrugged. "I have no clue," she said, leaning her face to his again and swiping a kiss over the top of his nose. "I'm certainly not denying anything anymore."

"You're not denying sex," he said, emphasizing the last word in ways that made her body thrum. "You're probably not even denying that you once loved me. But how do you feel about me now?"

She moved to stand, suddenly unnerved by his proximity and dizzy from the healing draft. The questions made her head hurt. And then there was the way he oh-so-casually mentioned the sex. How could she possibly think clearly when he kept reminding her about the sex?

"I think you're hot," she admitted.

He frowned, clearly fighting between annoyance and amusement. "I think I put too much of that powder in your soup."

She danced around him, fairly certain he was right. "I do, you know."

"That's great. I think you're hot, too. But apparently, lust isn't enough to get you your powers back."

She frowned, fully aware that lust wasn't a powerful enough emotion to regenerate her magic. "No, I need to love you again. Well, more than that. I have to admit it."

"So admit it."

"I can't," she said.

He grabbed her wrist, stopping her antsy movements. "Why not?"

The tone of his voice, fraught with both frustration

and pain, sobered her. Buzz or not, they didn't have time to fool around. Either she needed to get her powers back or they had to pillage the ancestral home for enough weapons to fight off what she knew was an impending attack.

"Why not?" he asked again, this time clutching her more tightly.

"I don't trust you," she admitted, then squeezed her eyes closed tightly and breathed steadily, trying to regain her equilibrium. "No, that's not right. I don't trust myself. Not with you."

"Because I hurt you."

"Because I let you hurt me," she explained, gently pulling out of his touch, needing space to process her emotions more clearly. Even if she had all the weapons in the world at her disposal, even if she had her powers back and more, fighting Movert was nearly inconsequential to putting her heart on the line. She had to face the truth, whether or not she regained her powers as a result. She couldn't heal until she came to terms with what had happened between her and Brock, from the beginning of their affair three months ago to their lovemaking last night.

"I manipulated you," he admitted. "You were the victim, Regina."

She scoffed at his choice of words. "Guardian witches are never victims, Brock. I was a willing participant. I was so starved for love and attention, I let you waltz right into my life without asking questions, without challenging you. I bought right into your smooth lines."

"You trusted me," he supplied.

"No, I don't think that's the point. I allowed myself

to trust you without having any basis for that trust except hot sex. I let my own need for intimacy override my good sense as a Guardian. Maybe I didn't lose my powers because I denied my love for you. Maybe I lost my powers because I didn't deserve to be Guardian in the first place."

A commotion outside put an end to their conversation. Regina motioned for Brock to cut the lights as she dashed to the sleeping bag she'd managed to shimmer along with her and Brock. She grabbed her wand and the Creed athame. Once the house was dark, they peered outside the window, through the sheer curtains that hid them from prying eyes.

A band of neighborhood teens were kicking a can down the street, wires from iPods hooked into their ears. The mesh of the old world and the new seemed perfect for this city, so intent on rebuilding in a place that would be forever associated with the old ways and destructive weather.

"Where are we?" he asked.

"Family home."

"I thought the Registry was your family home."

She smiled. At least the Hunters didn't know everything about her. She'd always guarded the location of this home, knowing the three-story manse just a few blocks from Bourbon Street in New Orleans could be the ultimate safe haven when times got rough. Like now.

"The St. Lyon clan came to this continent a long time ago, landing first in New Brunswick, Canada and then emigrating to—"

"Louisiana."

She nodded and they moved away from the

window. In the dark, the atmosphere within the ancient walls thickened. The scents of magnolia and night-blooming jasmine teased her nostrils while the sound of a mosquito buzzing near her ear reminded her of why she loved Arizona. She couldn't remember the last time she'd been to the French Quarter home, yet she knew she could navigate the furnishings in the dark, even without her powers.

She returned to the doorway near the kitchen, where the full moon threw silver slivers across the hardwood floors.

"You deserve to be Guardian," Brock said, bringing them back to the earlier topic. In the quiet of the night, his voice brimmed with an intimacy that frightened her. Late-night chats. Pillow talk. Sensual teasing between lovers. Not just memories anymore.

Possibilities.

"I'm not so sure," Regina said.

"Then that is what is holding you back."

His slid his hand around hers and in the darkness, she felt free to close her eyes and enjoy the sensation of being captured, held and supported. This is what Brock had given her before. This was the hole he'd filled. She'd become Guardian so young and while scores of Guardians before her had existed without a male support—her mother a prime example since her father had run off shortly after her sister's birth—Regina had dared to want more. She had wanted more than a lover, more than a friend. She'd been desperate for a life mate, someone who understood magic and wouldn't be frightened by the scope and breadth of her power and responsibilities. Brock had slid so easily into the role that she'd never questioned, never tested his loyalty until too late.

But in the last few hours, he'd been tested.

Had he passed?

Had she?

"I'm being a fool again," she said, leaning her forehead against his chest, hoping he'd envelop her in his embrace and chase away the shadows of doubt attacking her from all sides.

She wasn't disappointed. His arms encircled her and he crushed her close so that the sound of his heartbeat drummed in her ear. "You're exhibiting great caution."

"Caution could cost us both our lives."

He didn't respond. He didn't need to. Regina knew she'd spoken nothing truer in her entire life.

She looked up, her nose knocking against his chin. Laughter lightened the moment, but not for long. Staring straight into Brock's inky-black eyes, she made a decision that would either save her life or end it.

"I love you, Brock. I trust you. And I trust me to handle whatever comes our way, good or bad."

His smile could have lit the entire house. He swept her into his arms and kissed her hard. Sparks of need shimmered through her, then intensified to hot glory, practically catching the roots of her hair on fire. Their mouths and bodies melded, their skin practically fusing from the voltaic charge arcing between them.

With effort, Brock pulled away.

"Okay, I know you're a damned good kisser and I'm no slouch myself, but what the hell was that?"

Her skin still tingled and in the corners of her eyes, Regina caught sight of tiny flickers of magical light dancing around them, much like the protective ring she'd conjured last night. Her smile filled her entire body with anticipation.

"I think that was my powers coming back."

"Test it," he urged.

Regina took a deep breath, flattened her palm in front of her and concentrated on drawing in all the energy around her. A familiar warmth formed on her skin, followed by a flash of light and then a swirling round ball of lethal magic danced in the center of her palm.

Brock pumped his arm in the air. She smacked her hands together, dispersing the energy burst, then flung herself into his outstretched arms.

"You're back!" he shouted.

"No, we're back. But before we can celebrate our reunion," she teased, licking her lips suggestively, "let's go kick some Hunter King ass."

CHAPTER TWELVE

THE HUNTER'S LAIR was everything Regina expected. Dark. Dank. Stinking of stale magic and unwashed skin. Brock had allowed her access to his mind so that she could pinpoint the location of Old Movert's hideaway and with her renewed powers, she'd shimmered them near the entrance to a cave tucked deep in Barranca del Cobre, a canyon deep in the Sierra Tarahumara mountain range in the southwestern part of Chihuahua, Mexico. Around her, she could smell the presence of copper beneath the verdant ground and behind the massive rock. No wonder Movert made his base here. With so much of the healing metal surrounding him in its natural state, he could nourish the magic he'd stolen from the witches he'd murdered.

But here, she'd also be at her most powerful. Since her epiphany with Brock, her body tingled with renewed energy. When he took her hand and squeezed tightly, the strength within her surged. At one time, he'd been her lover, then her greatest enemy, now her most powerful ally. She'd never ridden such an emotional roller coaster, but she was sure that she and Brock had a real shot at a future together.

If they lived.

She stared briefly at the night sky. Streaks of purple

announced the coming dawn. They didn't have much time. At sunrise, Brock surmised, the Hunters that Old Movert sent out on recognizance under the shade of darkness would return. Their numbers would swell to an unbeatable level. She and Brock had to attack now.

Brock reeled her in close. The scent of his skin made her dizzy with need, but she blocked out her responses. Once the battle was fought and won, she would make sure they didn't leave her tower bedroom for weeks. But for now, she needed to stay focused.

"Where are your protection squads?" he whispered.

Regina shook her head. She'd put out a call, but so far, none of her warrior witches had responded. "They must still be busy with Movert's forces. They can't leave the coven unprotected. They'll be here eventually, but we've got to move now. If Movert goes another night without my head on his platter, he will start killing witches at the Registry indiscriminately, just to draw me out. He said as much in the cave."

"He'd never have gotten this far without me," Brock muttered.

Regina grabbed his chin and forced his gaze into hers. "And thanks to you, I now know about his hideaway and his weaknesses. I've never felt more powerful, Brock. Because of you. Now, let's do this."

While Regina would have loved to have the backup of her trained protection squad, witches adept at spells of war, she didn't mind not drawing any more of her kind into danger. On a deep level, she needed to face Movert alone.

Well, not alone. With Brock. Never in her life had anything felt more right, even if she was terrified that she might fail.

As planned, Brock bound her wrists. As gingerly as possible, he gagged her with a scarf they'd found in the St. Lyon house and after sharing a nod and swiping a quick kiss across her forehead, he led her inside the Hunter's nest.

Brock stopped abruptly at the first curvature in the cave. He glanced at the torches on either side and recognized instantly that the protection charms stolen from murdered witches and posted at the entrance to Movert's lair had been changed since his last visit. He glanced at Regina, who shrugged, unfamiliar with the spells. Okay, so he was going to have to think on his feet. Fine. He could do that. He'd do whatever necessary to save Regina. And that included breaking his blood oath.

Which gave him an idea. Withdrawing the coven of Creed athame from the sheath in Regina's jacket, he sliced his hand and then smeared the blood on the charms. They immediately flickered, then dimmed.

They were in.

Regina's eyes reflected her horror, but he reassured her with a pointed stare, wiped the blade and returned it to its hiding place. From this point on, they marched through the cave unchallenged, each time the charms recognized his blood oath to Movert and allowed them through. After twisting and turning through narrow passageways for what seemed like miles, they emerged into a cavernous den.

A fire burned in the center and various Hunters slumbered near the warmth. The smoke channeled out through a crack in the stone ceiling of the cave, but the smell of burnt wood and old clothing and charred meat struck him nonetheless. Seconds after he walked into the chamber, his skin tightened, as if someone was wrenching his flesh from his muscle and bone.

The pull of his master.

Taking Regina by the arm, he yanked her close to his side, traversing the rocky terrain toward the center of the cave. There he found Old Movert sitting on a rock near the fire, whittling what looked like an old bone into the shape of a witch's wand.

"I see you've returned to me, Brock Aegis," Movert said without looking up from his task.

"I might have come to you sooner if you hadn't hexed me with the *juju* last night," he snapped.

Movert glanced up, his sneer intensified by the firelight. "I couldn't trust you after what you'd done with the witch."

The Hunter King didn't so much as flick his gaze over at Regina, who was struggling against her bindings, as she and Brock had rehearsed. He made it clear that the conflict now was between Brock and Movert and everyone else was inconsequential.

"You have no idea what I did with the witch."

"You were naked and snuggling against her foul body when the magical spell she'd cast failed and we found you. Do you deny that she seduced you?"

"Yes," Brock said boldly. "I seduced her. But these are matters you have long forgotten, Movert. I swore a blood oath to you. Did you really think I'd fail twice?"

Regina's eyes, those beautiful lavender eyes, glossed with tears that dropped in two large splashes down her cheeks. With the continuation of her race on the line, she was clearly pulling out all the stops.

Movert's eyes darted between them, but he didn't

seem to buy Brock's story entirely. It didn't matter. They were close enough to attack. He only had to get Regina untied. And if he couldn't, he could reach the knife. Killing Movert himself would mean betraying his blood oath, a crime that would result in his death. But with Movert gone, Regina would live unchallenged. This sacrifice he was willing to make.

Though it certainly wasn't his first choice.

"Shall I proceed?" he asked, moving to unbind Regina's hands. Hunter code did not allow for witches to be bound before they were killed unless they were to be burned. It was one of the few rules they followed.

"No," Movert ordered, standing abruptly and throwing his carved bone to the ground, though he kept the sharp-bladed knife tight in his grip. "I shall kill this witch."

"What?"

A few of the sleeping Hunters awoke, but they kept a prudent distance. Brock did not release Regina's bindings, but stealthily tugged at the trick knot they'd hidden in the folds of the rope.

Movert's laughter echoed through the cavern.

"Yes, apprentice of mine. I shall kill the witch myself and yet remain here in the living realm. Did you think I didn't know about the consequences of smiting a Guardian witch? Did you think I sent you to do the deed without knowing you'd sacrifice your soul? That was, after all, the terms of your blood oath to me, wasn't it? Your willingness to sacrifice your life for mine?"

Brock took a step back, his arms curved at his side, his fingers relaxed, but itching to curl into fists. He had to hold back. Wait. Once Movert was close enough...

The old Hunter King twisted to the other side of the fire, out of Regina's range.

"This was a dilemma I've contemplated since your banishment to the middle realm, one I only recently solved when I found you in the witch's tower bedroom, bound by her containment spell. On the floor, I found this," Movert said, raising a platinum necklace high into the firelight. The alexandrite at the center glittered bloodred.

Her amulet. Ancient and powerful, Regina had enchanted the necklace to make her forget him. While she slept, he'd yanked the chain from around her neck to force her to face what he'd done and save her from her fate at Movert's hands. How could the Hunter King now use the magic against her?

Movert thrust his hand through the fire, his flesh protected by the myriad charms he wore pinned to his chest. "Put it on her."

"Why?" Brock challenged.

Movert's face curved into what Brock assumed he meant to show compassion. "Why break her heart as you slit her throat? This will make her forget you, will it not? Do it."

Brock knew Movert had something more up his sleeve, but he reached out and took the amulet anyway, holding the chain wide as if he intended to put it over her neck. Regina's eyes widened and she shook her head violently, stepping back, as if trying to stumble out of his reach. One of the dozen Hunters behind them pushed her forward. She crashed against his chest and in the dust cloud of dirt kicked up by the fight, released her hands. She had the athame in her grip and had rolled out from behind him when Movert shouted a one-word containment spell and she froze.

"This is perfect," the Hunter said. "She even has a weapon. Put the necklace on her, Aegis. I'd threaten your life if you refuse, but I gather by you coming here with betrayal yet again in your agenda that you care not if you live or die so long as your lover survives. So let me inspire you another way. Put the necklace on her or I will kill her slowly and painfully and you will watch each and every torturous moment."

Brock spun to face his master.

"What are you playing at?" Brock asked.

The Hunter King leveled his deadly, one-eyed stare at him. "I wanted to see what she was capable of, which powers I could steal from her beyond the energy burst she's yet to conjure, but I see she came here only with an athame. A weak weapon, or did the failure of the coven of Creed teach her nothing?"

"No," Brock said forcefully, "the coven taught her the athame was useless."

Movert arched a bushy eyebrow. "Then why raise it against me?"

Brock grinned. He glanced furtively at Regina, whose eyes portrayed her confidence.

"So I could do this."

He threw the necklace around his own neck. The moment the stone at the center hit his chest, his felt a shock not unlike cardiac arrest surge through him. He remained standing and held out his palm as Regina had taught him. In an instant, his hand filled with concentrated energy and without hesitation, he flung the burst at his former master.

The ball flew through the flames and hit its target.

Movert flew backward and with him down, his freezing spell on Regina dispersed. Free, she ripped the scarf from her mouth and between them, they felled the entire population of Hunters in the cave.

"I guess you didn't forget me," Regina quipped as they both dove for cover, anticipating that Movert was not yet dead.

"Impossible," he said.

Knowing Movert would want Brock to kill Regina in order to banish his traitorous apprentice to the lower realm forever, they'd come up with a way for Brock to attack his master and defy his blood oath by transferring her most powerful magical ability to him—a warlock trick, but without the killing of the witch. All he had to do was keep something that belonged to her close to his skin. The necklace notwithstanding, he had a lock of her hair tied on a string around his neck. They'd theorized that if he vanquished Old Movert with her power, he'd be spared banishment to the lower realm. It had been a risk, but one they'd taken. Together.

A bitter, raspy laugh drew their attention to the fire. Movert walked through, his limp more pronounced, his vest charred from the attack, his eyes blazing with hatred and determination.

The old Hunter grabbed at his chest, but the mojo to return fire had been destroyed. He tried to reach another stolen power, but Brock formed another energy burst that sent him flying again. Only then did Regina shimmer from one side of the fire to the other. Though Movert was nearly dead, she took no chances and thrust the athame into his black heart. He screamed out, his inky mouth widening as the horror of his twisted life faded from painful shout to pitiful croak.

And then, Brock heard no sound except Regina's heavy breathing and the crackle and pop of the dying fire.

EPILOGUE

THE ACT of returning the power he'd borrowed from Regina proved exceedingly more exhausting than Brock had ever imagined. Certain witches could be very creative—and very naughty—in their spell casting. Not only did he think he'd need to sleep for a week, but certain parts of his body might just be sore enough to make walking difficult, if ever he was sufficiently coaxed from her bed, which he doubted would happen anytime soon.

Regina, glowing in the sweat of their latest "power transfer," rolled off the mattress and padded to the dresser beneath her window, naked and beautiful. Brock couldn't help but fold his hands behind his head and grin from ear to ear.

"You're looking rather pleased with yourself," she said without turning around.

"Are you psychic now, too?" he asked.

She spun and gifted him with a saucy look. "No, I'm just getting to know you better." She retrieved two bottled waters from the cooler she'd stashed there so they rarely had to leave her room, tossed him one, then broke open the seal on the other.

He caught the bottle one-handed, enjoying the tingle of condensation that sprinkled across his face.

"Well, I can't deny that the power I have over your body is much more enjoyable to wield than any energy burst," he admitted.

She rolled her eyes. "Tell me about it."

Two days had passed since their victory against Movert, and yet they'd spoken very little about the incident itself. Brock had been surprised at how easily he'd reconciled his master's death as necessary, but then, he'd done the same with witches for years, under the mistaken belief that they were some sort of threat to humanity. He'd learned the hard way how what he'd been taught his entire life had been untrue. Now, he'd also learned that even the most powerful witches, like Regina, mourned the need to kill. Every so often, when the throes of passion had subsided, he caught the sadness in her eyes.

"You know that you did what you had to do, right?" Brock asked.

Regina frowned, then after a swig of water, winked playfully. "I'm not ashamed of anything I do in that bed if that's what you're thinking."

"That's not what I'm talking about."

Suddenly cold, Regina bounded back into bed and snuggled with Brock beneath the covers. The warmth of his skin immediately seeped into her body and when he shifted to wrap her tightly in his arms, she knew she could stay here for eternity. If the witching world didn't need her. Which, unfortunately, it would.

"Regina?"

"I killed Old Movert, Brock," she said, forcing as much finality into her voice as she could manage. "I know I acted in the only way I could."

"Doesn't mean you don't harbor regrets. Look at how you reacted when you banished me."

"I wasn't in love with Old Movert."

"Thank God," he said.

"And the goddess, too," she said with a smile. "Movert was a threat to me, to you and to the witches I'm sworn to protect. What's left of his Hunter force is now dispersed and the protection squads are after them."

"Will you kill them all?"

Regina thought carefully about how to reply. Twisted or not, the Hunters had been Brock's only real family for most of his life. "The protection squads will do what they must to ensure the safety of our kind. If the Hunters want to renounce their beliefs, we'll see what arrangements can be made. It'll be an issue of trust, I suppose. No one knows that more than I do."

Brock brushed a kiss along the top of her head and the contentment within her spiked. He truly was a remarkable man. Nothing like the men who'd come and gone from the lives of the former Guardians.

"What are you thinking?" he asked.

"Guardians have tried to love before, but few men could handle being with such a powerful witch. Most of them were witches themselves, but once in the presence of real power and sway, they wanted for themselves what they could not have. Here you were raised to hate what I am and when I gave you the power, you couldn't wait to give it back."

"Giving it back has been the most enjoyable time of my life," he said, chuckling as he dragged her naked body onto his. His muscles felt slick and hard and delicious beneath her. She hadn't thought she could make love to him one more time today, but maybe with a few spells for endurance, they'd manage. "I just wish I could help you with your responsibilities. You've been carrying this alone for so long."

She kissed him gently, their tongues twining and caressing, their mouths so in tune, hours could have passed before she finally came up for air. "You were willing to die for me, Brock. For my people. If our plan hadn't worked, you would have had to kill Movert yourself and with your blood oath, you would have died. And no amount of love on my part could have brought you back."

"You don't know that for certain," he said lightly, but Regina knew the truth just as well as he did. When she hugged him so tightly he groaned, he made a concession. "Okay, okay. I did what I knew was right. Truly knew. For the first time in my life. I have no regrets."

"Me, neither," she said.

"So," he said, glancing around the room as if bored. "How long do you think we can hang out here without any witching crises to interrupt us?"

Regina grinned. "Aunt Marion has done a very good job of running things and ensuring our privacy for two days. I'd say twenty-four more hours is a safe bet. She's indulgent, but she hat es responsibility and she has her limits."

"Do you?" he asked, his tone wicked.

She licked her lips. "Have limits? None that I can think of," she said, though a few possibilities skittered through her brain, all having to do with sex with Brock. Even in their former affair, she'd never experienced such utter abandon, such complete and total trust as she did now that they'd committed their hearts. He'd clearly earned his right to push the envelope, if he were so inclined. "What about you?"

With a pleasured moan, he pounded the pillow thickly, then grabbed her by the waist and tugged her against him. "You want me to tell you my love is unlimited, don't you?"

"Not if it's too corny," she said with a laugh, and a twinge of guilt because now that he mentioned it, such a devotional claim might be nice to hear.

"It is too corny," he decided. "But like many corny platitudes, it is also true. I love you, Regina."

"Will you fight at my side?"

"You know I will."

"Will you listen to my problems without trying to fix everything for me?" she asked, knowing this had been the downfall of many relationships before hers, both witch and mundane.

He chuckled. "I can promise to try. But I'm still going to want to help."

"And I'll need your help. The Hunters have scattered, but they're still a threat. Maybe some inside knowledge could help my protection squads be a little more prepared."

He grinned from ear to ear. "If it means spending more time with you as we train them, I have no objections."

Regina drifted back into his arms as Brock reached for the bottled water he'd set on the nightstand. His movements caused the amethyst necklace she'd hung on the lamp to swing and catch the light.

She reached across his body, inflamed when her

nipples scraped across his chest, and retrieved the amulet.

"Thinking you want to forget me again?" he asked. The nearly hidden worry in his voice made her laugh.

"The magic won't work anymore. I'm under a new spell now."

"Really? Which one is that?"

"The one you cast over me. The love spell. I can't resist you."

His chuckle turned into a sensually ravenous growl. "Now that's magic I'll believe in for as long as you'll have me."

Happily Regina knew she'd want him for a very long time.

DISENCHANTED?

Rhonda Nelson

* * *

For my novella mates, Julie Leto and
Mia Zachary. I've enjoyed building this magical
world with you and hope that our readers are every
bit as enchanted with these stories as I have been.

Dear Reader,

I hope *Witchy Business*—and "Disenchanted?" specifically—casts a spell on you! Romance, magic and a happily-ever-after—does it get any better than that? As a big fan of all three, I certainly don't think so. Working with Julie and Mia to build our magical world was a lot of fun. The idea of having a Betty Ford-type clinic for ailing witches and wizards was my brainchild, one I am particularly proud of, and we couldn't think of any better place than Sedona, Arizona, to set the stories. Having been to Red Rock Country many times, I know it's a truly enchanted place. I hope you enjoy your "visit" there.

I love to hear from my readers, so be sure to pop by my Web site, www.ReadRhondaNelson.com. I blog daily about the bizarre happenings that make up my everyday life—and believe me, there are many!

Rhonda Nelson

CHAPTER ONE

"STILL NO CHANGE?"

Refusing to look at his father's impassive face and his mother's ever-hopeful one, Benedict DeWin tightened his fingers on the Montblanc pen he held in his hand and gave his head a small, almost imperceptible shake. It had been the same answer to the same question for the past twenty-odd years. *Any luck with that charm I showed you, Ben? Incantation? Done any magic at all?*

No, no and no, Benedict thought, swallowing a bitter, beleaguered sigh.

And yet Isaac and Gloria DeWin never stopped asking, never stopped hoping that his powers would manifest. Benedict's lips twisted and he barely resisted the urge to slouch in his seat like a sullen teenager who'd been called on the carpet.

Unlike him, his parents—practical royalty amid the wizarding world—couldn't accept that their impressively combined genes had borne a child, let alone their *only* son, who didn't have an iota of magical prowess—an ordinary, in magical terms.

Gallingly his younger sister had inherited it all.

"Mom dropped the S word this morning," Vivi had warned him over breakfast, blithely conjuring the morning paper. She'd added pink highlights to her naturally platinum hair and a small diamond stud winked in her nose. Despite the built-in tension surrounding their situation, Ben adored her. In fact, she was his best friend.

At the time she'd issued the warning, Benedict had dismissed the Sedona threat as a murmur of hot air, but staring at his parents' gravely concerned faces right now, he was beginning to wonder.

Surely not, Benedict mentally scoffed, an unwelcome chill landing in his belly despite the warm fire crackling in the grate of his father's impressively appointed study. Sedona?

Sedona?

He glanced around the room, his gaze instinctively finding the portrait wall, where dozens of powerfully magical ancestors—most impressively, Merlin—stared back at him. Centuries-old heirlooms and relics held places of honor above the mantel and behind unbreakable glass. Armed with protective charms and enchantments, the very room whispered of imposing power, of ancient magic. Curiously he'd always felt a combined mixture of comfort and intimidation upon crossing the threshold. Hours of playing chess with his father inspiring the former, he imagined, and years of falling fathoms below the mark no doubt accounted for the latter.

Despite living in a household with the wizarding community's most elite, most legendary witch and wizard, Benedict never felt like he didn't belong... until he entered this room.

But Sedona? A family history buff, Benedict knew that no DeWin had ever set foot in Sedona—the last-ditch stop for witches and wizards who'd either lost their powers or had never recognized them to begin with—and he felt certain several of his ancestors would spin in their graves were he to actually go. The admittedly beautiful city with its ancient red rock formations and powerful vortexes was a haven for more than the magically disenchanted, but mundanes—ordinaries—flocked to the city as well, drawn by its energy.

The city housed the Registry for the North American region, a building with dusty parchment and scrolls containing the family trees of every wizarding family born in the last ten centuries and all of their pertinent information—powers, when they manifested, etc. It reportedly ran miles beneath the surface, a veritable treasure trove of magical history. In addition to the Registry, the complex also held Magecraft, the Betty Ford equivalent for ailing witches and wizards. It was a joke amid the people of his world and, were his parents to send him there, it would make them a laughingstock. Benedict breathed a small sigh of relief. Nah, he thought again, shaking off his worries. Not Sedona. They couldn't be that desperate.

"Still nothing," his father finally said, shooting a veiled look at his mother, who seemed to strengthen with some sort of hidden resolve. Her clear blue eyes glittered with equal amounts of determination and sadness, and her aging bejeweled hands appeared to tighten in her lap. "That's most unfortunate."

Benedict merely nodded, but didn't speak. Experience had taught him the less he said the better. His father would soon tire of the one-sided conversation and personally, he didn't enjoy this monthly rehashing of his shortcomings. He preferred to discuss the family holdings—impressive before he'd taken the helm of DeWin Diversified Industries, but he'd managed to almost double them, a feat he was particularly proud of. His father was proud of him, too, he knew. Benedict swallowed. Somehow it would have been easier to resent him for these monthly "magical report" meetings if he wasn't.

"The wedding is only two months away," his mother said, her voice smooth and practical as always.

As if he needed reminding, Benedict thought, his jaw inexplicably tightening. He wasn't likely to forget that, despite the fact that it was the twenty-first century, he'd be marrying a woman who'd been chosen for him before she was born—an *arranged* marriage.

In 2007. It boggled the mind.

Even his mind, even though it was a typical occurrence in his community. In order to assure their lines and continued magical successes, many old wizarding families had maintained the archaic custom of betrothing their children. They'd had to. Preservation and all that. Like his own parents, he and Portia Flynn had been promised to one another—firstborn son to firstborn daughter—since before his birth. Vivi, damn her lucky hide, as the second born, was safe.

As for how he felt about it… He'd been too big a disappointment to his parents to heap any more upon them. At twenty-eight he'd never been in love—though he'd experienced many degrees of lust—so he supposed it was best that he didn't know what he'd be missing. This was a business transaction, he knew, and nothing more. Fortunately business he understood. Business he excelled at. It was his thing, his passion, his saving grace and sanity.

Per tradition, he'd met Portia at last season's Enchanted Ball. While pretty, there was something distinctly…chilly about her. Her smile had been calculated—rehearsed, even—and never quite reached her eyes.

Vivi had instantly hated her, of course. "You're an idiot if you let them shackle you to that emotionless block of ice," she'd said and had once again accused him of being a martyr.

He wasn't a martyr, dammit—he was a DeWin, and he'd do what was expected of him. It was the least he could do, considering he'd never lived up to his expected potential.

"It's not the wedding I'm worried about," Isaac said grimly. "It's the Confirmation Ritual that has me most concerned."

No doubt, Benedict thought. The Confirmation Ritual required both the groom and bride to undergo a series of tests, so to speak. They were required to showcase their magical talent—charms, enchantments, spells, transfiguration and potion-making, just to name a few. It was the magical equivalent to a peek under the hood, a test drive to make absolutely certain each family knew exactly what they were getting into. And unlike past events, Vivi wouldn't be able to help him. She couldn't hover in the shadows and perform the necessary incantations and what have you.

He'd be on his own, and powerless.

Despite endless tutors, the fact that Benedict had never so much as levitated a feather had to have his parents more than mildly concerned. The mere thought had his guts twisting. The secret that his family had worked so hard to keep would become public knowledge. He'd become a joke, the idle gossip of cocktail parties and supermarket fodder, a stain upon the DeWin name, and even worse, pitied.

The thought acted like a hot poker applied to his ass and he leaned forward, suddenly desperate to escape the room. A grim shadow had fallen over his shoulders, cloaking him in the sort of knowing dread that made his palms sweat and his face burn. "Well, if we're done here, I've got some reports I need to go over. Business—"

"We're not done," his father said abruptly.

Benedict paused, tension camping in his neck. He leveled a careful gaze at his father. "We're not?"

His mother smiled sadly, making him even more uncomfortable.

And that's when he knew.

Son of a bitch.

"No, we're not, dear," she said.

Isaac cleared his throat. "In light of the Confirmation Ritual and your lack of—" He blushed and looked away. "Well, we think that a quick trip to Sedona is in order."

His father said it quickly and quite matter-of-factly, as if he'd just announced that he was sending Benedict to summer camp as opposed to sentencing him to Humiliation Hell. While the majority of his business acquaintances were outside the wizarding community, he'd lose all credibility with the ones who weren't. Years of hard business decisions and harder work…lost. His very identity gone in the blink of an eye. Even being a DeWin wouldn't save him. Panic and shame twisted his insides into a knot so tight it cut off the breath in his throat. Sweet mother of—

"I have spoken personally with Regina St. Lyon and have made arrangements to secure your anonymity," his dad continued, referencing the Guardian of the Registry. "Discretion is key here, I understand."

His mother's sympathetic gaze softened even more and she leaned forward. "We know this is hard for you, Ben, but not as hard as it will be if you fail at the Confirmation Ritual." She paused. "It's your last hope, you see?"

No, he didn't see. All he saw was another opportunity to fail. To disappoint them.

Because it wasn't going to work.

Nothing ever had and Sedona wasn't going to be any different.

"Vivi will be going along as well," his father continued. "For moral support, of course. She insisted." Isaac frowned slightly, no doubt worried that Vivi would more likely wreak havoc than help. Ben almost smiled. A very true concern. "Also, you'll be bewitched with an Incognito Charm so that you won't be recognized."

Having been touted as the late J.F.K., Jr. of the wizarding world—a flattering but overblown comparison if you asked him—Benedict imagined an Incognito Charm would definitely come in handy. Still…

"As added precaution, you'll be enrolled as Ben Martin as opposed to Benedict DeWin," his father continued. He paused and blew out a careful breath. "We wouldn't ask you to do this if we didn't think it was in your best interests, Ben," Isaac told him, still clearly uncomfortable with this conversation.

"And, of course, you can always refuse," his mother added. "This isn't mandatory." She chewed worriedly on her bottom lip. "But we do think that it's crucial."

Refuse? Benedict thought, smothering a snort. What good could possibly come of refusing? It would only exacerbate an already bad situation. Furthermore, his parents would always wonder if Sedona would have done the trick, turned him into the magical force their genes should have created.

No, as humiliating as it would be, he would go.

Because that was the only way he'd ever put an end to this galling cycle. And then, for better or worse, he'd move ahead with his life.

Whether he'd be married remained to be seen. Once the Flynns realized he couldn't do magic, he seriously doubted they'd want him for a son-in-law, DeWin or not.

One could hope, at any rate.

Benedict swallowed. "How long?"

His mother and father shared a relieved, cautiously hopeful look. "One week."

One week? Benedict barely smothered another laugh. One week to turn him into a magical force to be reckoned with when years of the finest tutors and instructors hadn't been able to awaken even the most basic wizarding traits?

It was almost funny, *almost* being the operative word.

Because he grimly suspected there wouldn't be a single thing the least bit entertaining or laughable about this damned miserable, demeaning trip.

CHAPTER TWO

BRYONY FLYNN, London transplant and head gardener at the Registry, stared at the enchanted fruit and vegetables in her garden and muttered a mutinous stream of obscenities that should have withered every plant in a five-mile radius.

"That bloody bastard," she said through gritted teeth. "This is the *last* straw." Gathering her evidence into the nearest produce basket, Bryony set off at an angry but determined clip toward her cottage. It was times like this when she seriously wished that she could *surface*—merely "surf" in magical slang, though it had nothing to do with riding an ocean wave in her world—but she'd long ago given up hope that she'd ever be able to do anything so powerful. Nope. If she wanted to move from one place to another, she had to walk, drive or ride just like the rest of the mundanes and ordinaries. Instantly appearing where she wanted to be had never worked for her.

And right now where she desperately wanted to be was in Regina's office, her obscene fruit and Richard Hornby—aka the Horn Dog—beside her. So that she could watch Regina fire him. Once and for all.

She clambered into her golf cart and hit the gas. Asshole, Bryony thought. Just because he could perform a few little charms he thought he was the gods' gift to witches. He was the Broomsticks Coach, for pity's sake, she thought, smothering a snort. Surely he could be easily replaced. Granted she'd never been able to make her own broomstick hover more than a couple of feet off the floor, but if push came to shove, she'd volunteer to teach the class herself. Richard, the sexist ass, was a blight and she couldn't wait to be well shod of him.

Still furious, Bryony clipped the curb as she pulled up in front of the Registry's main office. The weeping willow trees she'd planted on either side of the stone entry steps when she'd first arrived some four years ago were flourishing despite the poor soil and dry climate, and fall flowers blossomed against the cool stone walls, adding warmth and color to the interesting landscape. A carpet of lush green grass—the emerald in her crown, so to speak—blanketed the grounds, all the way to the rocky banks of the creek that ran alongside the property. Getting grass to grow here was no small feat and she allowed herself a few seconds to bask in the glow of her accomplishment.

This was home, Bryony thought, perpetually grateful that Regina had ultimately hired her and given her a place to stay. She frowned, grabbed her basket and climbed out of the cart. Going home sure as hell hadn't been an option. Once her initial course through Magecraft had been deemed unsuccessful—which was hardly fair considering she'd improved, dammit—her parents, afraid that her poor magical skills would jeopardize her older sister's impending marriage into the DeWin family, had basically encouraged her to stay in the States...and as far away from them as possible.

Though it stung and she missed the rolling hills of her native home, Sedona and the people here had become her new family. Frankly she felt more welcomed and loved here than she ever had in her parents' house. They'd been too concerned with grooming her older sister, their ticket into wizarding royalty, to be too concerned with her.

Frankly she'd always been an afterthought. She'd gotten Portia's hand-me-down clothes—which had always been a bit too tight—and her parent's leftover attention. Precious little, in truth, but like a hearty dianthus, with just a bit of care, she could bloom whereever she was planted.

Bryony wished she was closer to her sister, but taking a cue from their parents, Portia had always treated her like a second-class citizen. From the time Portia had been little she'd been groomed to be Benedict DeWin's future bride and, were Bryony to be honest, if she knew that gorgeous Hunk-O-Male was going to be hers, she undoubtedly wouldn't want a semi-magicless little sister to potentially ruin her good thing, either.

Her family fell strictly into middle-class territory—marrying a DeWin was the social equivalent of winning the lottery.

Because her family had been so obsessed with Benedict, Bryony had found herself intrigued by him as well. Until she'd moved to the States she'd pored over the society papers and gossip magazines, scouring the pages for snippets of news and grainy photos. It was natural for her to be curious about the man who was unwittingly shaping her life. At least she'd told herself that every time she'd lingered too long over a picture of him.

But then, how could she not?

The man was…

Mercy.

Hair as dark as a raven's wing, eyes that made obsidian look pale. Sharp, chiseled features, a bold nose and bolder brow, and a mouth so finely crafted the simple implication of a smile could send a shiver echoing through her midsection. That half grin held more potency than the fullest version any of the so-called Hollywood stars possessed.

He wasn't just sexy—he was *magnetic.*

What had begun as pure curiosity had blossomed into a rabid fixation she wasn't altogether proud of. Her family wanted Benedict because of his wealth and prestige. Bryony…just wanted Benedict.

Though it was completely unreasonable considering that, a) she'd never met him and b) he was her future brother-in-law, she nevertheless found herself completely infatuated with him, imagining scenarios where he was betrothed to her instead of to her sister. She had the whole Cinderella complex going, which was so far away from cool it was downright pathetic. Bryony could stand being many things—an embarrassment to her family, halfheartedly loved but mostly unnoticed, slightly curvy thanks to an incurable sweet tooth—but *pathetic* was intolerable.

And envious was even worse.

In two short months her sister would be marrying a man that, for whatever reason—mental illness, probably—Bryony *knew* she could love. Beyond odd? Possibly insane, considering she'd never met him?

Yes, to all of the above.

But…she knew him all the same. She knew the

exact slope of his cheek, the precise distance between his brows, the striking shade of his deep, deep eyes. She read mischief and longing—for what, she hadn't discerned exactly—integrity and confidence in those compelling orbs. She knew he had an endearing dimple in his left cheek, one that somehow softened the completely masculine lines of his face. She knew the difference between a genuine smile and one he'd conjured merely out of obligation. She knew that he had a wicked sense of humor and a noble sense of family duty. She knew that, despite coming from a wealthy blue-blooded family, he had an admirable work ethic. Most interestingly, she knew he was lonely. After all, she had enough experience with it to recognize it, didn't she?

Bryony released a small sigh. In the end, what difference did it make? Because the most important thing she knew about Benedict DeWin was that he was marrying her sister. Unrealistic pining was a waste of time and energy. Her gaze fell to the basket of perverted fruit and vegetables in her hands. Better that she spend her time on things she could actually do something about.

Like getting Richard canned.

Purpose restored, she pushed determinedly through the doors and made her way toward Regina's office.

"Whoa, dearie! What's the hurry?" Miss Marion asked her, meeting her just outside Regina's door. Looking cheerful as always, Marion's ancient cat's-eye glasses—bewitched today with silver stars to match her outfit—dangled from a pearl strand around her neck. A permanent fixture at the Registry, no one knew exactly how long Miss Marion had been on staff at Magecraft, but Bryony knew retirement was nowhere in her immediate future.

Despite the fact that she seemed to come off as a bit of a ditz, Bryony had learned long ago that assessment couldn't be further from the truth. A grin tugged at her lips. Miss Marion could throw down when necessary and had done so on her behalf more than once.

"I need to see Regina," Bryony told her, grimly gesturing toward the basket of corrupted fruit and vegetables in her hands.

Miss Marion's gaze dropped to the bundle in Bryony's arms and she let out a little gasp of horror. "Oh, dear. Don't tell me he's struck again?"

"Can you think of anyone else who's perverted enough to do this?"

Marion's lined face puckered into a scowl. "You're right, of course. But Regina isn't here." She winced in regret and a hint of worry clouded her gaze. "Off on Registry business again, I'm afraid."

Again? Bryony wondered, growing slightly concerned. Regina occasionally had to leave the Registry to handle things—the other Guardians were constantly meeting about one thing or another—but it seemed like Regina had spent a great deal of time away from the school lately. Bryony hoped it was nothing serious, but didn't doubt for a minute that Regina was more than capable of dealing with whatever had come up.

Regardless, her being gone certainly put a crimp in Bryony's fire-Horn-Dog plan. She smothered an impotent growl of frustration and muttered a small curse.

"Ah," Marion sighed knowingly. "Third time's the charm, eh? She's supposed to let him go this time, right?"

Bryony nodded and her eyes narrowed marginally. "And I was supposed to get to watch."

"No worries, dear," Marion soothed. "I'm sure Regina will take care of it when she gets back."

"Marion, my English cucumbers look like penises!" Bryony all but wailed, her frustration getting the better of her. She plucked one out of the basket and shook it for emphasis. "They look like they were cross-pollinated by the Jolly Green Giant, for pity's sake." She gestured wildly at the rest of the contents of her basket. "And just look at my pears." She pulled in a calming breath, which in no way made her feel any more relaxed, and swallowed a despondent whimper. "My pears have *nipples,* Marion. *Nipples.*"

"That's most unfortunate," an amused male voice said from directly behind her.

Bryony gasped, then closed her eyes tightly shut, mortification setting in.

Miss Marion chuckled. "Mr. Martin," she enthused, swiftly moving around her. "And I see you've brought your lovely sister with you."

"You must be Miss Marion," Bryony heard the man say, his voice a deep baritone drawl, despite the northeastern accent she detected. It was equally smooth and rough, with just the slightest hint of wickedness thrown in for good measure. For whatever reason, she got the weird impression that she'd heard it before. That she should recognize it.

"I am, indeed," Marion replied. "Regina told me to expect you and I've got everything in order. We don't allow couples to room together here at Magecraft—too many distractions of the romantic variety, we've found—but since you're brother and sister, I've put you in a two-bedroom cottage with a lovely view of the gardens. I hope you don't mind."

Intrigued, Bryony finally turned around.

And felt every bit of the air vanish from her lungs.

It didn't rush out in a *whoosh*, it didn't leak out in a little sigh, it simply…*vanished.*

Dark, almost black eyes and darker hair, six and a half feet of hard, toned, perfectly proportioned, designer groomed male. His lips were currently curled into a wicked smile that made her belly tip in a wild fluttering roll, and a deep dimple—which seemed out of place but curiously fit—cut a small slash into his lean cheek. She had the wild, unreasonable impression that she should know him—that she *did*—but for reasons she couldn't explain, she couldn't place him in past or immediate memory. It was the oddest thing, the strangest sensation. Bryony frowned, studying him.

A petite blonde with pink highlights bustled forward, shooting—Mr. Martin, was it?—an annoyed scowl. "Not at all," she assured Marion. "I'm Vivi Martin," she said, smiling warmly. Her amused gaze dropped to the fruit in Bryony's basket. "Nice fruit," she said. "Though I don't think you're going to find the right kind of market for them around here."

Bryony chuckled, startled out of her momentary haze. "Bryony Flynn," she told her, shifting the basket in order to shake Vivi's hand. "And no doubt you're right about that."

Vivi's eyes narrowed speculatively. "That's a lovely accent."

"I'm from London, but I've been here for about four years."

"Teacher, then?"

"Gardener," Bryony corrected. "And for the record, these racy fruits and vegetables aren't our usual fare. This was the work of a prankster," she said, barely keeping the edge out of her voice.

"Still edible, though, right?" the mystery man asked, plucking one of the pears out of the basket.

Bryony felt her lips twitch and experienced an inappropriate vision of his mouth attached to her own breast as opposed to the fruit. "Right," she returned breathlessly. She frowned once again and gave her head a little shake. "I'm sorry for staring," she apologized. "You just look so familiar."

He casually tossed the pear from one hand to the other and those dark, mesmerizing eyes probed hers. "I have one of those faces."

No, he didn't. He was about as ordinary as the fruit in his hand, but she wasn't going to argue with him. Instead she merely smiled. "Right."

"Well," Marion said, breaking the interesting moment. "Let's get you two settled. You'll actually be next door to Bryony here, so she'll be able to help you if anything comes up."

For whatever reason, the idea simultaneously thrilled and terrified her. Which made absolutely no sense. He wasn't a threat to her—he was a student, obviously. Which, due to their no-fraternizing rule, put him firmly in off-limits territory. As for the thrilled part… Bryony let go of a little sigh. Clearly being celibate for the past year had impacted her more than she'd realized.

"How convenient," Ben said, his voice a smooth purr that sent a tornado of heat swirling through her midsection.

Convenient? Er…she didn't think so.

CHAPTER THREE

"WELL, WELL, WELL," Vivi drawled, dropping into a comfy chair in their well-appointed cottage.

Benedict opened cabinets and checked the contents of the fridge, satisfied when he noted that his favorite brand of beer had been stocked. He pulled one out and nudged the door closed. He hadn't counted on the Registry and Magecraft facilities resembling a five-star resort, but was thankful all the same. Then again, anything other than a resort area would have looked completely out of place. Real estate was prime in downtown Sedona.

To keep unwanted visitors from wandering onto the grounds, the site had been bewitched with a Dementia Charm—as well as many other powerful cloaking spells—which made the trespassers immediately forget why they came there to start with. Instead interlopers developed a craving for enchiladas and salsa rojo and soon found themselves at Brujas, a Tex-Mex restaurant conveniently located right off Highway 89-A.

"Well, well, well…what?" Benedict finally asked, moving to the window to see if he could catch another glimpse of Bryony, the X-rated fruit bearer.

"Looks like we're not the only family with something to hide."

That had to be her cottage, Benedict thought, spying a slightly bigger version of the one they occupied. Flowers, vines, shrubs and ornamental grasses grew in carefully cultivated abandon around her house. Butterflies and pixies fought for prime blooms and a blindingly white unicorn with a silvery mane and tail grazed in her garden, idly nibbling at instantly replenishing ears of corn.

Vivi heaved a long-suffering sigh. "Ben, are you listening to me?"

He frowned and reluctantly turned away from the window. "What?"

She looked at him as though he'd lost his mind. *"Flynn,"* she said significantly.

Ben quirked a brow.

Vivi's eyes widened, presumably at his thickness. *"And she's British."*

He waited, still not following.

She blew out another beleaguered breath. "Just like your future wife, you nimrod! They're obviously related."

Stunned, Benedict felt the room tilt as the impact of what his sister had surmised suddenly slammed into him.

"Sisters would be my guess," she added speculatively, while he continued to reel. "There's a small resemblance there, though frankly I prefer this one to the one you're engaged to. She's…genuine."

Yes, she was, he thought, still thunderstruck. Genuinely beautiful, genuinely curvy, genuinely real in every sense of the word and most troubling of all, genuinely sexy. In fact, though he was no stranger to sexual attraction, he had to admit he'd never felt anything so potent in his life. One look into those lush green eyes—striking when paired with that wild mane of ebony locks—had stirred a curious sense of familiarity and longing so intense he'd narrowly avoided making a fool of himself.

He'd felt his body literally gravitate toward hers, but he had managed to mask the inappropriate behavior by selecting a pear from her basket rather than slipping the pad of his finger across that delectably plump bottom lip. He'd found himself equally intrigued and turned on in a matter of seconds and couldn't decide which initial reaction troubled him most.

Benedict had always prided himself on having good instincts and thoughtful restraint, both of which had served him well when it came to business. He'd learned to listen to his gut, but never give impulse his head. His gut reaction to Bryony Flynn had awakened an immediate caveman instinct to make her his and, had his sister and Miss Marion not been standing in the way, he knew beyond a shadow of a doubt that particular impulse would have had its way. He would have moved into seduction mode so fast she wouldn't have known what hit her.

Gratifyingly, though, he knew she would have liked it.

Because she was every bit as intrigued by him as he'd been by her. Apart from her initially shocked expression—the one that had, for the briefest moment, made him worry that the Incognito Charm hadn't worked—her eyes had dilated with interest, her pulse had fluttered wildly at the base of her throat and she'd moved marginally closer to him as well. In fact, the sexual attraction between the two of them was so strong it was a damned miracle Marion and Vivi hadn't been able to smell it.

But Portia's sister? Surely fate couldn't have delivered such an ironic blow.

Two months before he was scheduled to wed.

It would simply be too cruel.

Benedict turned to Vivi, who'd been scrutinizing him entirely too closely for comfort. "Portia's sister?" he asked skeptically. "That's a stretch, don't you think?"

His sister shook her head. "She has one, doesn't she?"

Benedict paused, searching his memory. Yes, she did. A younger one whom he'd never met. Then again, he'd only met Portia once. If the bride and groom were destined to hate each other, it was better to find it out later rather than sooner. Insurance, he supposed, so that the parties couldn't back out. Ultimately all that mattered was securing the bloodlines—of passing on something greater than oneself—and, barbaric and practical as it was, a couple didn't have to like each other to have sex and produce a child.

He supposed Bryony could be Portia's sister. All evidence seemed to point in that direction and it would be just his luck, wouldn't it?

"She does have a younger sister," Benedict finally confirmed. He dropped heavily into a nearby chair. "I've never met her, of course."

"She wasn't at the Enchanted Ball?"

"No. Not that I recall."

Vivi paused, her clear blue eyes thoughtful. "Seems like she would have been in attendance." She rolled her eyes. "God knows the rest of the Flynn clan was present that night."

A laugh rumbled up Benedict's throat and he nodded, silently admitting the truth of that statement. As though he were a prized stud on the auction block, the Flynns had turned out in force to get a look at their future in-law. Aunts, uncles, cousins, cousins three times removed—they were all there, gawking at him, snickering and nodding as he walked past.

Vivi was right. If Bryony Flynn was related to Portia, she should have been there. Unless they had something to hide.

"I'll check into it," Vivi announced.

"How are you going to do that?"

"Leave it to me," she said enigmatically. "You've got to concentrate on your awakening."

Benedict snorted, opened his beer and took a pull. "You know this is a waste of time."

"No, I don't, and neither do you, for that matter." She paused to look at him. "There's powerful energy here," she said, suddenly serious. "Don't you feel it?"

Benedict nodded. "From the moment I stepped off the plane, Vivi. But that doesn't mean that anything is going to happen."

She shot him a sympathetic but encouraging smile. "Give it a chance."

He released a pent-up breath. "That's why I'm here."

Nevertheless, powerful energy or not, Benedict knew better than to get his hopes up. Would he love to have his awakening? To finally gain his powers?

More than anything.

Being the perpetual disappointment to his family hadn't been easy to live with. Granted he'd tried to make up for his magical shortcomings in other ways, but at the end of the day…he was still flawed. Part of a family that loved him, but one that he never quite felt like he belonged to.

Of course, the only prayer he had of getting out of his upcoming wedding was by *not* receiving his awakening. Even the Flynns, desperate as they were to become part of the DeWin family, couldn't possibly want to contaminate their line with an ordinary.

But if they did, well…he supposed he had no other choice than to honor the arrangement. Letting his parents down again simply wasn't an option.

"She's quite beautiful, isn't she?"

"Who?" he asked, knowing full well who his sister meant.

Vivi's lips quirked. "Don't play coy. I saw the way you looked at her."

"I don't know what you mean."

Vivi threw back her head and laughed. "You were looking at her the same way you were looking at that pear—like you could have devoured her."

Benedict grunted, then took another pull of his beer. "You need to have your eyes checked."

"You need to keep your pecker in check."

He choked, startled. "You've lost your—"

"She's your future sister-in-law, Ben," Vivi said, cutting him off.

"You don't know that."

"But I strongly suspect it. And I'm usually right about such things."

It was true, he knew. Still…

Vivi sighed. "Dipping your wick before you marry the Ice Queen is one thing. Dipping it into her sister is another."

"You're being crass."

"I'm being blunt." She peered closely at him again, making him resist the pressing urge to squirm. "You generally like that about me. In fact, the only time it pisses you off is when I've hit too close to the mark."

"You're a mile off the mark," he lied, wishing it were true.

"Of course, having an affair with her sister would pretty much ensure that you wouldn't have to marry Portia, wouldn't it?"

"Vivi," he said warningly.

His sister shrugged innocently, but thankfully let the subject drop.

Which was just as well because the idea was too damned tempting, on more than one level.

Would that he were a bastard enough to do it.

CHAPTER FOUR

JUST BECAUSE she'd let the subject drop didn't mean that Vivi DeWin wasn't entertaining thoughts of interfering. In fact, that's the reason she'd insisted on coming along on this trip. Benedict might have resigned himself to marrying Portia Flynn, but there was no way in hell Vivi planned to let her brother do it. She mentally rolled her eyes. Someone had to look out for the self-sacrificing moron and, since her parents were laboring under the mistaken impression that marriage to Portia would be good for Benedict— er…*no!*—Vivi had nominated herself to take care of things.

Since Benedict had never been in love, Vivi had planned on conjuring a little potion—he'd thank her later—and hurrying Mother Nature along. Unfair to the object of his manufactured affection? Certainly. But the end would justify the means. Her big brother deserved better than to be married to an emotionless ice cube only interested in furthering her social status. He needed to have an inkling of what he'd be missing if he settled for Portia.

Thankfully, given his instantaneous attraction to Bryony Flynn, Vivi didn't think she was going to have to do anything at all, other than pulling a few little strings to make sure they spent as much time together as possible. Marion, Vivi felt sure, would be willing to help her. A romantic at heart, she'd been an ally up to this point and it was quite clear that she had a soft spot for Bryony Flynn.

Though she'd just met her, Vivi did, too. In fact, she'd instantly liked her. Wit and old soul wisdom sparkled in those pretty green eyes, and empathy and kindness was written in every line of her open face. When angered—like she was this morning—clearly she was a force to be reckoned with.

Which meant, she wouldn't be a pushover.

All in all, if Benedict had been slated to marry Bryony instead of Portia, Vivi more than likely wouldn't have interfered. For whatever reason, she had a feeling about the two of them. And typically her "feelings" were on the mark.

Furthermore, despite the fact that Benedict wasn't holding out hope for his awakening, Vivi had her suspicions about that as well. Her gaze slid to her brother, who was currently skimming through his class schedule. Occasionally he'd roll his eyes or snort, but he was at least making an effort.

According to Marion, typical ordinaries who'd never awakened either had never known love, had denied love, or had abused love. Benedict had certainly never abused love, and he had known love from his family. Vivi would have never considered his always staying one step removed from his emotions as "denying" love, but she supposed when it came right down to it, that's exactly what he'd done. It was all part and parcel of his I'm-not-good-enough-because-I-can't-do-magic attitude.

No matter how many times Vivi had tried to tell him that he was still worthy, she'd known that he'd never really believed her. It broke her heart, because he was more than just her brother—he was a good man.

If Benedict could just learn to accept love—to genuinely welcome it into his heart—then maybe his powers would manifest. Vivi knew he had them—she could feel them herself, hovering just beneath the surface. It was only a matter of fitting the right key into the lock.

And for whatever reason, she got the distinct impression that key belonged to Bryony Flynn.

CHAPTER FIVE

BRYONY PURPOSELY moved to the other side of the garden to avoid peering at Ben Martin's cottage. To her chagrin—and stupidity—in an effort to catch a glimpse of him, she'd been spending a great deal more time outside than what she ordinarily did. And that was saying something, as she was usually outdoors or in her greenhouses from dawn until dusk anyway.

No matter how much she tried to shake the sensation, she couldn't let go of the idea that she knew him. His name, she knew, was on the tip of her tongue. It was frustrating as hell.

Furthermore, her physical reaction to him had been completely beyond the realm of her experience. She'd taken one look at him and every cell in her body had sung with recognition and need. She'd been hit with an almost overwhelming urge to touch him, to slide her finger across his achingly familiar brow, then frame his face and offer her lips up for a kiss. Her nipples had tingled, a tornado of sensation had swirled through her belly and settled in her sex. Longings that had never known the light of day had suddenly rose up in her, manifesting themselves in her dreams.

In short, she was a wreck.

And he'd made her that way with a simple smile.

Were he to ever touch her, no doubt she'd be doomed, Bryony thought, equally hoping and dreading that the thought would come to fruition.

Which was crazy when she knew, as a student, he was totally off-limits.

No guy, even Ben Martin, was worth getting fired for. And she stood a lot more to lose than just her job. She'd lose her home as well. Could she find another job? Another place to live? Certainly. But she didn't want to. She loved it here, Bryony thought, carefully removing a ladybug from her arm. Did she get lonely? Long for a warm body in her bed and a baby in her arms? She frowned. With increasing frequency.

At the moment, though, those things just didn't appear to be in her cards. A firm believer in Fate, Bryony knew when the time was right—when the right guy came along—she'd know. Until then, she had a pretty sweet deal at the Registry and she didn't want to screw it up. Her lips quirked.

Literally.

In the meantime she was simply going to have to get the better of this fixation and, rather than trying to scope out Ben Martin, avoid him like the plague.

"Ah, there you are," Miss Marion called happily. "I thought I'd find you back here."

"Back here" was her personal herb and vegetable garden. To supplement her salary, Regina had allowed Bryony to grow and sell herbs and fresh produce to many of the shops and restaurants in town. Siobhan Silverhawk, who owned and operated Luminous in the beautiful Tlaquepaque Village, was a good customer. Bryony was busy harvesting a few things for her and planned to drop them off after lunch.

She straightened and turned around, surprised to find that Marion wasn't alone, but had Ben Martin and his sister, Vivi, in tow. Her heart skipped a little beat as her gaze tangled with his, and she experienced the same vanishing-breath phenomenon as she had the first time she'd seen him.

That couldn't be good.

"Hi," Bryony said for lack of anything better.

"I was hoping for a favor," Marion said, bustling forward. "How does your schedule look today?"

The same as it always did, Bryony thought, intrigued at Marion's request. "A favor?"

"Yes. Would you mind taking Ben and Vivi here out to the vortex at Bell Rock?" she asked. "Professor Huggins is feeling a bit peaked today."

Bell Rock? Already? He'd only been in courses for a day. Bell Rock and the other vortexes weren't usually incorporated into a student's curriculum until the second week of enrollment. Her confusion must have shown, because Marion suddenly moved to explain.

"Ben here is in a fast track program specifically designed by Regina." She smiled, though it seemed a bit off to Bryony. "He and Vivi are only here for a week, though Vivi seems to be coming along remarkably well from what I hear," she said, shooting Vivi a proud look. "Professor Guerrero was quite impressed with her wand work this morning."

Vivi tweaked a bright pink lock of hair and smiled. "I try," she said, not the least bit modestly.

Smiling exasperatedly, Ben nudged her shoulder with his. "Show-off."

Marion's gaze once more found Bryony's. "What

do you say? Could you take them up? Professor Huggins will owe you one."

She didn't care how many Professor Huggins was going to owe her. This had Bad Idea written all over it. Unfortunately she was an employee and Marion was in charge when Regina was out of pocket. In short, she couldn't refuse, not matter how much she might need to. *Need* being the operative word.

Bryony arranged her face into a facsimile of a grin and hoped it didn't look as forced as it felt. "Certainly," she said, nodding. "I'll need to make a quick stop in town first, though." She gestured to her basket. "Siobhan is expecting these today."

"That'll be fine," Marion said, pleased, her eyes sparkling behind her glasses. "After lunch, then?"

Bryony nodded, purposely looking at Vivi in a vain attempt not to notice her brother. She might as well have been trying to stop her heart from beating. She was hammeringly aware of him, could feel him pinging her like sonar, and every vital organ was affected.

"I'll, uh... I'll pick you up at one," she finally said, trying to pull her shattered thoughts into a semblance of order. Which was damned difficult when she literally felt his gaze trailing over her, lingering along her hips, then belly, breasts and finally, her mouth, which seemed to water and warm for him.

Not unlike other parts of her, farther south.

Ben peered into her basket and frowned. "No more nippled pears?" he asked, smiling.

Bryony felt the tops of her ears and thighs burn. "I have more, but they're evidence."

He quirked a brow? "Evidence?"

Bryony chewed the inside of her cheek. "It's a fellow staff member's idea of a joke. It was funny the first time. After the fifth, it got old."

Ben chuckled, the sound soft and sexy against her ears. It was the sort of laugh one would share in bed. "I can see where that could happen." He paused. "It was still good, though," he said, that dark gaze sucking hers in once more. "Quite juicy."

Was she the only one who heard the innuendo in his voice? Bryony wondered, barely resisting the urge to fan herself. She cast a glance between Vivi and Marion, both of whom wore placid expressions, though she thought she detected the slightest quiver on Vivi's lips.

Bryony mentally whistled, dismissing it as wishful thinking. Evidently she was the only one who heard anything remotely sexual in his smooth voice. Sweet Lord. What was she going to do? This was just terrible. Why did she always lust and long for unavailable, unattainable men? Benedict DeWin, her sister's fiancé, and now Ben Martin, out-of-reach student.

Who was only here for a week. To her knowledge, Regina had never fast-tracked a student before. What was so special about Ben Martin that he was getting preferential treatment? She filed the question away and made a mental note to press Marion about it later. There was a story there and she wanted to hear it.

"I'm glad that you enjoyed it," Bryony finally said.

Marion beamed at Bryony. "She has quite the touch when it comes to growing things," the older woman enthused proudly. "You should have seen this place before she got here. Oh, we could grow the usual stuff, but nothing like what Bryony makes bloom." She glanced around the backyard, gesturing to the weeping cherry tree currently dressed out in her finest blooms. "Well, who else could make a cherry tree blossom in the fall?" she asked, laughing softly. "And the grass. Now that's quite an accomplishment, particularly given where we are."

Vivi nodded. "It's impressive. Have you always been interested in horticulture?"

"For as long as I can remember," Bryony admitted with a soft sigh. She smiled, remembering. "Mom couldn't keep me out of the dirt."

And fortunately, she hadn't tried that often. As long as Bryony was outside and out of her mother's hair, Lucina Flynn hadn't cared what Bryony did. In retrospect, it had been a blessing. She loved gathering seeds, then planting them and watching things grow. More than anything, though, Bryony appreciated the significance of the earth and all she bore. Mother Nature fed the world, and everything was designed so purposefully and perfectly.

"Are your parents still in the U.K., then?"

"Yes. Yorkshire, specifically."

Vivi smiled as a turquoise pixie alighted on her shoulder and tugged at her pink hair. "Any siblings?"

"Just a sister."

"Sometimes I wish I'd had a sister," Vivi said, shooting a comically dark look at her brother. "Does she share your love of gardening?"

Bryony couldn't smother a laugh. "Er...no. Portia's more into manicures than manure."

Vivi suddenly lost her balance and fell against her brother's shoulder, causing the pixie to fly off with a high-pitched shriek of outrage.

Ben grunted and righted her. "Are you all right?" he asked, his voice oddly strangled. Honestly, he looked like he wanted to strangle *her*.

Vivi cleared her throat and nodded. "The sun was in my eyes," she mumbled, a flimsy excuse even to Bryony.

She studied the pair, aware of a curious undercurrent suddenly swirling around them. "Well," she said, deciding it was time to wrap this up. "If you'll excuse me I need to get back to work."

"Sure," he said, steering his sister toward their cottage. He shot Bryony a smile, causing her foolish heart to jump into an irregular rhythm. "I'll look forward to it."

And God help her, against her better judgment and ordinarily good sense, she did, too.

"You look funny, dear," Marion commented, an odd sparkle in her eye. "Are you all right?"

"Fine," Bryony lied. "Just fine."

CHAPTER SIX

AFTER ENDURING Vivi's I-told-you-so's for the past hour, Benedict couldn't have been happier than when Bryony finally pulled up and drove them into town. Tlaquepaque Village was a beautiful arts and crafts area, which had been authentically crafted after a true Mexican village. Beautiful tiles, fountains and grottos, cobbled streets, vine-covered stucco walls and soaring, twisted sycamore trees, intricate wrought-iron work and lovely arches created a unique hideaway for local artists and sculptors.

Benedict considered himself well-traveled, but had to admit he'd never seen anything so charming. Nestled against the banks of the Oak River, the village name translated literally to "the best of everything." Benedict certainly couldn't argue with that.

Vivi, of course, was instantly enchanted. "I'm not going to a damned vortex when I can stay here and shop," she muttered under her breath, careful that she wouldn't be overheard.

"Yes, you are," Benedict snarled back through a smile, as they meandered through Luminous. As much as he would love to be alone with Bryony, he knew— particularly now that they'd confirmed that she was Portia's sister—he couldn't trust himself.

The short drive down to the village had been bad enough. Bryony drove a small SUV with a sunroof, which she'd conveniently opened, he supposed, to torture him. He'd had to watch that long, ebony hair whip around her head, clinging to her mouth and occasionally a single lock would curl around the soft curve of her breast. Thanks to the idiot who'd charmed her fruit, Benedict couldn't look at her breasts without comparing them to those ripe, juicy pears.

To make matters worse, her particular scent seemed to have invaded his senses in such close proximity. She'd smelled like sunshine, freshly mowed grass, clean rain and lavender.

In a word—mesmerizing.

He'd caught her shooting him little puzzling glances during the short ride and he'd found himself alternately flattered and worried. If this damned Incognito Charm failed, he was doomed. Vivi, damn her hide, had scurried into the backseat before he could, thereby forcing him to sit next to Bryony. Honestly, despite Vivi's whole dipping-his-wick speech, Benedict had gotten the distinct impression that she'd purposely forced their proximity. And now she wanted to bail on the vortex outing?

He didn't think so.

"I'm not altogether sure what your game is, Vivi, but you're here to help me." He pinned her with his gaze. "You're not helping me," he said through gritted teeth.

Vivi winced and patted his cheek. "Now that's where you're wrong." She suddenly turned to Bryony. "Look, do you mind if I skip the vortex and stay here?" she asked, putting on her best hopeful face.

Bryony frowned. "I don't think—"

But before she could finish the sentence, his sister muttered a little incantation and Bryony's face wreathed into a smile.

"—that would be a problem," she finished. She blinked, clearly surprised that those words had come out of her mouth, but ultimately she didn't question them.

Witch, Benedict thought, ready to throttle his sister as, smiling, she twinkled her fingers at him and walked away. "Hit me on my cell when you're on your way back," she called.

Bryony watched Vivi walk away, still evidently bemused by the charm she'd just received. She turned and looked at Benedict. "Well," she said, letting go of an endearingly nervous little sigh. "Are you ready?"

He suspected not, but nodded anyway. "Sure." He followed her back out to the car, making idle chitchat along the way.

Benedict slid into the passenger seat and donned his sunglasses. "Where are we going again?"

Bryony pointed to one of the huge red rocks that thrust toward a beautiful cobalt sky. "Bell Rock, so named because…"

He grinned at her. "Because it looks like a bell?"

She returned his smile and a bit of the tension that had been dogging them lifted. "Right."

"So what's the significance of Bell Rock?"

"It's one of the most powerful vortexes in the area. You don't just feel it—you can see it."

Benedict frowned. "What do you mean?"

"You'll see," she said enigmatically, a soft smile turning her lush lips. She wheeled the SUV into an unpaved lot, then shifted into Park. "It's a short hike," she said, climbing from her car. She snagged a couple of bottles of water from a cooler in the back and handed one to him. Benedict murmured his thanks and set off behind her.

"Do you feel it?" she asked over her shoulder, leading him onto a worn trail.

Actually…he did. He'd felt the energy from the instant they'd arrived in the area, but right now… Right now the hairs on his arms were standing on end and he felt lighter on his feet, yet firmly grounded to the earth. It was odd, to say the least.

"I do," Benedict admitted, feeling his fingers tingle.

Bryony's lips slid into an answering smile as she made her way farther up the side. "My skin always prickles when I come here." She pointed to a nearby juniper tree. "See how twisted the branches are? The energy here is so strong it makes them grow like that. They respond physically, growing in an axial twist. The lines of growth follow a slow helical spiral along the length of the branch." A delighted grin tugged at the corner of her mouth. "Pretty cool, eh?"

Benedict studied the branches and nodded, impressed. "Yeah, it is. Do you come here often?"

Bryony paused, fingering a leaf. "I used to," she said, a faraway look in her clear green gaze. "When I first came out here, I would visit the vortexes every day."

"They made you feel that good?"

A sad smile shaped her lips. "Hoping for a miracle, more like."

"Ah," Benedict sighed, inclining his head. Another piece of the puzzle. From the sounds of things, that miracle had never happened. Why stay, then? Benedict wondered. Why hadn't she gone home?

"Anyway," she said, releasing a long breath. "They have helped. Though I've never had my awakening, I can tell that my gift is stronger than it was, and getting stronger every day."

At least she had that, Benedict thought, slightly jealous. He'd never felt anything remotely resembling what he'd been told his awakening would be like. He'd never felt the room spin, or an electrical current run the length of his body and settle in his fingers. He'd never felt so energized that every muscle in his body had gone rigid with power.

Could he feel the power of the vortex? Certainly. And the closer they got, the more intense the sensation became. But he wasn't holding out hope that a quick trip to Bell Rock was going to make him the wizard he'd been born to be.

Other than a single woman surrounded by various crystals—quartz, in particular—the area was deserted. Bryony wandered over to what he assumed was her favorite spot.

"What are we supposed to do now?" Benedict asked, joining her. She'd closed her eyes and a soft smile played over her lips. The ends of her hair swirled gently around her head, not from the wind, but from the energy. He could literally feel the hairs on his arms swaying. His belly gave a little jolt of surprise as a bubble of…something whirled through him.

"Now we wait," she said, sighing as the energy moved into her. "Let it come. Think about a tornado," Bryony told him. "What does it do?"

"Destroys trailer parks."

Eyes still closed, a startled chuckle broke up in her throat, causing him to smile as well. "That's not exactly the visual I was looking for. But, since we're there, *how* does it destroy trailer parks?"

"Do you want a technical answer?" he asked.

"Never mind," Bryony said, feigning irritation. "The energy from the wind acts like a magnet, pulling things in. The funnel becomes a vacuum cleaner, sucking things up, right?"

"Well, I'm not a meteorologist, but that sounds pretty accurate."

Another chuckle broke up in her throat. "Has anyone ever told you that you're exasperating?"

"No, but Vivi has told me that I'm a pain in the ass."

Bryony chuckled. "At the moment, I would have to agree with that assessment."

"You're my teacher. You're not supposed to insult me."

"Anyway." Bryony sighed heavily, clearly ready to continue her lesson. "The vortex acts in much the same way. The energy reacts with your own internal power source."

"What if you don't have one?" Benedict asked, not to be difficult, but out of true concern. He couldn't help but wonder, after all.

"Everybody has one," Bryony told him, her voice gentle with understanding. "Even mundanes have one. It's just a matter of unblocking negative energy and re-placing it and recharging it with good energy."

"Do you believe it works?"

"I know that it works. Now stop talking and *feel*. Let the energy move through you."

Benedict sucked in a deep breath, then released it

through his nose and closed his eyes. Every once in a while he could feel Bryony's hair whip against his sleeve and that scent—*her scent*—seemed to be magnified here. It circled his senses, slowly drugging him.

Though he knew he shouldn't, he opened his eyes, aware of more than one kind of energy working its way through him. Could he feel the power of the vortex? More than he would have imagined. The arches of his feet prickled and the sensation moved upward, encircling his spine.

Unfortunately that power was aiding and abetting another power—one of the sexual variety.

Though it was more than likely wishful thinking on his part, Bryony seemed to be leaning closer to him. Her eyes were still closed, long lashes painting crescent shadows on her creamy cheeks, but her mouth was slightly parted and her bottom lip glistened, evidence that she'd recently wet them.

With her tongue.

Another surge of energy hit, making his palms itch and his dick strain hard against his zipper. Portia's sister, his mind kept repeating. Bad, bad, bad. He should step away, put as much distance between them as he could. Kissing her—regardless of how much he wanted to—spelled doom in the worst kind of way. He knew it. Knew it with every fiber of his being and yet…at this precise moment, he didn't care.

Which was odd in and of itself, because he'd never been ambivalent about anything in his entire life. If anything, he'd always cared too much about doing the right thing. If he didn't know any better, he'd be convinced he was under a spell.

And he was, he suddenly realized—hers.

Bryony chose that precise moment to open her eyes. Eyes so clear and green they resembled a flawless cabochan emerald he'd once seen. Her gaze dropped to his lips, then bumped up to his once more. Desire and regret clouded her gaze and she let go of a little whimper that strongly mirrored his own desperate longing and good intentions gone bad.

"Mr. Martin," she said haltingly.

He sidled closer to her, slipped his knuckles down the smooth curve of her cheek, sending another powerful jolt of energy through him. She gasped and her eyes widened, telling him that she'd felt it, too. "Call me Ben," he said, putting his lips ever closer to hers.

"What are you doing, Ben?" she asked, her breath whispering over his mouth.

"Thinking about kissing you."

Though she clearly had reservations of her own, her gaze dropped to his lips again and lingered. "Are you usually so ruminative?"

Ben chuckled. "Only when I'm trying to be good."

"Kissing me would be bad?"

"No," he said, laughing softly. "Kissing you is going to be magic. It's the consequences I'm concerned about."

She made a moue of understanding. "Is going to be?" she asked. "What does that mean?"

"That means I've weighed the options and decided the risk is worth the reward," he said, his voice a bit rusty to his own ears. He bent his head and whispered a soft kiss over her lips, just a sampling before he laid full siege. He was giving her an out, should she so wish to take it.

Bryony gave a little sigh of supplication, then pushed her hands into his hair and pressed her body against his. "It better be," she said grimly, before she pressed her lips to his.

Benedict wrapped his arms around her, aligning her small curvy body against his and felt every bit of breath leave his lungs as a burst of energy suddenly flared inside him. He felt his hair stand on end, his knees quake and his insides vibrate from a force he had absolutely no experience with.

Bryony groaned into his mouth, leaning even closer to him—practically hanging on to him—and deepened the kiss. Her ebony locks lashed his face and he cupped the back of her head, drawing her more closely to him. Her sweet tongue darted in and out of his mouth, that plump bottom lip gliding purposely across his. He could feel little pebbles and debris bouncing off his calves, but the puzzling thought was no sooner borne than abandoned as Bryony's flavor exploded on his tongue.

She tasted like maple syrup and mint gum, like nights at home and hot sex. She tasted better than anything he'd ever had in his life, Benedict realized.

She tasted like...forever.

Which was crazy considering he'd just met her. But he couldn't shake the sensation that she should be his—that she belonged to him. A Neanderthal-like longing rose up in his chest and he was hit with the ridiculous but pressing urge to haul her off to the nearest cave.

Breathing hard, her pretty eyes dilated and lips plump from their kiss, Bryony finally drew back. A small smile trembled across her lips. "It was," she said.

Benedict blinked, confused. "Was what?"

"Worth it," she told him. "Come on." She threaded her fingers through his and squeezed. "We've got to get back."

Right, Benedict thought. Because the sooner they got back to the cottage, the sooner he could have her on her back. Reckless? Inconsiderate? Foolhardy? Just plain stupid?

Yes, to all the above.

But like he'd told her, the risk was worth the reward.

CHAPTER SEVEN

VIVI HAD PICKED up a book on Sedona Schnebly, a member of one of the first homesteading families in the area, as well as the town's namesake, and was pretending to read it while Benedict finished his homework. He seemed preoccupied and he glanced at the clock every few minutes. She knew why, of course.

He was having dinner with Bryony.

Vivi squelched a pleased smile and idly flipped another page, the chakra bracelet she'd bought in town sparkling on her wrist. Leaving them alone together had clearly been the right call. After all, time was of the essence here.

Naturally Vivi had pressed Benedict about what had happened the minute they were once again alone and, though he wouldn't give her any details, he did confirm that he'd kissed Bryony. Vivi smothered a snort. Like she'd needed that confirmation. Bryony's lipstick had vanished and Ben's mouth bore a manufactured sparkle that wasn't exactly masculine.

Furthermore, Vivi had watched Ben watch Bryony and that had been the most telling thing of all. He didn't just look at her—he didn't seem to be able to *not* look at her. This went well beyond mere intrigue. It was genuine interest exacerbated by something innate and powerful. Yin and yang and the whole shebang. The idea warmed her heart in a way that nothing else could. Her brother deserved this happiness, deserved to love and be loved.

In truth, Vivi firmly believed that if he hadn't fallen already, Benedict would be head over heels in love by the end of the week.

And there was no way in hell he'd willingly marry Portia if he was in love with her sister, family duty or not.

She blithely turned another page and smiled. Things were turning out rather nicely, if she did say so herself.

SHE'D KISSED a student.

Bryony fastened the purple quartz pendant around her neck, then nervously smoothed a nonexistent wrinkle out of her dress.

And now, rather than realizing her mistake and taking the prudent path—one that would keep her away from him—she'd agreed to have dinner with him. Her lips twisted.

Obviously that trip to the Bell Rock vortex this afternoon had sucked the brain right out of her head.

All joking aside, though she'd been to Bell Rock dozens of times over the years, she'd never felt the sort of energy she had felt today with Benedict at her side. When they'd kissed, she'd felt the bottoms of her feet gravitate slightly off the ground. At first, she'd merely deemed it fanciful thinking, but there'd been nothing fanciful about the successful augmentation spell she'd used on her tomatoes this afternoon.

She was getting stronger.

And for whatever reason, she believed that Ben Martin had helped her.

Bryony didn't make a habit of lying to herself, so she hadn't even tried to pretend that she was going to draw a halt to their budding relationship. Something about Ben Martin tripped every single one of her triggers. That nagging sense that she knew him kept bugging her, but it was more than that.

Looking at him made her chest ache. Watching his mouth move as his lips shaped words was the most erotically mesmerizing thing she'd ever seen. Today on the drive back from Bell Rock, she'd become fixated on his hands. He had strong hands, with blunt tipped fingers. Hands that knew how to kick ass and love a woman. They were sensual and competent and the idea of him putting those hands on her had made her womb clench with an achy kind of heat she'd never experienced before.

Bryony wasn't a virgin. She'd had a few lovers over the years—only one since moving to the States—but no one had ever made her feel quite like Ben Martin did. Ben affected her on a cellular level. She could feel him beneath her skin. Wanted him with an intensity she'd never experienced before. The sexual attraction combined with this hauntingly familiar sense of knowing him made for a cocktail of longing she couldn't begin to understand.

Ultimately it didn't matter.

If there was ever a time for her to dip her toe into the Naughty Pond, it was now, while Regina was still out of town. A quick conversation with Marion had confirmed that her boss wouldn't be returning to the Registry for several more days. Bryony couldn't help but be greedily thankful for her own good fortune.

Tonight she and Ben were going to dinner—a nice

little place located in the Tlaquepaque Village that was known for its dark ale and ribs. Frankly they could have been going to a fast food restaurant and she would have been just as excited. She just wanted to be with him.

Also, in another stroke of luck, Professor Huggins was still under the weather and not expecting a quick recovery, so Marion had asked Bryony to accompany Ben to the other remaining school-authorized vortexes. She'd readily agreed, pathetically grateful for the time she knew she'd get to spend with him. Again, for reasons she couldn't explain, she felt like an alarm clock was set on their relationship, creating a pressing sense of urgency. She wanted to breathe the same air as him as much as she could. Crazy? Definitely. But nothing about the past couple of days had been normal, anyway, right?

And come Friday, it would all be over with anyway. He would go back to… Bryony stilled, realized that she didn't know where he'd go back to.

A knock sounded at her door. Releasing a quick breath, she walked over and let him in.

"Where are you from?" she asked.

Ben blinked. "I'm sorry?"

"Where are you from? It just occurred to me that this is something I should know, considering."

A slow smile kicked up the corners of his lips and he sidled closer. "Considering what?"

"The improper nature of our relationship. If I'm going to get canned for fraternizing with a student, then I at least want to know from where that student hails."

Ben drew back, a line emerging between his brows. "Get canned? What are you talking about?"

"It's against school policy for staffers to become romantically involved with students," Bryony told him. She offered a smile. "But since my boss is out of pocket this week, I've—" She paused, purposely looking speculative. "What was it you said? Decided the risk was worth the reward."

He continued to frown. "Are you sure you want to—"

Bryony silenced him with a kiss, giving him her unspoken answer. When she drew back, he was grinning, looking completely pleased with himself.

"You like me," he said, eyes sparkling with wicked mischief.

"Yeah, well, you like me, too, so we're square." She laced her fingers through his and pulled him toward the door. "Come on," she said. "We've got reservations, remember?"

Ten minutes later they were seated on a cool stone balcony with an open fireplace. The sun was slipping slowly onto the horizon, painting the landscape—and the rocks, specifically—in a bright golden glow.

Looking relaxed and elegant in a pair of khaki pants and navy-blue shirt, Ben leaned back in his seat and let go an appreciative sigh. "I'll bet you don't get tired of looking at that."

Bryony sipped her ale. "No, I never do. Not to say that I don't love Yorkshire—I do. But it's different here. I can breathe better, if that makes sense."

A waitress brought the wine Ben had selected, then took their order. When she moved away, Ben caught her gaze once more. "Don't you ever miss your family?"

How much to tell? Bryony wondered, compelled to

bare her soul when any other time she knew she would have simply lied, said what was expected of her. Then again, what was the point? Who was he going to tell?

She toyed with her napkin, darted a look at him from beneath her lashes. "Truthfully, no."

Ben's eyes widened and he smiled. "Honesty," he drawled. "I like it."

"It's not that I don't care about them," Bryony said. "It's just—" She let go of a breath. "My older sister is marrying into a powerful family and my mother and father have always put her needs before mine." She took a drink of wine. "I'm an ordinary, an embarrassment. In fact, they've pretty much advised that I stay in the States until after my sister is wed. I suppose they're worried about his family backing out due to my inabilities."

Benedict swallowed, seemingly unsure of what to say. "That sucks."

"Yeah, it does. But it's not a hardship. I don't want to go back. I prefer being here. I'm applying for citizenship and I'm staying in the States." A thought struck. "You never told me where you're from," she admonished.

Ben feigned innocence. "Did you ask?"

Bryony chewed the inside of her cheek. "You know I did, you great fraud. Tit for tat. Time for you to do a bit of sharing. Where are you from? What do you do? Apart from Vivi, what other family do you have?"

A soft chuckle rumbled in his throat and firelight painted golden light over his dark hair, making him look lethally sexy. Those dark eyes tangled with hers. "Don't want to know much, do you?"

"Just the facts," she quipped.

"I'm from upstate New York," he said. "My family has property there. I'm CEO of our family holdings and I dabble in a little bit of investment banking. Apart from Vivi—the perpetual bane of my existence," he teased, "I have a mother and a father who are far too interfering in my personal life, but who want the best for me all the same." He paused, took a sip of wine. "We don't always agree about what's best for me."

Bryony winced. "I can see where that would be a problem."

"Yeah, well. When you've been a disappointment to them your entire life, the guilt generally propels you to go along with whatever they say."

Her heart ached at the resignation she heard in his tone. "Ben," she said, his name an entreaty. "They can't possibly want that from you."

He smiled sadly and cocked his head. "That's what makes it so easy to do it."

"What makes you so sure you're a disappointment?"

"I'm here, aren't I?"

"Just because you're an ordinary doesn't mean that you're a disappointment. And for what it's worth, I think you deserve better."

He stilled, considering her. Those dark as sin eyes caught and held hers. "For what it's worth, I think you do, too."

The compliment left his lips and settled warmly around her heart. "Vivi obviously worships the ground you walk on, otherwise she wouldn't be here when it's painfully obvious that she doesn't need to be."

Ben chuckled. "What tipped you off?"

She settled against the back of her chair. "That little

charm this afternoon. After my head cleared, it became quite clear what she'd done. Imp." Bryony laughed. "Does she always try this hard to play matchmaker."

"She's *never* tried to play matchmaker."

Bryony nodded succinctly, disproportionately pleased. "Then I'll be flattered rather than pissed." She paused. "Did the trip to Bell Rock help any?" she asked.

"Something happened," Ben told her. He paused while the waitress deposited their food. "But I'm not sure how much of it was vortex energy or our kiss." He lingered over the word, making it as hot and intense as the actual act had been.

She was wondering if it was a combination of both and after a moment said as much. "I successfully performed a spell this afternoon that I've tried countless times. I don't know what happened, but I feel stronger."

Ben smiled at her, seemingly genuinely pleased. "So you think me kissing you helped?"

"It's possible," Bryony admitted, smiling. She knew exactly where he was going with this line of questioning.

"Then you can count on me to continue to *help* you the rest of the time I'm here."

"Don't put yourself out," Bryony said, her voice droll with humor.

"Marion mentioned that you'd be taking me to the other vortexes as well, so I should have ample opportunity to help you," he continued to needle.

"Yeah, well. Maybe I'll be able to help you as well."

Ben shrugged magnanimously, his dark eyes glimmering with wicked humor. "Knock yourself out, baby. Feel free to help the hell out of me."

Mercy, Bryony thought, her toes curling in her shoes. Now there was a tempting thought. Her. Helping herself. To him. Until her eyes rolled back in her head.

Heaven help her, she was in trouble.

CHAPTER EIGHT

"WHAT ARE YOU GOING to do?"

Benedict looked up from yet another roll of parchment and gazed innocently at his sister. Playing dumb would only stall her for so long, but it was better than the alternative, which was having this conversation right now.

He knew what he had to do…he just hadn't figured out a way to do it yet.

And time was running short. In fact, he was leaving Sedona tomorrow afternoon, and the idea of walking away from Bryony had become more and more distasteful. In fact, he wasn't altogether certain he could do it.

When he wasn't in class, he was with her. Yesterday they'd visited another vortex, this one out by the airport, and the same thrilling sensation had taken hold of them again, this time even more powerful than the first.

Though he hadn't experienced a true awakening, Benedict was beginning to feel what had to be his magic hovering just beneath the surface. The increased energy flowing through his veins made his fingers itch to pick up a wand. He hadn't, of course, more out of fear of disappointment than anything else. But he knew it was only a matter of time. Were he to stay here—with her—Benedict fully believed that his powers would finally manifest.

Something about this place and her, specifically, made him feel more alive, more in touch with who he was meant to be than anything ever had.

"Benedict, stop ignoring me," Vivi said, unconcernedly filing her nails. "You know what I'm talking about."

He did, dammit. Marrying Portia when he'd become so emotionally invested in her sister was simply out of the question. And "emotionally invested" didn't begin to cover it. He grimly suspected he was falling in love with her, but reason told him that it couldn't be the case. It was too soon. He'd only just met her. And yet… Benedict felt like he'd known her forever, that a part of him had known a part of her…always.

And when he was with her, he lost all track of time. They laughed and talked and kissed, shared secrets and divulged dreams. He'd almost spent the night with her last night, but something had held him back. Benedict imagined it was the truth. He couldn't make love to her until he'd told her who he was. In retrospect he should have told her who he was from the very beginning, from that first kiss, so that she could walk away if she'd wanted to. But he'd been a selfish bastard and now—Well, now he was merely a cowardly one.

Vivi heaved a dramatic sigh, signaling that she'd completely run out of patience. "When are you going to call Mom and Dad?"

"Tomorrow," Benedict lied. Actually, that was a conversation that needed to be handled in person, not over the phone.

"You're pathetic," she scoffed. "You know I can tell when you're lying to me."

"Drop it, Vivi," Benedict finally told her. "I'm going to take care of it. Your nagging doesn't make it any easier."

"I should think you'd be happy. Instead of marrying someone you don't even particularly like, you can marry someone you love. The Flynns will be happy enough, so long as they become part of our family. It's a win-win situation."

His lips quirked sardonically. "Except for Portia, whom I don't imagine will be happy with the new status quo."

"She'll recover," Vivi said flatly. "Bryony's the one who matters."

"I know that, dammit," Benedict snapped. "Don't you think I know that?"

Vivi paused, studying him. Then her eyes rounded. "Oh, my God! You haven't told her who you really are yet, have you?"

"It hasn't come up yet, no," he admitted.

"You moron!" she shouted, outraged. "Have you completely lost your mind? You've spent every evening with her this week. You've had ample opportunity to tell her and yet—" Her mouth dropped open again, as another thought suddenly occurred to her and she sprang from her chair. "You haven't slept with her yet, have you? Because as a woman, I can tell you, you will have royally—and I mean *royally*—screwed up."

"Not that it's any of your business, but no," Benedict told her. "Jeez, give me some credit. I care about her, okay?"

"Benedict, you have got to tell her," she said gravely. "Tonight."

"I'm going to."

"You have to."

"I am," he insisted, exasperated, more at himself than at her for pressing.

Tonight he and Bryony were heading out to Cathedral Rock, the last of the vortexes he would visit. Bryony had suggested going in the evening, when fewer people were around so that they could fully absorb the energy without any interference. She would need more intensive *help*, she'd told him, alluding to the fact that she wanted to take their relationship to the next level. He did, too, but he couldn't until he leveled with her and when he did so he was afraid he'd lose her forever.

No matter which way he tried to spin this, in essence, he'd still lied to her. Simply coming clean might not be good enough. One could hope at any rate, Benedict thought, releasing a heavy sigh.

The alternative was unthinkable.

RATHER THAN FOCUSING on the fact that Ben was scheduled to go home tomorrow, Bryony had decided to concentrate on the positive.

Like tonight.

Despite the fact that Horn Dog had been doing what could only be described as spying on her and Ben, Bryony hadn't let that keep her from spending time with him. She'd deal with the consequences later, she'd decided. In for a penny, in for a pound. She might as well enjoy the time she had left with him, little as it was.

For whatever reason, Bryony knew Ben had been holding back on her—why, she couldn't imagine, because the one thing she was absolutely certain of was how much he wanted her. She could feel it every time he kissed her, every time his hand slipped up and cupped her cheek. It was more than need, though that was certainly fabulous, but something so foreign to her it had taken her a little while to place it.

Affection.

He truly cared for her.

The idea made a lump of emotion well in her throat. She knew that Miss Marion was her friend, that Regina had a lot of respect for her. But Ben Martin... Well, if she didn't know any better, she'd think that he loved her.

That's what it felt like, at any rate. Every time he threaded his fingers through hers, every time he smiled at her. Every time he touched her. It was a different kind of energy, of feeling, and like a rose coming off a weeklong drought, she drank up every bit of his attention. And with every passing moment spent in his company, she could feel herself growing stronger as a witch. While her powers hadn't fully emerged, she knew they were there, waiting to burst free.

Ben Martin, for whatever reason, was a big part of that.

Bryony loaded the picnic basket she'd prepared for their dinner and enough pillows and blankets for a comfy seduction into the back of her car, then drove the short distance over to Ben's cabin. Vivi, looking unusually pensive, was sitting on the porch charming fireflies when Bryony pulled up.

"Is everything all right?" Bryony asked.

"Sure. I'm just moping." She frowned. "You and Ben are having all the fun and I'm stuck here alone."

True, Bryony knew, but that wasn't really what was bothering her. She'd improvised well, though, so Bryony played along. "Horn Dog is alone," she joked. "I could hook you up."

Vivi's lips curled into a distasteful grimace. "There's a reason Horn Dog is alone, not the least of which is why he has that horrible nickname." She shuddered delicately. "Thanks, but no."

"Is Ben ready?"

"He was finishing up an essay for Potions," Vivi told her, jerking her head toward the door. "Go on in. I'm sure he'll be ready in a minute."

Smiling, Ben stepped out onto the porch and pressed a gentle kiss to Bryony's temple. Warm shivers eddied over her. "No need. I'm ready now." He glanced at his sister. "Try to behave."

"You, too," Vivi said ominously.

Intrigued by the comment, but too happy to ultimately care, Bryony laced her fingers through his and tugged Ben toward the car.

This was their last night together…and she was going to give him an evening neither one of them would ever forget.

VIVI WAITED until Bryony and Ben pulled out of the driveway before calmly snagging her cell phone from the clip at her waist. Just because Ben wasn't ready to tell his parents about Bryony didn't mean that it wasn't time to let them know. Granted, she should probably let him do it himself, but…

But he didn't seem inclined to do that as swiftly as

she thought he needed to. Naturally she'd decided to interfere. Again. And he'd thank her later.

She keyed in her parents' number and waited for her mother to pick up. Her father considered the phone a nuisance and rarely answered it.

"Hello."

"Mom, it's Vivi."

"I know who you are, dear," came her mother's smooth voice. "Is everything all right?" She gasped. "Has Benedict had his awakening?"

"No," Vivi told her. "It's something better."

"Better?"

Vivi released a pent-up breath. "He's in love."

Her mother, a romantic at heart, let out a little shriek of happiness. "Oh, that's fabulous! Just fabulous! Our Ben, in love. Why I don't know when we've had such good news. I—"

Vivi waited for her mother to catch up.

She stopped short, then, "Oh, dear. He's in love," she said, the enthusiasm leaking out of her voice.

"That's right. Bad news for his future bride, eh?"

"This is no time to be glib, young lady," her mother scolded.

"And I haven't even told you the kicker."

She groaned and Vivi knew from experience her mother was massaging her brow. "Out with it then. What's the kicker?"

"He's in love with Portia Flynn's little sister."

Her mother gasped again. "No!"

"Yes."

"What's she doing there?"

"She's been here for four years. She's an ordinary like Ben. Her family shipped her off to the States to keep us from finding out about her. Evidently they were afraid you'd call off the wedding."

Her mother tsked. "Oh, that's terrible."

"It's not terrible for Ben. Like I said, he's in love with her." Vivi paused, letting her mother sort things through.

"Does she care for him, too?"

"Most definitely."

"Well, this is a sticky widget, isn't it?" Gloria sighed. "Why are you calling? Why didn't Ben call?"

"I'm calling because Ben doesn't know how to tell you." She sighed softly. "He doesn't want to disappoint you again, Mom."

"Oh, Vivi," her mother said, regret and sadness in her voice. "He's never been a disappointment."

"Then now's the time to prove it, Mom. You and Dad need to let him off the hook. He'd be miserable married to Portia."

"No parent wants their child to be miserable."

"Then cancel the wedding."

Silence stretched across the line. Then, "I'll see to it."

Vivi's lips slid into a relieved sigh. "I knew you would."

"Make sure he brings her home, dear. I want to meet the woman my son has finally given his heart to."

"I will," Vivi promised.

There, Ben, she thought. *Now you're free.*

CHAPTER NINE

HER HEAD NESTLED against his chest, Ben idly stroked Bryony's arm and gazed up at a starry night sky. It was a deep, dark blue, an ocean of inky darkness punctuated with sparkling white lights. Bryony had pulled a blanket and pillows out of her car and spread them on the ground along with their picnic and they'd alternately feasted on food and on each other.

Benedict had been waiting for the right moment to tell her who he was, but so far the opportunity hadn't presented itself. Bryony, he knew, wanted everything to be perfect tonight. She kept making little comments about this being their last night together—how their time was getting small—and he hadn't wanted to ruin the evening.

Nevertheless, he knew he had to tell her.

He really did.

"Bryony?"

She hummed under her breath, slipped her hand beneath his shirt and caressed his belly. "Yeah?"

"Do you buy into the whole denying love, never knowing love and abusing love as the reason ordinaries never receive their powers?" Benedict had mixed feelings about it. Magecraft presented it as fact, but if that was the case…then where did he fit in? To his knowledge, he'd never experienced any of those things.

"I do," Bryony said, leaning up to peer at him. A small frown emerged between her smooth dark brows. "Why? Don't you?"

"I don't know." He chuckled. "I guess I'm just having a hard time figuring out where I fall in all of that."

Bryony snuggled back down against his chest and chuckled softly. "Oh, I can tell you that."

Startled, Ben glanced at the top of her head and scowled. "You can?"

"Sure."

He waited. "Well?"

"Oh, you want me to tell you?" she asked, feigning innocence.

Ben chewed the inside of his cheek. "Yes, that would be nice. You know. Since you know, and I don't and all."

"You're guilty of denying love."

"What?"

"That's it."

Ben's first response was "horse shit" but he stopped short and snorted derisively instead. Nevertheless, his heart had kicked up in his chest and there was something curiously disturbing about her insight. "I don't think so," he replied skeptically. "Who have I denied love from?"

"Everyone would be my guess. It's all part of your guilt complex."

"I have a complex?" Interesting. He wasn't aware of it.

"You do. But if I had to guess, I'd say you were guilty of denying love to yourself."

This time he did laugh, though he'd become curiously nauseous. "How do you deny love to yourself?" He asked the question indulgently, as though her answer didn't matter, when nothing could be further from the truth.

She doodled on his stomach, unwittingly making his belly flutter. "Well, when someone like you has a guilt complex, then they start to believe that they aren't worthy of anyone's love. So even though they might accept it from their parents or siblings, they still can't quite make themselves accept their own worthiness from within." She leaned up and pressed a kiss to the underside of his jaw. "In short, you don't love yourself because you don't think you deserve it."

She pressed another kiss to his jaw, moving up so that she caught the corner of his mouth. Meanwhile, Ben felt like he'd been hit in the stomach with an anvil. Though every part of him resisted what she said, Benedict knew, deep in a place where insecurity dwelled, that it was true.

"But you do," she said. "You deserve all of that love and more." She whispered another achingly sweet kiss on his lips. "Will you deny me?" she asked softly. "Or will you let me love you?"

Will you let me love you?

That simple request was his undoing. Benedict answered her in the only way he knew how. He tunneled his fingers into her hair and slanted his lips over hers. Yes, he thought. *Love me. Make me believe that I'm good enough. Make me believe I matter.*

And forgive me later for being who I am.

ETTA JAMES'S "At Last" playing in her head, Bryony smiled against Ben's lips and felt her nipples pearl behind the thin fabric of her bra. Finally she thought. All night long she'd been dropping hints, waiting for him to make the ultimate move, but for whatever reason, he'd hesitated. Bryony didn't know what sort of doubts he'd had and had chalked up his caution to being a gentleman.

Being a gentleman was nice, but tonight she wanted a lover.

She wanted to make a memory that would last her a lifetime. She wanted to make love to him beneath a blanket of stars, at one of the most sacred vortexes—one of the most powerful—in Sedona. Even now she could feel the energy twirling around them, tugging at her hair, enervating every particle in her being.

She'd purposely waited until the majority of foot traffic had waned before she'd brought him up here, then found a secluded spot where they wouldn't be disturbed. Now, as Ben gently tugged her shirt up over her head, Bryony knew her careful planning had paid off. She shimmied out of her pants, shucking her panties and quickly shedding her bra before snuggling back under the blanket with him. Ordinarily more modest, Bryony didn't seem to mind undressing for him. She was comfortable, she realized. Unafraid of being rejected.

Ben Martin, eyes dark and heavy-lidded with need, gazed at her appreciatively. He was about to rock her world, she realized, her toes curling. He was going to *help* her, Bryony thought with an inappropriate smile, until her back bowed off the blanket and she sang the orgasm song.

"Are you laughing at me?" Ben asked, kissing each of her eyelids in turn.

"No," Bryony told him. "I'm just looking forward to being helped."

A sexy chuckle rumbled up his throat. "Ah. You need some assistance, then?"

Bryony reached for the snap at his jeans and slipped the button from its closure. "I thought I'd made that obvious."

Gratifyingly, a stuttering breath leaked out of his lungs. "I'm st-starting to get the p-picture."

"Here," Bryony said, taking the full length of him in hand. "Let me put things in Technicolor for you."

She bent and kissed him again, working the hot slippery skin against her palm. She growled low in her throat, enjoying the feel of him in her hand. Before she could settle in for a long siege, he rolled out of reach and removed his clothes. A second later he joined her, fully naked—every glorious inch of him—beneath the blanket.

Skin to skin. Soft, supple muscle, his masculine hair abrading her in the most delicious way possible.

Heaven, Bryony thought, as Ben's mouth latched onto her nipple. He pulled the aching bud deep into his mouth, causing a bow of delight to alternately unravel and tighten deep in her womb. Her sex wept and she arched shamelessly against him, desperate for the feel of him deep inside of her. She was dimly aware of a sudden wind, which had swept around the cathedral, but the pleasure mounting inside of her left no room for cognitive thought.

Ben shifted to the other breast, sucking so hard he flattened the crown of her breast against the roof of his mouth. "You taste so good," he murmured, gently sliding a hand down her belly to part her curls. His fingers brushed her clit, ripping the breath from her lungs. "And I bet this will taste even better."

Before she could process the thought, Ben's mouth was attached to her sex, eating her as though he was a starving man and she his last meal. His tongue abraded her, working the little hood of sensation like a combination he needed to crack. Bryony fisted her hands in the blanket, groaned as pleasure bolted through her. He slipped a finger deep inside and hooked it around, accurately finding that patch of cells that would make her fly apart.

She could feel it rising up inside of her, her orgasm hovering just out of reach. "Not like this," Bryony gasped. "Please," she pleaded. "I want you inside of me."

For whatever reason, this seemed unbelievably important. Imperative even. Another rogue wind tore around them, tugging at the blanket, but Bryony held it tight. If she didn't, she felt like she'd fly right off into the sky.

Honoring her request, Ben positioned himself between her thighs, the engorged tip of him nudging her quivering folds. "Which are you?" he asked roughly. "Denying love, abusing love, or never known love?"

"What?" she asked, unable to focus on anything but the point where their bodies met.

"Denying love, abusing love, or never known love?" he asked again, barely restraining himself. His shoulders shook with need, his face a fierce mask of pure masculine desire.

God, he was beautiful.

Bryony smiled sadly. "You know my history, Ben. Which do you think?"

"Never known love?" he accurately guessed.

She nodded, not understanding why this was so important right now. A storm had blown up. In about five minutes they were going to get soaked.

Ben's gaze softened and he bent and pressed an achingly soft kiss against her lips. "Not anymore," he said, slowly sinking into her. "You're loved."

Tears welled behind her lids. "Ben," she breathed, moved beyond anything she'd ever experienced.

Unable to hold back any longer, he drew back and thrust again. Bryony lifted her hips, a silent invitation to draw him farther into her body. He pounded into her, harder, faster, then harder still. He angled deep, his tight balls slapping against her aching flesh. She clamped her legs around his waist and tightened her feminine muscles around him, reveling in the delicious draw and drag created between their bodies.

Ben's lips peeled back from his teeth and she felt him tense, knew that the same mindless sensation that was on the brink of tearing through her was working the same magic on him. She bent forward and nipped at his neck, then licked the spot she'd hurt.

An instant later, she came. Hard.

Her vision blackened around the edges, the breath tore from her lungs and her back arched so hard off the blanket she feared it would snap.

A low keening howl ripped from Ben's throat and he buried himself inside to the hilt. She convulsed around him, each contraction bringing another sparkler of intense relief. Just when she was certain it was over, another sensation took hold. Lightning hit her spine—a charge so powerful every muscle in her body went rigid—and her fingertips tingled with a sensation so intense she fully expected her nails to fly off.

She looked up into Ben's startled eyes and realized something similar had happened to him. He froze above her, every muscle taut with some unnamed force. The storm bore down around them, whipping the area encircling their blanket into a mini-tornado of energy that lifted them completely off the ground. She clung to Ben, a wild laugh bubbling up in her throat as she realized what had just happened.

They'd awakened.

Together.

Life, Bryony realized as she and Ben settled down onto the ground once more, didn't get any better than this.

CHAPTER TEN

THE NEXT MORNING Vivi awoke to discover a giant pitcher of water levitating over her bed and her brother's beaming face across the room.

In the instant it took to realize that her brother shouldn't be able to levitate a pitcher of water—a trick she'd mercilessly played on him when they were kids—he nodded and tipped the spout, showering her with water.

Vivi shrieked and bolted out of bed straight at him, not even bothering to dry herself off with a quick Inferno Charm. "Ben!" she squealed, absolutely thrilled. "When did it happen?"

Her brother, showing remarkable competence, quickly dried them off with a quick flick of his wand. "Last night."

Unable to contain herself, she hugged him again, then did a wild little dance around the room. "You know what this means, don't you?" she asked.

Ben smiled. "It means Mom and Dad were right about Sedona."

"No." She darted to the dresser and grabbed her own wand. "Now it means you can fight back." She tossed a hex at him, which he ably blocked.

"I don't have time to fight now, Vivi." He grimaced.

"I've got to call Mom and Dad and let them know that the wedding is off."

"Done," she said, hoping that he wouldn't be pissed.

A line emerged between his brows. "What do you mean done?" he asked darkly.

"I called Mom last night," she admitted. "I was afraid that you wouldn't do it."

His lips slid into a grim smile and he passed a hand over his face. "Afraid I wouldn't care enough about my own happiness? That I didn't love myself enough to think I deserved any?"

Vivi blinked. That's exactly what she thought. She flushed guiltily.

Ben sighed. "It's all right," he said. "You were right. Until last night I didn't think I deserved to be happy. I was an ordinary, a constant disappointment."

"So you think getting your powers has suddenly made you a better man?" Vivi asked, outraged. "Because that's pure bullshit, big brother."

Ben looked out the window toward Bryony's cottage. "I know," he told her, swallowing. "I had to realize it before I had my awakening, otherwise…"

Otherwise it would never have happened. Vivi nodded in understanding. "So you told Bryony who you are then?"

A red stain slid over his cheeks.

"Ben!" Vivi pushed her hands through her hair. "I told you—"

"I know what you told me, but the timing was off."

She scowled darkly. "I don't give a damn about the timing, Ben. You are going to ruin the best thing that ever happened to you if you don't go fix this right now." She poked him hard in the chest. "The wedding is off. You're free. Now go get yourself engaged to the right Flynn before she gets away."

A slow smile spread across his lips and the kind of happiness she'd never seen in her brother's eyes glowed in his dark gaze. "I wasn't the only one who experienced an awakening last night," he told her.

Vivi gasped, delighted. "No!"

"Yes." He shrugged. "She's amazing, Vivi. I'm in love with her."

"I know that, fool. Now go tell her."

THE LAST THING Bryony expected was to be summoned to Regina's office at the crack of dawn, but the Guardian had her own time schedule and the rest of the staff at the Registry and Magecraft simply had to fall in line.

This was shaping up to be a wonderful day, Bryony thought. She'd get to tell Regina about her awakening, then collect on Regina's promise to fire Richard Hornby. To make things even more fabulous, Ben had agreed to stay on in Sedona indefinitely. He could manage the bulk of his business as easily from here as he could from New York, he'd told her, much to her delight.

Though last night couldn't have been any more perfect, she'd sensed a curious unease from Ben after they'd made love. Did he regret it? No. She instinctively knew that wasn't it. What, exactly, remained a mystery. Rather than press him on it, she'd decided to go on as they were. A couple of times he'd started to tell her something, but had stopped short. It had been strange, considering that they'd just made the most beautiful love any couple could ever dream of making, and they'd both had their awakenings.

He'd been her key and vice versa, Bryony had realized. He was the half to her whole, the last tumbler in her lock. He was hers, she'd realized last night. Her honest to goodness, bona fide, genuine soul mate.

It wasn't a myth.

And he loved her.

Her heart warmed and did a little pirouette in her chest at the mere thought. *You are now,* he'd said. Meaning that she *was* loved. By him.

Bryony turned around as Regina entered her office. "Sorry you had to wait," her boss said. "I've been a bit busy lately."

She'd noticed, but didn't say anything.

Regina paused. "Bryony, Richard Hornby flagged me down last night as I returned and shared what I hope is a false rumor with me."

A knot of tension formed in Bryony's belly and her mouth parched. "Regina—"

Her boss inhaled a startled breath. "So it's true, then? You've been seeing a student?"

"I have," Bryony told her, unwilling to lie. "I—"

Regina's eyes widened and she pushed back from her desk and considered Bryony with what could only be dubbed disappointment. "Honestly, Bryony, I'm surprised at you. I never thought that you would abuse our rules here, and given who you've been seeing…" She shrugged. "Well, suffice it to say that I knew you didn't particularly care for your sister, but I never thought you'd have an affair with her fiancé."

Bryony felt the room shift and her ears rung. "I'm sorry?"

"Benedict DeWin," Regina said. "Isn't that who you've been seeing?"

"I—"

The door opened and bounced off the wall as Miss Marion came hurtling into the room. Pink rollers marched in perfect rows across her scalp and she bent at the waist, breathing hard. "She doesn't know, Regina," Marion said, gasping a lungful of air. "Incognito Charm."

Benedict DeWin… Incognito Charm…

And suddenly she knew.

Her gaze flew to Marion's. "Marion," she said, feeling utterly broken and betrayed inside. "You knew?"

Marion's lined face crumpled. "It's not what you think, dearest."

"And you let me?" she asked, realizing how much her supposed friend and confidante had duped her.

"You don't understand. Vivi and I, we thought—"

Vivi, too, Bryony thought, her lips twisting with bitter humor. Professor Huggins was ill, my ass, Bryony realized now. It had all been a ruse, a way for them to play matchmaker. That was excusable. Vivi loved her brother and, if Bryony had her guess, didn't want him to marry Portia. Like her, Vivi had to have known that Benedict would never have been happy. When push came to shove, even Marion could be excused. She was a notorious romantic who would have jumped at the chance to instigate a little *amore* between Bryony and Benedict.

But Benedict…

Benedict had known who she was the entire time, and had kept her in the dark beneath the Incognito Charm to protect his identity.

Bryony felt her throat tighten and a rueful laugh got

caught in her throat. No wonder he looked so familiar. No wonder she'd fallen so easily in love with him. She'd been halfway there to start with.

She'd deduced Vivi and Marion's motives in this, but Benedict's were still a mystery. Angry and hurt, Bryony left her chair and walked determinedly out the door.

Perhaps he'd be willing to *help* her with that.

BENEDICT JUMPED as the door to his cottage burst open.

"You bloody bastard," Bryony said, her voice vibrating with angry emotion.

Vivi looked from Bryony to him and smiled. "I told you she'd be pissed."

"Put a sock in it, Vivi," Bryony told her. "I'm not exactly thrilled with you at the moment, either."

Vivi smiled, then looking pleased with herself, settled into the nearest chair. She conjured a bowl of popcorn. "I knew she wouldn't be a pushover."

"Just exactly at what point were you planning to tell me who you were, *Benedict DeWin?* Right before you walked down the aisle with my sister? Or better yet, was I just supposed to find out at the wedding?"

"Who told you?"

"Regina. Richard ratted us out. I got called into her office this morning, I'm assuming to get fired, and she let it slip. Evidently she was under the impression that I knew I was sleeping with my sister's fiancé. It wasn't fun," she all but growled.

Benedict swallowed, unsure of where to start. He settled on the most damning thing against him. "I'm not marrying your sister, Bryony."

Benedict imagined the small part of her brain that

wasn't a mass of anger appreciated this, but the pissed-off side was still craving a row. "When were you going to tell me?" she demanded. "Considering everything that's happened this week—considering that you've implied that you love me—" Her voice broke, making him feel like the bastard she'd called him. "I think I have a right to know, don't you? *Help* me out with it, Ben," she said, sarcasm coating every word. "Help me out with that one, why don't you?"

"I was going to tell you last night," he said, looking away.

She hummed impatiently. "Would that have been before or after we had sex?"

"Both, dammit," Ben finally snapped. "I just couldn't. I let it go on too long and there was no easy way to say it. There was never really an opening for 'Oh, by the way, I'm engaged to your sister.' And I needed to tell my parents that I was breaking the engagement and, I don't know." He gestured wearily. "I'm sorry, Bryony," he told her, realizing it was completely inadequate. "What do you want me to say? I screwed up. I admit it."

"Tell her you're an idiot," Vivi supplied helpfully. "That love made you stupid."

Bryony shot Vivi a look. "Do you ever shut up?"

"No," Vivi told her unapologetically. "It's part of my charm." She tossed another kernel of corn into her mouth. "But you heard him. He isn't marrying your sister. He wants to marry you."

"Oh, for the love of God, Vivi, I can propose myself," Benedict snapped. "Go!" he ordered. "*Now.*"

"Jeez," his sister mumbled, unfolding herself from the chair and setting her snack aside. "You finally get your powers and you turn into an egomaniac."

"Vivi," he said warningly.

Benedict waited until Vivi closed the door, then took a cautious step forward and was heartened when Bryony didn't retreat. "I'm sorry," he said, his gaze searching hers. "I was an idiot." He sidled closer. "I'm… I'm in love with you, Bryony."

A reluctant grin caught the corner of her ripe mouth and her hopeful gaze tangled with his. "You've really backed out of your engagement?"

Ben nodded. "My mother and father have already broken the news to yours."

"They'll blame me, you know," Bryony pointed out.

"Do you care?"

She shook her head. "No."

He slipped a finger down the side of her cheek. "I think it's poetic justice considering the way they've treated you."

She nodded. "I suppose."

"Do you want to invite them to our wedding?"

A stuttering breath leaked out of her lungs and those clear green eyes suddenly watered with what Benedict hoped were tears of joy. "Are we getting married?"

"If you say yes, we are." He kissed her lids, sipping up the single tear that slid from her eye. "Will you marry me, Bryony Flynn?" he asked, his voice rough with emotion.

She laughed and wrapped her arms around his neck. "I could be persuaded. With a little *help*."

Benedict muttered an incantation and instantly the blinds fell and the room went dark. Candles suddenly glowed and music drifted from the stereo speakers.

"Oh, I can help you," he assured her, chuckling softly, then sealed the promise with a purely magical kiss.

SPIRIT DANCE

Mia Zachary

* * *

This one is for Rachel Robinson. Without your blue, light-saber-wielding construction guys, this story wouldn't have been written. Go gnomads!

ACKNOWLEDGMENTS

Thanks as always to my creative partner Melissa James for pushing her comfort level, and special thanks to Robyn Grady for reading above and beyond on short notice.

Dear Reader,

I believe in fate. But I also believe in being prepared and making your own opportunities. I originally came up with the premise of this novella more than six years ago (with the ghost as the heroine!). The story didn't sell, and I think it's because I wasn't prepared and the right opportunity hadn't arrived. Fast forward to 2005 and a "fateful" dinner with an editor at an RWA conference. Suddenly I was offered the chance to combine two story ideas into one great premise!

Hereditary witch Siobhan Silverhawk has always known she's different, or at least that she is supposed to be. Despite the many classes she's attended at the "magic rehab center," she feels like a fraud. Helicopter pilot J. B. Pendleton thinks she is one, too. The last thing J.B. wants is "different," since he has his wife's ghost and his grieving son to deal with. But then he lets his son talk him into drinking one of Siobhan's "love elixirs." The crazy cocktail must really work, because suddenly he can't stop thinking about her.... And when opportunity knocks, the doors to their hearts swing wide open!

I hope you enjoy Siobhan and J.B.'s romance. I had a good time with them. And it's no coincidence that my son is the same age as Ben, which made writing that little boy's scenes all the more poignant. I hope "Spirit Dance" makes you laugh, and maybe cry a little. But most of all I hope it inspires you to make an opportunity in your own life.

I wish you luck, I wish you success and most of all I wish you joy!

Mia

CHAPTER ONE

"YOU DON'T *LOOK* LIKE a bitch, Sisi."

"Excuse me?" Siobhan Silverhawk blinked twice at the six-year-old earnestly studying her with dark satin eyes.

"Benjamin Joseph…"

The boy's father, John Bradley Pendleton, crossed his arms over his broad chest. His imposing height and muscular build, combined with serious hazel eyes and a commanding air, should have made him appear intimidating. But Ben simply ignored the glower.

"What? Mommy called her a bitch whose magic power is stealing men's hearts. I just wanna know if it's true 'cause I'm kind of a man and I *need* my heart and—"

"That's enough, Ben. I never want to hear you use that word again." J.B. pointed for emphasis. "Apologize to Siobhan."

"Saw-ree." The boy's expression made it clear he didn't understand what he was sorry for. "So *are* you a…you know?"

"Yes, I am, kiddo." She reached out to ruffle Ben's soft curls. "But that's witch with a 'W,' okay?"

"You don't look like a witch, either. You don't have a pointy hat or green skin or tentacles or anything."

J.B. choked back a laugh. "Tentacles?"

Ben nodded. "From *The Little Mermaid* movie. That witch was like an octopus on the bottom."

Heat tinted her cheeks as J.B.'s gaze slowly traveled the length of her legs, from her ankles to the short hem of her floral sundress. Then he looked at her and winked. "Nope, no sign of tentacles."

"No green skin, either. I do, however, come from a family of powerful magic users."

J.B. cleared his throat, his expression closing. "I know you have to play a certain role for the tourists looking for entertainment, but I've told Ben the truth."

"And which truth is that?" She barely kept the sarcasm from her voice, already knowing the answer.

"That there's no such thing as witches or ghosts except on TV, that there's nothing magic except for tricks at birthday parties."

Ben cocked his head to the side. "Hey, Sisi. How come I've never seen you do card tricks or make stuff dist-appear?"

"I'm waiting to get my own show in Las Vegas."

She kept her tone lighthearted. There was no way either the man or the boy could have known how deeply their offhand remarks about magic wounded her. But, inside, Siobhan suffered the familiar inadequacy.

Her family tree was one of knowledge, of healing and of foreseeing. She was directly descended from the great wizard Taliezar on her mother's side and from Walks With Thunder, the legendary medicine man, on her father's. The power of ancient bloodlines spanned centuries and should have come down to her, as it had her older sister, Sîan, and the youngest, Shona.

She wanted to be a healer, a medicine woman in the tradition of the Díne, her father's people. She wanted to be able to ease pain and take away hurt and cure illness. But desire meant nothing in the face of destiny. Though she knew it wasn't possible to heal everyone, she had never been able to heal *anyone*. At least not with magic.

However there was a small measure of hope. If a witch hadn't come into her powers by the age of twenty-five, or had lost control of her gift, she could check into the Magecraft Treatment Center in Arizona.

And so Siobhan had moved to Sedona, a place of enchantment, a center of power, a haven in the high desert. In this rare city where the idea of Old World magic and New Age mysticism was not only tolerated but openly encouraged by the tourism office, all were welcomed who sought what was lost. Or merely hidden.

Although she was technically a Novice, the five years she'd been devotedly attending classes at the Center had earned her the privilege of attending Invocator-level seminars. However, she'd taken every class available to no apparent end. Despite her heritage and unwavering dedication, she hadn't exhibited the tiniest hint of astral energy.

Her teachers swore that she had the Gift. But she wasn't sure how much longer she'd be allowed to attend the Center before the Guardian, Regina St. Lyon, placed the silver O beside her name in the Archive, forever marking her as ordinary. If Siobhan had a magical gift, it must be so deeply hidden that she needed to accept that her destiny didn't include witch-craft.

Instead she drew on centuries of herb lore and years of study to create body lotions and bath salts, healing in her own small ways. Luminous, her herbal product shop, successfully catered to the New Age hobbyists and the vacationers. And though her customers swore she had a "magic touch," in this city where the paranormal was an accepted norm, she felt like a fraud.

Siobhan chose a bright red fruit from the basket on the counter and slyly offered it to Ben along with her best cackle. "Can I tempt you with an apple, my precious?"

"Sure, thanks." Oblivious to the *Snow White* reference, he took as big a bite as he could manage without one front tooth. "But, Daddy, you *know* you're wrong about ghosts. Mommy visits me all the time."

She watched grief, frustration and worry chase across J.B.'s features before he forced a little smile. "Imaginary friends are a lot of fun, aren't they? But ghosts are different—they're not real."

"They are so real, Daddy. One time, I heard Grandma say she's not surprised about me coz you used to talk to *your* great-grandma after her heart attacked her and—"

"Hey, sport, we'll talk about all this later, okay? Why don't you go over there and pick out a nice gift for your aunt Lissa's birthday."

"Okay," Ben replied around a half-chewed bite of apple. "I'm gonna smell all the purples and pick the bestest one."

As he trotted around the herb solarium in the center of the shop toward the displays of candles, J.B. gave a heavy sigh.

Siobhan spoke casually, though her heart ached for both of them. "He's still not adjusting, huh?"

"I just don't understand it. Gabrielle's been gone almost two years." His brows furrowed over his troubled gaze as he watched Ben from across the room.

"Well, for him to lose his mother at such a young age—"

"Yeah, I know." His reply sounded both impatient and tolerant, like he'd heard this too many times before. "That's not what I meant. It'd be one thing for Ben to still be grieving, but he doesn't seem to understand that she's dead."

A drunk driver had instantly left J.B. a widower and single father. Both his and Ben's lives were ripped apart, but J.B. had handled it better. He'd had no choice. Ben was still so grief-stricken that he constantly talked to his mother, acting as though she were alive and with him.

When a former army buddy offered him part ownership in Airstar Adventure Tours, J.B. had jumped at the chance. Thinking it best to get away from Baltimore and the memories haunting them, he'd quit his job and transferred to Sedona. Where, unfortunately, nothing had changed. Living in a place renowned for vortexes and harmonic convergences didn't make it easier to ground Ben in reality.

Her pale gaze reflecting compassion, Siobhan briefly touched his forearm. The heat of her fingertips tingled along his skin, exciting and calming him at the same time. "I don't know what you're going through, having never lost someone I love, and I know you're taking Ben to a child psychologist. But maybe this is what he needs to do."

"I understand that, part of me really does. But 'his

mother' has disrupted the class a couple of times and he's started acting out at home."

"What do you mean?"

Scratching the back of his neck, J.B. glanced over to make sure Ben was out of earshot. "He's not making friends in first grade. The other kids think he's weird for talking to invisible people. And he's breaking things or hiding them around the house. When I try to talk to him, he swears his mother did it."

"Oh, dear. What does his doctor say?"

"That because of his age and what little time he remembers with Bri, this is the only way he can deal with the loss." He smirked without much humor. "Basically stuff that's bound to have me paying his hourly rate for another few years."

She offered a comforting smile but to his disappointment didn't touch him again. "A lot of kids have imaginary friends and they grow up just fine."

He noted her defensive tone with a grin. "Are you talking about yourself?"

"Um, actually, I had, uh, three invisible playmates. Flora, Fauna and Merryweather."

"Interesting names."

Embarrassment tinted her cheeks. "They were the fairy godmothers in *Sleeping Beauty,* one of my favorite movies."

When he moved closer, her pupils dilated and her full lips parted slightly. She was tall and lithe, with shining ebony hair that fell straight down her back. From a distance she looked every inch a Navajo princess. Up close, however, Siobhan had the creamy skin of her Celtic ancestors and startlingly pale green eyes.

Taking secret pleasure in her reaction to his near-ness, he lowered his voice to an intimate level. "Can I tell you a secret?"

"Of course," she whispered, angling her face toward his.

"I had an imaginary friend, too."

She gave him a little shove and rolled her eyes. "Sure you did, J.B."

"I did. Being a military family, it seemed like as soon as I made a new friend, one of our fathers got reassigned and we had to move. But I always had Super Spot."

Siobhan crinkled her brow, obviously trying not to giggle. "Um, 'Super Spot'?"

J.B. shrugged, hands spread. "Hey, Dad wouldn't let us get a real dog so…"

"Super Spot. More powerful than a teddy bear, able to leap tall bed pillows in a single bound."

The sensation of warm contentment spread over him as he listened to her musical laughter. That had been the first thing he'd noticed about her when he and Ben had moved into the house next door. Her grace and stately posture belied a down-to-earth nature that fascinated him.

He'd used humor to get Siobhan to open up to him over the past six months. She'd been a good neighbor to him and a great babysitter for Ben the few times he'd flown sunset tours. He sensed her interest but, other than coffee and conversation, there'd been nothing more.

That didn't stop him from trying, though. "You know, I might think you've cast a spell on me, but you're too beautiful to be a witch."

Oddly that brought a scowl to her features. "Do

you honestly think witches look like ugly, hunch-backed old hags with gnarled fingers and warts?"

"*You* look like exactly what you are—a gorgeous and very desirable woman." Her expression hovered somewhere between flattered and annoyed. "What? Didn't you think I'd noticed?"

She ducked her head, a smile curving her lips. But before she could respond, Ben called out, "Daddy! C'mere, c'mere. Let's get this one!"

J.B. winked at her. "Excuse me a minute."

"THE ONLY EXCUSE for letting that man walk away is the chance to stare at his butt. That ass is seriously fine."

Siobhan yanked her gaze away from J.B.'s denim-covered derriere and turned to her best friend and store manager. She bit her lip when she noticed V'Leria's latest hair color. The turquoise-blue streaks were actually an improvement.

"Tell me again why you haven't ridden that hunk-cycle yet?"

"Shh! Will you stop it, *Valerie?*"

V'Leria nudged her in the ribs with a sharp elbow. "Will you start? You live right next door to that gorgeous morsel of manhood. He's obviously hot for your bod—he flirts with you every chance he gets. So, what are you waiting for?"

Acceptance. Someone to believe in her, especially when it was getting harder and harder to believe in herself. Her past relationships had only led to heartache. The wizards she'd dated couldn't abide her lack of powers, fearing the deficiency would be passed down to their children. Meanwhile mortal men couldn't stand the idea of her being a witch.

It would have been one thing if she just dabbled in the Craft or acted a part for tourists, but an actual spellcasting, magic-wielding witch? They thought she was delusional. Apparently that included J.B. He often flew helicopter tours through the most challenging gorges and canyons. But apparently his daring didn't extend to the supernatural.

Which was a real shame. J.B. was sexy and funny and handsome in a rugged, life-weathered way. He had somber hazel eyes tempered by a quick, boyish smile. Judging by the way his ranger T-shirt stretched across his chest, she had to agree that his body was "seriously fine." She liked him, a lot, and it would be an easy decision to see where this attraction led.

But they were neighbors and there was Ben to consider if things didn't work out. She watched J.B. laughing with his son while they smelled different candles. Although he seemed so open and carefree, she easily saw the shadows across his heart. And frankly she had enough emotional baggage of her own.

"J.B. flirts with every woman he sees, Val." At that very moment, he was winking at an older woman as he held the front door for her. "See what I mean?"

V'Leria propped one hand on her bare midriff and thrust out a leather-clad hip. "He doesn't flirt with *me*. He doesn't lean in close or gaze into *my* eyes or whisper in *my* ear."

Siobhan held her tongue, knowing better than to say that, with all of her piercings, a man would have trouble finding V'Leria's ear. "It doesn't matter. There's no point in pursuing an attraction when he's got his hands full with a troubled child."

"Sure, honey. Keep telling yourself that the kid is

what's holding you back." With a condescending pat of the shoulder, V'Leria walked over to help the new customer.

Siobhan ignored her and smiled as J.B. and Ben approached with a basket of scented tea lights and bath beads. "I see you found something you like."

"Yep. Now Aunt Lissa will smell like a honey garden."

She glanced at the calligraphy on the label to see that she'd written Honeysuckle Gardenia. As she tucked the label into the basket, J.B. moved next to her. He rubbed a few strands of her hair between his fingers then held them to his nose.

"You, on the other hand, smell more earthy. Like fresh-cut grass and sunshine."

Her pulsed tripped. His skin always had a warm, slightly musky scent. Like summer nights and pheromones. She wondered if he smelled that way all over. How would his skin feel beneath her hands? How would his hands feel on her? How would he taste—

"Um, is there anything else you need?" She dragged her eyes away from J.B.'s amused gaze. "Or are you guys all ready to check out?"

"I'm thirsty," Ben complained.

She chuckled, a little envious that it was so easy for children to ask for what they wanted. She glanced at J.B. from under her lashes. Then she crooked a finger at Ben. "Come on over to the juice bar and let's see what we have for you."

J.B. accepted the basket Ben thrust into his stomach. "How about some apple juice, sport?"

"Nah." The boy scrunched his forehead, sounding out the menu. "What's a fruit in-foo…infoo-something?"

Siobhan chose a clean pitcher from the rack. "An infusion? It's different fruit juices mixed with brewed teas or blended with herbs."

"Like a magic potion?"

"Sort of. They're supposed to make you feel good. I can either make hot ones or turn them into frozen smoothies." She tucked errant strands of hair behind her ear and pretended to be indecisive. "Gosh, I can't figure out which you'd like better."

Ben's eyes lit up. "I want the smoothie kind!"

"Manners."

He sighed at his father. "Please. An orange one, Sisi."

"One Creamsicle coming up, sir." She filled the pitcher with ice cubes, then poured in orange juice and milk. She added a quarter cup of lemon balm tea for calming and relaxation then turned on the blender. "What about you, J.B.?"

He teased her, dramatically arching one eyebrow. "Aren't witches supposed to mix their potions in a fiery cauldron under a full moon or something?"

She replied with thinly veiled sarcasm, "Actually I use stainless steel pots and sterilized glass bottles in accordance with Arizona's state health regulations."

"You sound more like a scientist than a witch."

She topped Ben's smoothie with whipped cream and a straw, then handed it to him with a smile that fell away when she looked back at his father. "The difference between magic and science is a matter of a few centuries. It wasn't that long ago people went to the village witch for their remedies and cures."

J.B. scoffed. "I'll stick to modern medicine, thanks. It's got a better track record than hocus-pocus and snake oil."

From over by the bookcases and reading chairs, V'Leria gave a low whistle. "Ooh. *Now* you've done it."

"Hocus-pocus, huh?"

This was the sort of prejudice that drove her mad. They were living in the twenty-first century, for heaven's sake! This was Sedona, not Salem during the Burning Time. And while science could explain a lot, miracles happened every day. Siobhan got another pitcher and started grabbing bottles from the small refrigerator.

"Well then, since I don't have any magical powers, you shouldn't have any problem drinking something I make, right?"

Ben held out his nearly empty cup. "Mine is pretty good, Daddy. Wanna sip?"

"No, thanks, sport."

Siobhan banged the ice tray with unnecessary force. "What's the matter, J.B.? Scared I'll put a hex on you? Worried that I'll turn you into a frog?"

"You can *do* that? Cool." Ben started hopping around. "Turn Daddy into a frog, turn him into a frog!"

"No, she can't do that." J.B. dropped a hand onto his son's shoulder in an attempt to quiet him. "Siobhan isn't a witch. There's no such thing as witches or magic potions."

"Double, double toil and trouble," Siobhan muttered sotto voce as she gave the drink a final stir. Then she handed him the frothy pink liquid. "Bottoms up, Pendleton."

He reluctantly accepted the plastic cup, aware that every pair of eyes in the place watched him. He didn't believe for one second that Siobhan had magical powers—or that she might poison him. But there was something about the wicked gleam in her eyes that had him worried.

Feeling ridiculous for hesitating, he took a small sip. It wasn't bad, a little sweet maybe. But to amuse Ben, who was staring at him with wide-eyed anticipation, J.B. made his voice tremble. "What's in here anyway?"

"Mango, cranberry and passion fruit juices. Along with some other stuff." Siobhan's wide grin was pure challenge. She made a beckoning gesture. "All of it."

He took an exaggerated breath and made a show of gulping it down just as V'Leria gave a theatrical yelp. "Siobhan! That wasn't one of your *love potions,* was it?"

He choked for a second, but managed to drink the rest of the juice. When the cup was empty he set it on the counter but didn't say anything. Instead he pretended to sway a little on his feet, one hand pressed against his belly.

Ben goggled at him, his voice hushed. "Well, Daddy? Did it work? Are you in love yet?"

J.B. gazed at Siobhan, meeting her challenge with one of his own. He wasn't sure about love, but lust? He'd been in lust from the moment he'd seen her over the hedgerow separating their backyards. He promptly recalled the sight of her body in shorts and a tank top as she bent herself into a yoga pretzel and the way her full lips had parted in surprise when she'd noticed him…

He finally broke the stare and looked down at his son. He twisted his face into several grotesque expressions then suddenly croaked like a frog. Over Ben's hysterical giggles, he declared, "It worked! Siobhan must really be a witch after all, kiddo, 'cause I'm suddenly crazy about you."

As J.B. scooped Ben up for a bear hug and some tickling, Siobhan laughed along with them. But, inside, she felt her chest constrict with sudden yearning. How long had it been since she'd felt a man's arms around her? How many times had she imagined holding a child's soft body against her own?

Now, watching J.B. with Ben, she had to admit her longing involved that child and that man specifically…

After J.B. and Ben had left with the gift-wrapped basket, V'Leria sidled up to her with a sly look. "So, how long do you think it will take?"

"I don't know what you're talking about, Val."

"Really?" She cocked her head to one side. "Because unless my eyesight is going, I saw you add rosemary and verbena teas to J.B.'s drink. I got top marks in Miss Delilah's Potion vs. Poison class. Aren't those two herbs known for opening the recipient to new love?"

"Are they?" Siobhan crossed her arms and feigned innocence.

"You know they are."

She offered her friend a cynical laugh. "It won't work anyway. Miss Marion looked so disappointed this morning when I was the only one in class who didn't levitate the feather. I'm telling you, Val, I'm *this close* to being labeled a no-mag."

V'Leria smirked. "I don't think so. From the look on J.B.'s face just now, you're *this close* to getting laid."

CHAPTER TWO

NO WAY SOME FRUIT pulp and weeds had the power to control his thoughts and feelings.

However… That woman had been making him crazy—crazier than usual—for the past eight days.

During the day he couldn't get Siobhan off his mind. He found himself wondering what she was doing, missing her company and her kindness. At night he had vividly detailed dreams of being with her. Of seducing her and making love until she cried out his name. He'd been so distracted by a glimpse of her leaving the house this morning that he'd poured apple juice on Ben's cereal by mistake.

J.B. guided the helicopter on a steady course over the south rim of the Grand Canyon, giving the six passengers behind him a clear view of Kaibab Plateau, the world's largest ponderosa pine forest. The recorded narrative playing in the guest earphones offered facts about Horseshoe Mesa and the Hopi Watchtower as they passed overhead. At the edge of the forest, the plateau gently dropped away and a spectacular panorama of the entire canyon came into view.

Glaring afternoon sun lit up the rusty orange-striated cliffs and the mesas carved by wind and water and time. The Navajo Indian Reservation became visible to the east as he approached The Confluence, the point just below Cape Solitude where the Colorado and Little Colorado Rivers joined. Having flown the same basic route five or more times a day for the past five months, J.B. put himself on mental autopilot.

The rumble of the engine and hum of the rotors created a kind of white noise that allowed his thoughts to drift. J.B. instinctively pressed the left rudder down and angled the cyclic control to bank the chopper west, still thinking about his sexy neighbor. In the week since he drank that "love potion," he'd been doing all kinds of stupid stuff.

He'd gone to work with his T-shirt on inside out and backward; locked his keys in the car twice and left the grocery store—after wandering the aisles for an hour—without getting anything on his list. And he'd looked for Siobhan every chance he'd gotten. He'd taken to going out on the bedroom balcony after Ben fell asleep. There he stood silently watching Siobhan, secretly wanting her.

Most nights he recognized the different stances of her yoga routine. Other nights, though, she performed graceful tribal dances and the sound of her chanting had drifted up to him on the evening breeze. Then, long after Siobhan had gone inside, she danced through his dreams.

Her dark hair fell loosely over her bare shoulders, coyly hiding her breasts, making his fingers ache to stroke the silky tresses aside. Desire made her pale eyes glow a darker green as her moist lips parted. She reached out for him, beckoning, welcoming him into her arms—

A couple of rough taps on the shoulder broke his

reverie. Flipping on the headset microphone, he addressed the passengers. "Is there some kind of problem?"

"Yeah, we've been trying to get your attention! The tour guide thing is playing for the third time. Shouldn't we be going back now?"

J.B. realized with a start that they were over Point Imperial, the highest summit on the North Rim, heading toward Dragon Head once more. He'd been flying around in a huge circle. What should have been a forty-five minute tour was now into its second hour, burning extra fuel and putting the rest of his flights behind schedule. He scrubbed a hand over his face. This was one hell of a way to start the week.

She'd distracted him *again*.

"THANKS A LOT, Siobhan. I mean it."

He'd ended up calling her to beg a favor. There were one or two other people he might have asked. But a part of him had known that she wouldn't hesitate. He trusted her to keep Ben after school until J.B. could get to her—er, pick him up.

"It was no trouble at all. In fact, Ben was a big help at the shop."

"Really? What were you doing, sport?" He looked at his son.

Ben shrugged, his voice flat. "Just putting a bunch of stuff in bags."

Siobhan laughed. "A lot of stuff into a lot of bags."

When he looked at her for an explanation, his breath caught at the sight of her sparkling eyes and flushed skin. In an instant he knew this was how she'd look after making love... Blinking, he tried to remember what they'd been talking about. "So, uh, you were busy today?"

"It was incredible—one of the best sale days Luminous has had! I couldn't keep enough body lotion or massage oil on the shelves, and I completely ran out of face cream. Robin and her friend Leanne, two of my regular customers, apparently told every woman they know about my 'miracle cream.'"

J.B. smiled. "Miracle cream, huh?"

She made a comical face. "I know, that was my reaction, too. But Robin swears the moisturizer she bought on Monday cleared up her daughter's acne almost overnight. And Leanne says it made her look ten years younger."

"And did it?"

"Well, she *did* look really pretty today, but I would have called her the most beautiful woman in the world to thank her for all the new clients she brought me!" She laughed, then laid a hand on Ben's shoulder and rubbed his back. "Good thing you were there to help at the register."

His return smile was halfhearted, though. J.B. looked at him more closely. Ben's face was drawn and a little pale, the lines around his mouth tight, like he was coming down with something. He sighed inwardly. Elementary school was a germ and virus breeding ground.

He gave Ben a one-armed hug. "Come on, little guy. Let's get home so I can fix you some dinner."

"Can't we stay here? Sisi said she'd make chicken tacos."

"The chicken is already cooked. I just have to shred and season it if you want to stay." Siobhan wanted them to stay. He could hear it despite her casual tone of voice.

But J.B. looked at her with genuine regret and shook his head. He mouthed, "I think Ben's getting sick," before saying, "Thanks for the invitation but—"

Siobhan felt a twinge of disappointment, followed by a rush of confusion. She'd actually looked forward to having dinner with him— Them, she meant them. But her gaze was fixed on J.B.'s pure-sex-appeal smile and intelligent eyes. His sandy-brown hair was tousled, leading her to guess he'd driven home with the top down on his Jeep. She barely resisted the urge to reach out and comb the strands with her fingers.

Her disappointment grew stronger. She didn't know what had gotten into her lately, but J.B. had been on her mind a lot. If she didn't know the truth about her abilities, she might think her "love potion" had backfired. She'd even found herself inventing reasons to run next door. But it wasn't likely a single father would have cream of tartar or vanilla extract in the cabinet.

"Can we stay, Daddy? Please?"

J.B. shook his head. "Not tonight, sport. We've imposed enough for one day."

"It wasn't an imposition at all and, I promise, we'll have our taco dinner very soon." Siobhan smiled reassuringly and reached for the aluminum tin on the hall table. "Don't forget the snickerdoodle cookies we made."

Ben sighed dramatically. "Thanks, Sisi."

"That sounded real heartfelt, kiddo," J.B. commented. He reached down to heft Ben's school backpack and sling it onto one broad shoulder. He opened the front door, then stopped abruptly and bent down. "You've got a delivery, Siobhan."

She walked up behind him to see what he held. Their hands brushed as he passed her the two packages, sending a jolt of awareness and longing through her body, making her ache with sudden need. Oddly it was a need to comfort as well as seduce. She looked up into J.B.'s eyes and knew that he felt it, too. An invisible force seemed to draw them together as they held the intimate gaze—

"What'd you get, Sisi? What's in there?"

Dropping her gaze, she accepted the boxes as J.B. stepped back. Siobhan checked the first packing label and grinned. Her smile widened with delight as she saw the return address on the second box. "It looks like birthday gifts from my grandmothers, four days early."

"Cool!" Ben finally seemed cheerful. "Open 'em—"

"Gee, I guess since you claim to be a witch—" J.B.'s humor had a cynical edge "—your birthday has to be on Halloween, right?"

Siobhan concentrated on the packages, refusing to allow his jibe to bother her. "It's the day before actually."

"Open 'em, open 'em—"

"Ben, that's enough." J.B.'s stern warning had little effect, however.

"Now we can stay, right, Daddy?" He gazed up pleadingly, one hand tugging on the hem of J.B.'s T-shirt. "It's *no fun* opening birthday stuff by yourself so we have to stay and keep Sisi company and since we're gonna be here anyway we can eat tacos, right?"

She started to extend her invitation again, but felt

hesitant to interfere between parent and child. Not an easy thing to do since Ben was peering at her with great big angel eyes. How did J.B. manage to resist those on a daily basis?

"Wrong. If Siobhan wants, she can tell us what she got later. Right now, we need to get home."

"But, Daddy!"

J.B. assumed his Father Face, arching one brow and thinning his mouth. "No 'buts.' Tell Siobhan thank you for keeping you and then say goodbye."

Recognizing, as any smart child would, his father's tone, Ben stuck his lower lip out. "Thank you and g'bye."

"You're welcome, sweetie. I liked spending time with you."

"I wish we could spend more time." He was still pouting but now his voice was oddly quiet. J.B. placed an ushering hand on the boy's back when Ben dug his sneakered heels into the carpet. "I wish we could stay the whole night."

Her cheeks warmed at the thought of who would spend the night in which bed… She carefully avoided looking at J.B. "I'll see you soon, I promise."

"Thanks again, Siobhan." J.B. followed Ben out. "What's the matter, sport? You feeling okay?"

"Mommy was really mad 'cause she couldn't come in Sisi's—" The door closed behind them.

Siobhan frowned as she shifted the boxes and turned the dead bolt lock with the other hand. What an odd thing for Ben to say. He'd been a little upset when she first brought him home from Luminous, wanting to go into his house instead. But once she'd explained that she didn't have keys, and she offered to bake cookies, he'd seemed fine.

She walked through the house toward the kitchen, planning to make a dinner salad now and put the rest of the chicken in the freezer for another day. Ben's parting words really puzzled her. Were there rules of behavior for make-believe friends? Hers had never had any. Merryweather, Flora and Fauna were omnipotent within the confines of her imagination.

So why had Ben said his mother *couldn't* come in, instead of that she didn't want to?

Siobhan put the packages on the island counter while she got the scissors from the drawer by the back door. As she reached inside, she glanced out at her yard. The late evening sunlight set the flowers ablaze. Then for some reason her eyes focused on the door frame. Specifically on the object over the door frame…

Tiny icicles prickled her gut. She slowly turned to look at the front door.

Over every entry into her house—every window and doorway—she'd hung silver wire-wrapped chunks of polished obsidian. She routinely "smudged" the rooms with sweetgrass and white sage smoke for the same reason. To maintain a calming, nurturing and positive environment. To keep out negative energy…

Was it possible that Ben's mother wasn't a figment of a grieving child's imagination after all?

CHAPTER THREE

HER GRANDMOTHERS appeared just in time for dinner. Siobhan had made a chef salad of field greens, some deli meats, beefsteak tomatoes and crumbled goat cheese, and she'd poured a glass of sauvignon blanc. Before she sat down to eat, though, she'd wanted to get started on the chamomile and ginger tincture for a client suffering from morning sickness.

After stripping the leaves from the chamomile flowers and slicing the peeled ginger, she filled a glass pot with water for simmering the roots. As soon as she lit the gas burner on the stove, a vision projection of Anita Ten Horses emerged from the blue flames. Used to these visits, Siobhan didn't even startle.

She inclined her head to the stove. "Hello, Grandmother Anita. How are you?"

Her Navajo grandmother was short and sturdy with the round, wrinkled face of an apple doll under center-parted gray hair. But she was far from cuddly and Siobhan had always been intimidated by her. Anita Ten Horses was a revered medicine woman and her black eyes were solemn and filled with ancient wisdom.

"I'm fine, thank you. We have come to—"

"Excuse me, Grandmother. We?"

Just then the water in the pot she was still holding

began to ripple and another image materialized. Charlotte Gryffon, her Welsh grandmother, was tall and thin with waist-length blond hair and a regal bearing. She was a renowned and respected Seer, however her fun-loving personality and the merry twinkle in her green eyes would never intimidate anyone.

Siobhan set the pot down on a different burner. "Hi, Granny Char. What are you all dressed up for? It has to be, what, four in the morning your time?"

Charlotte gave her a cheeky grin. "I'm just about to wake your grandfather for a spot of fun. After I see you open your pressies, of course. Lucky for me you favor glass pots, eh?"

Siobhan turned to get the two boxes from the kitchen table. She'd removed the mailing wrapper and packing earlier only to find notes asking her to wait before opening the gifts. "I was surprised that you sent them so early. Usually they arrive on the day."

"This year is different," Anita said.

"Special," Charlotte agreed.

"You will need time to prepare."

Siobhan smiled ruefully. "Yeah, I guess it's not every year a gal turns thirty."

"More importantly, Granddaughter, it is not every year that a woman discovers who she is."

"We've got a secret," Charlotte sang with delight.

"What is it, Granny Char?"

She simply shook her head and smiled as Anita spoke. "Open the larger box, then all will be revealed."

Siobhan had set them on the counter farthest from the open flame. Now she reached eagerly for the larger of the two. She pulled it open to reveal a soft brown tube secured with braided cornhusk. Untying it, she found a sueded piece of buckskin about two foot square. She looked at the stove.

"This deer hide is to be used for the Blessingway ceremony on your birthday, for the creation of a sand-painting of Changing Woman." Anita's dark gaze seemed to glow with significance. "The *íikááh* must be completed by sundown and destroyed by sunrise for the restoration of health and harmony."

"I understand, Grandmother, and I thank you."

After bowing her head slightly, Siobhan carefully rerolled the buckskin and placed it on the countertop. At the bottom of the box was another piece of deer hide, this one crafted into a sheath. She lifted it and gasped as she slid out the knife.

The gleaming steel blade had a curved edge that came to a dulled point at the end. The wooden handle was inlaid with polished shards of stone depicting a Medicine Wheel. The four spokes of jet, mother-of-pearl, turquoise and red jasper representing the cardinal directions lay within a wide circle of silver decorated with four silver feathers.

"It's beautiful." Siobhan breathed the words.

"It was used for cutting and preparing herbs. However, on your birthday, you will use it to cast the ceremonial circle." Anita's voice became even more formal. "Siobhan Silverhawk. From middle daughter to middle daughter, this blade comes to you through generations of shamans. Use it wisely and use it well."

Siobhan tucked the knife back in its sheath and returned it to the carton with the buckskin. "I'll honor your instructions and the spirits of my ancestors. Thank you again, Grandmother."

"Right, then. Open mine next." Charlotte's tone made it clear that her patience had all been for show.

Siobhan opened the second box to find a folded sheet of fabric. When she shook it out, she saw that it was a white silk cloth. The four-foot-long rectangle was embroidered in silver thread with a continuous border of Celtic knots.

"It's an altar cloth, obviously," Granny Char said before Siobhan could ask. "But this one is for the October 31 Samhain ritual. Not nearly as essential as Annie's buckskin, but you can't honor those who have gone before with just any rag, so there you are just the same."

Siobhan thanked her with a laugh and reached back inside the box. This time she held up a heavy silver chalice. The base was textured like grass or dirt and the stem was actually a woman whose naked body had a bark pattern. She knelt on one knee with her face and both arms raised, her hands supporting the bowl of the goblet.

The shallow, wide-mouthed cup had been etched with the Celtic Wheel of Being. In this pattern, four overlapping circles represented the elements while the fifth circle ringing the "floral cross" symbolized balance. In the center of each knot were cabochons of garnet, citrine, amethyst and tourmaline.

"It's gorgeous. Thank you so—"

"Yes, yes. You're very welcome. Obviously you're to use it on All Hallow's Eve, the beginning of our Celtic new year." Charlotte's words became formal but her voice sounded a little anxious. "Siobhan Silverhawk. From middle daughter to middle daughter, this chalice comes to you through centuries of oracles. Use it wisely and use it well."

"I will, I promise." She ran her thumb lightly over a worn spot on the bowl. "Why didn't this go to Mum? She's your middle child."

"Aye, but because of your uncle Daffyd, she's not a middle *daughter.*"

Siobhan carefully repacked the cup and cloth and placed the box with the other. "And what about you, Grandmother? I thought Great-Aunt Carla was your only sister."

The flame died on the burner for a second before blazing back to full strength. She was going to hate to see her natural gas bill next month. Then she focused on her grandmother. The old woman's face was shadowed by memories. "I had an elder sister. Barbara. She died of malnutrition, as did many on the reservation in the 1930s."

It was obvious from her pained expression that she didn't want to discuss it, so Siobhan changed the subject. "Why don't the cup and knife get passed to the oldest daughter?"

Anita's tone was that of a teacher to a particularly slow student. "Three is a sacred number, for many reasons. It is representative of cycles. For example, past, present and future; youth, adulthood and old age and the three stages of the Goddess as maiden, mother and crone."

"That's right." Char nodded, sending ripples across the water's surface. "Two alone cannot enclose a space. Only with three can a plane be formed and three dimensions are needed to form a solid. Therefore three stands for that which is solid, substantial and complete."

Anita cast an exasperated look at Charlotte's pot.

"As I was saying. The midpoint of all these cycles is the strongest and most conducive to healing magic."

Siobhan looked at both of them in turn. Despite their differences, they were definitely two of the strongest women she knew. "So, what did you mean about my discovering who I am?"

"Don't you see?" Anita seemed to lean out of the fire. "You are inheriting these artifacts—and their endowment—from a middle daughter *on both sides of your family.*"

Charlotte silently clapped her hands. "Just think on it, poppet. This is your Power Year. Once your birthday arrives, you'll finally attain your abilities. And more than that, you'll come into both healing and foreseeing."

"I can't believe this. Why am I just now hearing about the Power Year thing?"

Anita frowned, adding more wrinkles to her face. "Your parents and I have been advising you for years to be patient, explaining that your time would come."

"I was actually closer to thirty-one when I got mine. We're often late bloomers in the Welsh lot." Charlotte shrugged good-naturedly. "Did they not tell you at the Center?"

"No, they didn't. Huh." Siobhan scoffed, shaking her head. "So that means I've wasted the past five years trying to coerce powers that I wasn't meant to have until now."

"Learning is never wasted, Granddaughter."

"Oh no," Charlotte protested. "In fact, it means with the studies you've done, on top of the power you'll inherit—"

"You have the potential to be one of the most gifted

shamans of your age," Anita interrupted. Then, to Siobhan's surprise, her normally stoic grandmother actually smiled.

"WHY DON'T YOU believe me?"

Ben's distraught plea still echoed in J.B.'s memory two hours after their argument. He slouched farther down on his lounge chair and closed his eyes. Raising his second beer to his lips, he took one swallow then set the bottle down. He scrubbed a hand over his face, feeling like the worst father in the world. His son had cried himself to sleep. Again. But this time he, not grief or temper, had been the cause.

After telling Ben to study the words for his Tuesday morning spelling test, J.B. had gone to the kitchen to fix dinner. Since he still hadn't managed the grocery shopping, there hadn't been much to choose from. So after whipping together something that involved canned soup, cheese and slightly stale bread, he'd gone to tell Ben it was ready—

And then stopped dead in his tracks.

The living room had been ransacked. Every drawer and cabinet in the entertainment center hung open, the DVDs and videotapes spilling onto the floor. Sofa cushions were strewn around the room along with most of the books. And Ben had been standing in the middle of it, torn magazines in each hand, his little face pale with guilt at being caught.

J.B. opened his eyes and tipped his head to stare up at the night sky. Ben had denied everything, claiming he was trying to clean up the mess. But J.B. had been tired after a long day and in no damned mood to deal with yet another case of acting out.

"I didn't do it, Daddy. Honest! I told you Mommy was mad. Why won't you believe me?"

What the hell was he supposed to believe? That his dead wife was the one who kept wrecking the house? That Bri had somehow broken the glazed ceramic pot Siobhan had given them as a housewarming gift, and hidden his computer war games? Yeah, right. This wasn't some Hollywood movie and Ben didn't have a sixth sense.

His thoughts moved to Louisa the Great, his nickname for his late great-grandmother. He didn't remember the details. Apparently he'd once claimed to see Louisa and she spoke to him. His parents had firmly convinced him that she wasn't real. Because of their reprimands and lectures, he'd stopped talking about Louisa the Great.

His parents had been right. Ghosts didn't exist, no matter how much you missed the person who'd died.

J.B. sat up, swinging his legs off the chair, and rested his forearms on his knees. He knew Ben missed Gabrielle and he did, too. Though he had to admit his grief had tapered off with time. They'd had a good marriage those first couple years. Until her need to climb the company ladder had meant less and less time together.

He'd been thrilled when she accidentally got pregnant, thinking they would become closer with a child to share. But Bri had wanted to get back to a job she loved more than motherhood. He hadn't blamed her and, besides, they'd needed her income to make it. But their relationship had suffered.

And while that worthless drunk was solely to blame for the accident that had taken her life, if she hadn't insisted on driving to D.C. for a meeting on her day off…

J.B. sighed heavily. There was no use in rehashing it all—his focus needed to be on helping his son. Life went forward and they had to move on with it.

Hearing the soft strains of instrumental music begin, he smiled. Siobhan had come outside and turned on her portable CD player. She liked to listen to Asian or Latin pieces for her exercise sessions. He stood up and went to the railing, leaning his elbows on the ledge.

Several times she lifted her arms in a curve and lowered them to her sides. Then she raised them overhead, bent forward and placed her flat palms on the ground. Stepping back with one leg, she lifted her torso, then spread her arms to the side and held her balance. Dropping her hands back to the ground, she repositioned her body and moved into the next pose.

Siobhan's skin was damp with effort, but her face never lost its expression of serenity. Unlike Bri, hers was a quiet, unconventional beauty. Her sensual mouth and bedroom eyes balanced her sharp cheekbones and hawkish nose. She moved like a dancer and her body had muscle definition and strength.

J.B. watched, mesmerized by her grace and flexibility. The words could also describe her personality. He felt wanted around her, welcomed and appreciated, as well as desired. *Bewitched,* he thought with a smirk. The smile instantly turned into a silent groan as she raised her hips for a back bend. She would be amazing in bed. His own body grew hard at the thought of being next to hers, of being inside her.

When she finished, Siobhan stood utterly still for a

few moments, her elbows out and her palms pressed together at a ninety-degree angle, meditating he guessed. Then she took a deep breath and lowered her arms. After turning off the music, she walked toward the house.

Just as she was about to disappear from view, she stopped and angled her ear in the direction of his balcony.

"Good night, J.B."

Damn. She'd caught him. She'd probably heard his heavy breathing as he watched her routine. Nothing for it now except to admit his presence. But instead of speaking, J.B. croaked like the frog she'd threatened to turn him into. Her musical laughter hung in the air like starlight—

Then something behind her caught his attention. J.B.'s heart skipped a beat as adrenaline flooded his system.

"Siobhan," he whispered fiercely. "Don't move!"

She froze, her brows raised in confusion. "What's wrong?"

"Keep still. Just keep still."

Some kind of animal—no way that thing was a dog—had appeared through the hedge at the back of Siobhan's yard. When it crept closer, he could see gray and white hair bristled all over its large, lean body. As he stared at the golden-yellow eyes, his mind scrambled to figure out how he would get to Siobhan in time.

The thing growled softly in the back of its throat and she spun around with a startled cry. "Oh!"

Acting without thought of the ten-foot drop, J.B. rushed to the side of the balcony and vaulted the rail.

He knew coyotes sometimes came down from the hills to supplement their diets with gourmet garbage, but wolves? As he'd hoped, he landed in the shrubs and not on the concrete patio. Gaining his feet, he clapped his hands and yelled to draw the animal's attention.

It seemed to work because the wolf looked over at him, but then so did Siobhan. She started toward him, concern tightening her features. "Are you all right, J.B.?"

"I'm fine."

Actually there were scratches all over his arms and one hell of a bruise forming on his right shin, but the injuries were minor compared to what that wolf might do to her. He tugged her outstretched hand. When she was close enough, he shoved her behind him. He spoke quietly and looked around for some kind of weapon.

"Don't move again, okay?"

As if it knew he was talking to Siobhan, the wolf walked a few paces forward. She leaned around J.B. and spoke in a high-pitched voice usually reserved for babies and the elderly. "Go home. Go on. Obviously this is not a good night to visit."

J.B. frowned at her tone. It wasn't a cocker spaniel, for crying out loud. He stared at her, nonplussed. "*Why* are you talking to that *thing?*"

The wolf growled again, louder and almost annoyed.

"He didn't mean it." She smiled apologetically.

J.B. eyed the animal as it bared its teeth. "Yes, he did."

"No, I was telling Rey that you didn't mean it."

"Rey?" His gaze bounced back and forth between her face and the wolf's. "You *named* it?"

Siobhan kept her attention on the Wolf King, moving around J.B. to crouch on the grass. She kept her voice too low to be overheard. "You need to go back to my sister. Whatever you did, just apologize to Shona and—"

Rey narrowed his golden eyes and curled his upper lip back.

"Don't bother snarling at me. You can't stay here and put me in the middle of your latest argument." He grumbled and gnashed his teeth, but he must have been feeling guilty because after a moment he nodded. She stood up and pointed her finger. "Now go home."

"Um, yeah." J.B. waved his hand vaguely. "Beat it."

The closest thing to a smirk crossed Rey's lupine face as he cocked his head to one side and flicked his tail. She rubbed a hand over his soft fur and chuckled softly. He nuzzled her arm then disappeared through the hedges. Siobhan turned back to confront J.B.'s stunned expression.

He looked pale beneath his tan and he kept glancing at the shrubs. "So, uh, what just, uh…"

"It's okay. I've seen him before and he's harmless."

J.B. frowned, his mood going from confused to irritated over the perceived danger. "Harmless? Siobhan, that was a *wolf,* a wild creature."

"He's only half-wild, trust me. And he's only half wolf." She stepped close to him and wrapped her arms about his waist. She might not be an intuit, but she recognized a man who'd been denied the opportunity to flex his muscles. "Thank you very much for protecting me. I felt a lot safer with you here."

He continued to glower while she gave him her most adoring look, then his face cleared and he held her tightly. His voice was gruff with a blend of humor and sarcasm. "Sure thing. Always glad to save a little lady from a big bad wolf."

Siobhan rested her cheek against his shoulder. He felt strong and reliable and oh so warm. The heat of his body seeped into hers. And he was getting hotter by the second. So was she. The embrace had started off as a means of comfort, but now it felt more like the promise of a night in his arms.

She sensed an echoing change in J.B. from the way he held her and the acceleration of his pulse. Her nipples beaded against his chest and tension throbbed between her thighs. She wanted him. Oh, how she wanted him and damn the consequences and considerations, at least for the moment.

Siobhan turned her face up and met his gaze. Even in the semidarkness of the yard, she could see the gleam of longing in his eyes. She felt desire burgeoning against her hip and coiling in her own belly. As J.B. slowly lowered his head, their breath mingled, their hearts drummed in unison, and she parted her lips for their first kiss…

"Daddy!"

They froze, their mouths mere centimeters apart, eyes already filling with regret.

"Daddy? Where are you?"

J.B. stepped back, sliding his fingers along her bare arms with a thin smile. "I have to go."

"I know."

He sighed, pressed his mouth to hers in a kiss that was all too fleeting, then limped back to his own house. He paused in the kitchen doorway and glanced over his shoulder. Then with a small wave, he went inside. Siobhan remained where she was, rubbing her hands over where he'd touched her arms, feeling the loss of his warmth as well as the opportunity. She had little doubt that kiss was still to come, but Ben was a consequence they couldn't fail to consider.

CHAPTER FOUR

A LOUD BANG was quickly followed by plumes of pink smoke. Instruction at the Center was held in carefully separated, spell-protected brick cottages dotted around the estate. The Registry's founders had soon regretted the original wooden lecture halls. Incantations and spells had frequently mixed with explosive results... and one unfortunate case of permanent blue facial hair.

"Don't worry, Evan dear. I'm fairly certain those stains will come right off in a matter of, um, days."

Miss Marion reached up to pat the tall, lanky young man's shoulder. Gathering his books, Evan left for the infirmary to have the nurse look at the splotches decorating his face like so many port wine birthmarks. She turned to the rest of the class with an encouraging smile.

"Now, let's not give up, shall we? Remember, magic is the use of natural elements combined with force of will to affect a change." She slid her cat's-eye glasses onto her nose and waved her hands randomly about the circular cottage.

The sheer multicolored scarves draped over the closed windows began to flutter in the spontaneous breeze. Flames shot up from the wicks of the vanilla-scented candles and the overstuffed floor pillows in the lecture area started dancing across the terra-cotta tiles.

In response to the scattered applause, Marion modestly inclined her head and levitated her assortment of crystal balls into the air. After showing off just a bit more by making them spin, she set everything aright. "Transmogrification simply takes a bit more will than most magic. Changing one thing into something else is a difficult skill."

Her many rings glittering in the candlelight, she wiggled her fingers over the eight fat, purple grapes on her desk. They instantly turned into a glass of red wine and then back again. "But, if you concentrate, I have every confidence that each one of you can turn your fruit into goblets of wine."

Marion ambled nearer the east windows, stealing a gaze through the leaded glass. The air outside glistened with rainbow-hued fairy dust from the spells that kept the property hidden and protected from ordinary folk. Any no-mag who did happen to wander onto the grounds immediately got an urgent craving for enchiladas and salsa roja.

Brujas, a Tex-Mex restaurant run by witches from the Center, had been conveniently placed near the Registry's turnoff on Highway 89-A for that very reason.

Marion smiled at the rare sight of a golden unicorn near the creek. In the centuries she'd lived and taught here, she never tired of the stunning views. Towering high above the Coconino Forest, the deep crimson rocks of the Magenta Cliffs marked the edge of the canyon. The breathtaking sight of ancient earth formations crouching beneath a cobalt sky gave her strength and a sense of peace, as it had to so many before her.

Generations of Hopi, Apache and Navajo had jour-
neyed to Sedona on their vision quests. Shamans still
came to Oak Creek Canyon, along with Druids,
Shintos, Wiccans, Romani, Santeros… All types of
mages, both human and extrarealmer—the elves,
nymphs and fairies.

Marion turned back to observe the class. She knew
better than to form attachments when the average student
spent less than a month here, the majority never to return.
But after five years, Siobhan Silverhawk was a not-so-
secret favorite. The girl should have been one of her
most promising students, however her magic remained
blocked.

Every week anxious Neophytes came to the Center
expecting instant power without learning the responsibility that went along with it. Despondent Invocators
came seeking quick, easy solutions to a problem only
they themselves could resolve.

Any time a witch's powers were obstructed, the
cause could only be one of three possibilities—the rejection of love, the misuse of love or the forsaking of
love. It was this last reason, Marion suspected, that
kept Siobhan and several other students from reaching
their potential. They'd been rejected too often to open
their hearts.

But try telling that to a bunch of impatient, de-
pressed magic initiates.

Marion sighed yet again, frustrated by the many
times she'd offered her insight only to be dismissed by
younger witches as sweetly scatterbrained. Well, who
wouldn't be scatterbrained, what with all of her admin-
istrative duties for the Guardian of the Registry, as
well as teaching so many classes, and really…

Really, she needed to concentrate on what her students were doing.

She turned back to the class. For the next fifteen minutes, Marion swept up and down the narrow aisles between pedestal tables in the practicum area. "Don't be discouraged, Siobhan. Aurora, mind where you point, dear. Sabrina, a small glass is better than no glass."

"Well done, Harry. Extra points for crafting a sparkling wine." As was typical in her experience, the Novices were doing better than the Invocators. Feeling insecure was a way of forsaking love—in this case self-love—and therefore those new to magic were quicker to learn than those rediscovering it.

"Glinda? Oh, no. Glinda!" Over at one of the tables nearest the west windows, a student was holding a bulging goblet with both hands. Marion scurried forward the instant she realized the peevish Invocator's impatience had gotten the best of her again. "You're only meant to use *eight* of the grapes!"

Instead an entire bunch of grapes had started exploding and fermenting inside the cup. Glinda was concentrating hard, as though to contain the growing mess but, before Marion could vanquish the errant magic, the glass shattered. Glinda dropped the goblet and held up her bleeding hand. "Ah!"

Siobhan had been working—without perceivable result—at the neighboring table and so was first to Glinda's side. She yanked a scarf from the curtain rod and grabbed for the other woman's wrist. "That looks bad. Let me help you wrap it."

Marion heard a collective gasp as she pushed through the crush of bodies around the injured woman.

When she finally got through she drew in a squeaky gasp herself. The cut had clearly been quite nasty. *Had been.* Because right before everyone's eyes, the palm of the hand Siobhan held was slowly closing, the ragged ends weaving together to form healthy skin.

The entire class was murmuring in amazement while Glinda stared at her hand as if it belonged to someone else. However, no one looked more stunned than Siobhan herself. Mouth slightly agape, she slowly turned her pale face and startled gaze in Marion's direction.

"What's happening?"

"Isn't it obvious?" someone whispered. "You're healing Glinda's hand!"

Siobhan visibly swallowed. "They told me but— I can't believe this. It's still two days before— This is just so unbelievable."

"Quite the contrary, my dear, dear girl. I *always* knew you had it in you." Marion smiled proudly. That silver O would not be written next to Siobahn Silverhawk's name in the Archive now!

"BY THE TIME I LEFT the Center, it seemed like everybody was talking about it. Miss Lilian wants to interview me for her textbook. I went from showing no promise in her Restoration class to this. But I have no idea how I did it. I just wanted to help and it…happened."

Siobhan took a sip of her prickly pear cactus iced tea. She only worked at Luminous for a few hours on Wednesdays, so she was having lunch with V'Leria at one of the outdoor cafés in the Tlaquepaque shopping center. A Sedona landmark, the arts and crafts village was an authentic replica of a Mexican pueblo with stucco walls, cobblestone walkways and courtyard gardens among the distinctive boutiques and galleries.

"Well, I'm jealous." V'Leria spooned more salsa roja onto the enchiladas she was eating. "I mean, I'm just a psychic but I kind of liked being the special one in this relationship. Now you've gone and ruined it by turning out to be this wunderkind witch. Way to go, Silverhawk." She rolled her eyes dramatically.

"Being such a gifted psychic, I would have thought you'd see this coming, Val." Siobhan batted her eye-lashes teasingly. V'Leria was actually a short-term psychic—she could only predict things that would happen within a few hours. But her humor quickly evaporated on a sigh. "I sure didn't anticipate this, despite my grandmothers' reassurance."

"Why not? Isn't, like, everyone in your family a witch?"

At the mention of her parents and sisters, Siobahn experienced the familiar twinge of pride—and envy. Her father, Jacob Silver Dawn, was a cardiac surgeon who had never lost a patient. Her older sister Sîan had followed in his footsteps to become an oncologist. Fiona Goshawk, her mother, was a prominent psychologist while her younger sister Shona worked as a futures trader for a brokerage firm.

"Yes, they are, which is why I always wondered if I'd been adopted."

In a family that was decidedly different, Siobhan had always stood out because she *wasn't*. Her sisters had attained their powers at puberty, while the only change she'd gone through was the one all women experienced. Growing up in a family that used magic as easily as cutlery, she'd felt overshadowed, ordinary and inadequate.

She'd never felt more hopeless than the day her friend Laurel's life had changed forever. They'd gone hiking in the Sangre de Cristos mountains, planning to reach the summit of Wheeler Peak. Halfway through the high-altitude climb, Laurel had fallen on the steep trail and shattered her leg.

No matter how hard Siobhan had tried to visualize the damage, no matter how much she'd prayed to the spirit guides for help, she hadn't been able to heal the injury. They'd had to wait hours until another hiker contacted the park rangers, who'd called in a medevac helicopter. To this day Laurel walked with a crutch and quietly endured persistent pain.

Siobhan had applied to the Arizona State University's biochemistry program while Laurel was still in rehab. She'd left Taos and the associated disappointment right after high school graduation. Her family had been saddened to see her go, but they understood her need to find her own place in the world and discover what her part in it would be.

V'Leria spoke around a mouthful of enchilada. "So what else has happened? Have you had any visions or anything?"

"No, nothing. I guess I shouldn't really expect it, since my birthday isn't until Friday. But to be honest, I'm not really sure when or if my powers will come."

"Well, I'd say it's pretty obvious that you're getting at least some of them, right?"

"I guess so." She toyed with the straw in her glass, stirring the tea in circles. "But maybe that's all I'm getting. Or maybe what I did get won't last."

Val held up a palm. "Um, excuse me, but this is Sedona and I'm pretty sure that negative thoughts are outlawed by the city ordinance. Seriously, don't dismiss what's happening. The moon is waxing, gaining energy, and it'll be full on your birthday. How could you *not* come into your own under those conditions?"

Siobhan combed her hair back over her ear. "My sisters have had their powers for most of their lives, while I've waited and studied and practiced in vain. So I think you can understand my reservations."

"But the love potion is working. You can't deny that."

"Yes, I can." Her contradiction was immediate, but so was the heat in her face.

V'Leria pushed her empty plate away with a shrewd look. "Very convincing. Have you thought about a career in theater?"

"Just because there's some mutual interest has nothing to do with a fake elixir. In fact, I was attracted to J.B. long before—" Siobhan abruptly closed her mouth. When Val grinned, she shrugged and grinned back. "Okay, I admit it. I like him."

"Do you just like him? Or do you 'like him' like him?"

"What is this, junior high school?" She made a face but she knew what her friend was asking. "I really *like* him, Val. I think I may even be falling in love with him. And I know he's attracted to me as well. But Ben might not be the only one having trouble letting go of Gabrielle. So I don't know that these feelings will lead anywhere."

"They will." V'Leria nodded to emphasize the certainty in her voice.

Siobhan thought about the men she'd dated and how quickly attraction had turned into rejection. "How can you be so sure?"

"Hello? Psychic? So trust me—trust your feelings—and then I want to hear every single detail about the long, slow, deep, wet kiss J.B.'s going to give you tonight."

"In my dreams," she muttered as her friend got up to order dessert. V'Leria was always sincere and enthusiastic in her predictions, but didn't often come close to being correct. All the same Siobhan allowed herself a tiny smile of anticipation, just in case this one came true.

J.B. SQUARED his shoulders and marched up the walkway to Siobhan's front door. He'd done it a hundred times before—okay, maybe a couple dozen—so there was no reason for the tension in his neck or for the giant, razor-toothed butterflies in his stomach. No reason at all.

He rang the bell and waited. Listening to the shouts of laughter behind him, he glanced around to watch Ben and some other kids riding their bikes in front of the town house complex. Should he ring again? It was Wednesday. Siobhan usually worked in the morning on Wednesdays so she should be home... He knew her exact schedule. He shook his head, acknowledging that his infatuation was now official.

A moment later Siobhan came to the door and held open the screen. "Hi, J.B. How are you?"

"Good. I'm good. I, uh, have something for you."

She tipped her head. "Oh, did the mailman deliver to your address by mistake again?"

"Um, no. This is from me." He held up the small white box.

Siobhan smiled shyly and opened the door wider. "Thank you. Would you like to come in?"

He stepped into the foyer but didn't walk any farther. "I need to keep an eye on Ben."

"Of course. We can see him through the screen." She glanced from his face to the box and back again, looking as nervous as he felt. "So… What's that?"

The box felt like it had suddenly increased tenfold in weight. What would she think about the fact that he was giving her jewelry when he'd never even asked her out on a date? Did jewelry imply the desire for a commitment? Was that what he wanted? Was it too soon, or about time?

Instead of giving it to her, he rolled it between his hands. "Ben's working on a special birthday project in his art class at school. He's really anxious to give it to you on Friday and I don't want to steal his spotlight."

"That's so sweet of you, J.B. You're a good father."

"Sometimes," he said. Thinking about last night's tears still pierced his heart. "Anyway, this is for you."

She accepted the gift with dignity, but her eyes were dancing with the same glee as Ben's did on Christmas morning. Siobhan tugged the ribbon free and pulled open the box. Inside, on a bed of satin, lay an Irish metalwork necklace. The pendant was a pewter disc with garnets and a bronze sun in the center.

"J.B., it's lovely. Where did you find it?"

"I was just walking by Fresh Eire and thought you might like it." He shrugged, but actually the place was a custom design jewelry studio and he'd spent two hours trying to choose the perfect piece.

"I do, very much. Will you help me put it on?"

She handed the necklace to him, turned around and lifted her hair to one side. As she did he caught a hint of her shampoo, something that smelled like spring-time. Her skin felt warm against his wrist. He took his sweet old time hooking the clasp of the silver chain.

"Thank you so much."

Siobhan turned again, her fingers lightly brushing the pendant, and looked into his eyes with a smile. Tipping her head back, she puckered her lush mouth and leaned forward. J.B.'s heart hammered inside his chest as he lowered his head to meet her kiss. As their mouths touched, he felt her lips soften beneath his, felt them part on a sigh.

The kiss was gentle and very, very nice. He brushed his mouth slowly over hers, savoring the moment. J.B. traced her upper lip with the tip of his tongue, before slipping it inside to sample her fully. She tasted like honey, literally as well as figuratively, and he wondered what she'd been eating before he came to the door.

She returned the kiss, deepened it. The sweetness of it sang through his veins and made him hungry for more. He lost himself in the moment, in feelings of tenderness and something deeper. But even as the thought crossed his mind, he shied away from it, con-centrating instead on the lust coursing through him.

Though only their lips were touching, he felt the electricity arcing between them down the entire length of his body. The kiss had escalated from nice and sweet to hot and passionate, making desire throb in his veins. Her response was eager, inviting.

But he couldn't exactly take her on the carpet right

in front of the screen door. So with genuine regret at
having to give up her mouth for even a second, J.B.
gently ended the kiss. The irises of Siobhan's pale
eyes were dilated and her fair skin was flushed. He
licked the taste of her from his lips and cleared his
throat.

"So, that means you like the necklace, huh?"

She laughed, breaking some of the sexual tension.
"Yeah. It's okay, I guess."

"If that's what your ambivalence is like, I can't wait
for you to be sure." He gazed at her intently, letting her
see the heat in his eyes. Though his tone was teasing,
there was a real question behind his words.

Siobhan reached out a soft hand to cup his stubble-
roughened cheek. As her gaze searched his, he
watched the play of emotions on her face and grinned
at what he saw. She returned the smile before pulling
his head down for another kiss. This one skipped past
nice and headed straight for naughty so fast he thought
his zipper might split.

When they finally pulled apart, breathing heavily,
J.B. saw Ben out of the corner of his eye. He sat on his
bike at the bottom of the steps, watching them. Siobhan
noticed, too, and took a step away from him, her fingers
covering her mouth as if to hide what they'd done.

J.B. tensed, bracing for his son's reaction to seeing
him kiss a woman other than his mother. But to his
surprise, Ben had a goofy smile on his face and seemed
okay with what happened— Until he suddenly jerked
his head to one side like something caught his attention. Then Ben ducked his chin and his mouth turned
down as if he might cry. But before J.B. could call to
him, he rode off down the sidewalk.

"Maybe…" Siobhan looked at the floor and spoke hesitantly. "Maybe this is not the right time for us to start—"

He tried to smile but doubted it reached his eyes. "It hasn't been the right time for the past six months. But I know Ben really likes you and he'll get used to the idea."

"And what's that?"

"The idea that I really like you, too."

CHAPTER FIVE

"The Power of the World does everything in circles. Mother Earth is round and Father Sky curves around her. The winds spin and the waves roll in circles. The moon rises up and the sun lies down in circles. And so it is where power moves."

Firmly grasping the inlaid knife, Siobhan spoke in Navajo as she traced the protective shape around an area of her yard. Dressed in traditional knee-length moccasins, a tiered cotton skirt and matching blouse, she began the ritual. The turquoise flowers of her "squash blossom" necklace and the silver "storyteller" discs of her concho belt jangled as she danced in the pale light of daybreak.

When the circle was complete and outlined in sea salt, she laid the buckskin hide in its center. She used a charcoal stick to carefully sketch the design she'd practiced late into the night. Taking a cleansing breath deep into her lungs, she asked the Creator for guidance and began the first song of the chant.

"Haiya naiya yana, yo wo yowa lana ya, na'eye lana heya 'eye…"

The Blessingway represented everything that was positive in the world—happiness, harmony and health. The ceremony was a paradigm for the ordered universe, emphasizing the "place home." The stanzas of the chant told the origin myth of how the Navajo people were given the Blessingway by the *díyin diné*, the Holy Ones.

As she sang the second of many verses, she reached for the clay dishes of colored sand, ground cornmeal, crushed flowers and other materials she needed for the dry painting. Flipping one of her thick braids over her shoulder, Siobhan knelt facing the east. Using her right hand, she scooped up some gypsum and let it trickle between her thumb and index finger to begin creating the image of Changing Woman.

As the sun rose higher into the sky, she continued working out from the center, covering any mistakes with fresh sand and beginning that section over again. She took only short breaks for water and a bite to eat. It was too important that she perform the ceremony perfectly to stop for long. If the Holy Ones were planning to finally gift her with full healing abilities, she would honor them as best she could.

She finished the *íikááh* just before dusk and with the last of her voice, Siobhan sang the final verse of the chant. *"Behind her, before her, it is blessed. Beneath her, above her, it is blessed. All around her, everywhere, it is blessed. Sa'ah naaghéi, bik'eh hózóó."*

Siobhan sat back on her heels, ignoring the ache in her thighs from kneeling for so long. Physically exhausted but feeling light of heart and spiritually energized, she waited. Surely there would be some monumental event now. An electrifying surge of energy, or even a real lightning bolt from the sky. Something to accompany the jolt of power that would pour into her any moment now.

Something. Anything. Any minute. She waited while the evening painted the sky in vivid orange and red and purple. She waited while evening gave way to night and the first stars appeared. Finally Siobhan creaked to her feet, wincing at the pins and needles in her calves.

After all of the anticipation and promises and ceremony, she didn't feel any different than she had yesterday.

So much for her Power Year birthday.

"MACARONIS IS A LOT better when they're cooked. We had it for lunch in the cafeteria." Later that evening, Ben admired the construction paper decorated with glued-on dry noodles and tempera color.

Siobhan glanced from his masterpiece to his face. "How did the paint taste once it was cooked?"

"Mostly like cheese." He mimicked her deadpan expression for a second before dissolving into giggles.

She pointed to the pasta in the "sky."

"This part must taste like blue cheese then, huh?"

"You're silly, Sisi."

"And *you* are quite the artist. I'm going to hang your picture right here on the kitchen wall." Siobhan pinned the noodle paper to the corkboard near the fridge. After making a production of positioning it exactly, she turned to J.B. "So, are you ready for those chicken tacos?"

The three of them sat around the dining table, sharing stories about their days. It wasn't the first time she'd spent a meal with them, but this felt different. Everything felt new and different and somehow right since she and J.B. had exchanged that first—and second—kiss the other day.

She had classmates and friends, and kept in close touch with her sisters, but she'd been ignoring how lonely her life had become. Past experience had taught her that casual sex was a mistake. From her first boyfriend, a boy she knew from the neighborhood, to her last, a wizard from the Elysian Isles, they'd all made her feel inferior—not really a witch, not fully a woman.

So she hadn't dated again until now. If sitting on the grass and making out after Ben fell asleep could be called dating. Either way, J.B.'s hot kisses and sensual touches were going a long way to change her self-image. At least, the womanly part. She still wasn't really a witch.

She looked over at J.B. as he laughed at an elementary joke Ben told, her heart swelling at the sight of their matching dark blond heads, light brown eyes and dimpled chins. She was enchanted with both of them. But how could they ever accept what she was supposed to be? Especially when she couldn't accept that she still was not. Where was her magic, her legacy?

Frustration and disappointment threatened to bring tears to her eyes. J.B. caught the expression that flitted across her face and arched his brow. She smiled to reassure him, feeling better for his silent concern. Pushing her negativity aside, she focused on enjoying her guests' company.

After dinner, Siobhan turned on the kids' channel for Ben. "You can watch TV while I clean up the dishes. Then I'll make us some popcorn to go with the movies I rented."

His face lit up. "Cool! This is just like what my classmate Justin does on Fridays with his family."

Almost as soon as the words left his mouth, Ben's cheeks turned a hot-red and the excitement bled from his expression. "Butcept we're not— You know. 'Cause Mommy is still my mommy..."

"It's okay, sport," J.B. said quietly, his voice filled with love but also a hint of impatience. "Even though your mom is dead, nobody can take her place, okay?"

Despite understanding what he meant, and knowing their relationship was too new, Siobhan felt a tiny stab of hurt. She wasn't trying to replace anyone; she just wanted to be included. Conjuring up a smile for Ben's sake, though, she rested her hand on his shoulder. "We're friends and—"

The instant she touched him, she experienced a weird kind of double vision. She saw Ben in front of her and at the same time lying on the floor. His eyes were closed and a dark-haired woman stood over him. Then, as quickly as it happened, the second image vanished, leaving her feeling light-headed. She tried to remember what she'd been saying.

"Um, we're friends, right?"

Ben refused to meet her eye. "Yeah, I guess so."

"Well, friends watch movies together all the time. But first I have to clear off the table, so you go on and I'll be right in."

"Go on, sport. I'll help Siobhan so the job goes faster and we can watch those movies." J.B. smiled until Ben had left the room, then he scrubbed a hand across his mouth. "I probably shouldn't have said what I did. At least not so harshly. But I'm getting tired of always having Gabrielle in the room with us."

Siobhan concentrated on gathering up the dirty

plates and cutlery. "You mean between you and Ben? Or between you and me?"

"Hmm. Both, I guess. You're the first woman since— Well, anyway. Ben's fantasies get so elaborate sometimes, I feel like I should include his imaginary mother in the conversation." He picked up the serving dishes and followed her into the kitchen.

Her neck and shoulders tensed as she debated whether to say what was on her mind. In the end she did, though. "J.B., what if this isn't Ben's imagination?"

"What are you talking about?"

Bracing her hand against the countertop, she inhaled softly. Even knowing it was a mistake, she pressed on. "It's possible that Gabrielle is real."

"Yeah, that's what the shrink says. Not to demoralize Ben since his mother is very real to *him*." J.B. placed the baking pan into the bottom washer rack.

"I know you're going to have trouble with this." Siobhan tapped her fingers nervously. "But the past couple of nights, I've felt like… I think someone's been watching us."

"Nobody's been watching. Except for maybe that old guy in the last house across the way. He's got a thing for all the pretty women in the complex."

"I'm being serious. Even though I don't have full powers, I'm sure I've felt some kind of presence—"

"Hold it right there, Siobhan." He closed the dishwasher harder than necessary. "That witch nonsense is fine for the freaks and New Age nuts. But don't try to pass it on to my kid, okay?"

Siobhan bit her lip and told herself it shouldn't matter. J.B.'s vehement disbelief in magic was hardly a surprise—she'd certainly encountered it plenty of times before. But more than the dismissal of her longed-for identity, it hurt to have her concern for Ben tossed back in her face. She cared. About both of them. So she had to set her own feelings aside and do what she could for J.B. and his son, even if that was only friendship.

She wanted to wrap her arms around him and remind him that once upon a time he'd had a creative imagination, too. Instead she spread her palms in acquiescence. "He's your son and you, of course, have to do what you think best."

J.B. hung his head. "Look, I'm sorry I snapped at you. It's just that Ben is already out of hand. And I honestly don't know how much longer I can deal with this." He stepped in front of her and took hold of her wrists. "Let's not spoil the evening."

Siobhan accepted his kiss and struggled to let it go. For now. Keeping quiet about her supposed legacy wasn't deceit; it was self-defense. So she wouldn't bring up her suspicions again. But that didn't mean she wouldn't try to find out what she could about earthbound souls.

When she walked into the living room ten minutes later, J.B. was on the larger sofa with his legs stretched out on the ottoman. Meanwhile Ben sat on the carpet facing the TV, but his eyes were downcast. She set one of the bowls of buttery popcorn next to him. "Here you go, sweetie."

"Thank you." His tone was subdued.

Siobhan inserted the first movie into the DVD player then looked around for the remote control. J.B. had it, of course. She walked over to join him on the sofa. He slipped his arm over her shoulder but she wriggled a few inches away, worried about Ben's reaction. J.B. simply grabbed her around the waist and pulled her to his side.

He shot her a pointed look when Disney's *The Sword and the Stone* came on the screen, however he didn't make any comment. Siobhan smiled and offered him some popcorn. In front of them, Ben was quiet at first, as though he were still upset. But he was soon giggling at Merlin and Arthur's magical high jinx.

After a particularly funny scene with the talking owl, Ben glanced over at them with a laugh. Siobhan tensed, bracing for a childish outburst. But he just smiled shyly before turning his attention back to the movie. Only then did she relax and let herself take real pleasure in the moment. It was strange to be sitting here like this, as if the three of them *were* a family. And yet it felt very comfortable, very right.

Sometime around the midpoint of the second movie, Ben fell asleep. Siobhan got up to move his popcorn bowl and cover him. As she turned with a light wool shawl, she looked down at the small body sprawled on the floor. With a sudden flash of déjà vu, she laughed at herself. So much for her foresight. *She* was the dark-haired woman in her premonition.

J.B. watched Siobhan lovingly place a blanket over his son and felt his chest tighten. What he'd started to say earlier, but hadn't, was that she was the first woman he'd had feelings for since Gabrielle died.

About a year after Bri's death, he'd gone on a few blind dates and had a disastrous friends-with-benefits thing with a coworker. Those women had been very nice, but he hadn't fallen for them.

Not the way he was falling for Siobhan.

It was way too soon to express what he felt, and much too complicated. So when she came back to the sofa he simply opened his arms. Settling her on his thighs, he slid one hand beneath her hair to cradle her neck. He gazed into her eyes and smiled, hoping she saw what he couldn't yet say. Then he drew her closer until their lips met. Siobhan folded her arms over his shoulders and parted her mouth in welcome.

He brushed his lips across hers, enjoying the warm velvet feel of them. She moaned softly against his mouth and slipped her hand beneath his shirt to stroke her fingers over his back. He kissed her hungrily, running his palms slowly along the curves of her hips. As they tasted and touched and teased, time seemed to both fly and stand still until he lost complete track of it. All he knew was her.

Finally, though, he realized they'd gone as far as they were going to under the circumstances. J.B. ended their kiss with great reluctance, though he didn't ease her off his hot, aching lap. Not yet. "I hate to do this, I *really* hate to, but I have to get going. A group of clients requested an early flight in the morning."

"Part of me hates for you to go."

He arched his brows. "Only part of you?"

She smiled apologetically. "The other part kept waiting for Ben to wake up."

"That kid? It would take an earthquake. But I understand and I promise we'll have some time to ourselves very soon."

Siobhan laughed. "My backyard or yours?"

"How about my bed?" When she hesitated, he

clasped her fingers. "It's *my* bed. I bought a new furniture set when we moved here from Baltimore."

She lowered her eyes. "That wasn't my concern. But it does relate to what I was wondering."

"And what's that?"

"Whether this is the right thing." She looked up at him. "I'm not interested in an affair, J.B., but I realize that you may not be ready for anything more. Your decisions don't affect only you. So don't start anything we can't continue, okay?"

Her assertion should have scared him off. Was he ready for a genuine relationship with Siobhan? Yeah, he thought he was. Even though Ben sure as hell wasn't. But she was someone special, someone worth making an effort for. Part of the army ranger creed was *"One hundred percent and then some."* That's what she deserved and so that's what he'd try to give.

J.B. reached to cup her face, rubbing his thumb along her cheek. He looked deeply into beautiful green eyes, hoping she saw his sincere affection. "I'm ready, lady. You're not getting rid of me that easily."

CHAPTER SIX

HE DIDN'T REMEMBER those being there before.

J.B. shifted the fifty-pound deadweight on his shoulder so he could close the door behind him. He'd carried Ben out of Siobhan's house, across the front lawn and up the steps. The kid hadn't stirred once. After flipping on the foyer light, J.B. had started toward the stairs. Then the glint of something in the living room caught his eye.

A bunch of Ben's matchbox-size metal cars were scattered on the floor. J.B. frowned. He thought he'd cleared up all the toys earlier. When had Ben had time to take them back out? He looked closer, knowing something was odd about the layout, but not sure what.

The cars were lined up, forming two lanes of traffic on the wooden floorboards. They sat a uniform distance apart. Ben's play areas were never that neat. J.B. took a few steps closer, the crease in his forehead growing with his unease. Between the precise lines of vehicles lay chaos. The five cars in the center were upside down and on top of each other. As if they'd been in an accident…

He clenched his jaw, breathing heavier as his heart rate accelerated. He tightened his hold on Ben, gripping him with both arms now. The heat from his little body did nothing to melt the ice crystals forming in J.B.'s gut.

Then the logical part of his brain clicked into gear. He'd been anxious to go over to Siobhan's when he got home from work, not paying much attention. Ben must have done this. He just hadn't noticed. Willing his pulse to slow, J.B. kicked the toys out of the middle of the floor toward the wall. He'd tell Ben to clean them up in the morning.

In the meantime, he'd better find the thicker blankets for the beds. It felt damned drafty in here.

"DON'T YOU WANT to go trick-or-treating, sport?"

They'd eaten an early dinner, though he'd had to coerce every single bite Ben had swallowed. Now he was trying to get the kid into his costume so they could get the candy begging over with. But Ben just sat on the edge of his bed, swinging his bare feet and staring at the carpet.

He didn't understand what was going on. Ben had been fine all day. J.B. had taken him along for a couple of canyon tours, and then left him to play with Cole, the office secretary's kid. He'd seemed happy enough. But as the day came to an end, Ben's mood had grown more and more solemn. The closer they'd gotten to home, the quieter he'd become.

"Daddy, I *do* want to go…" He fidgeted with the buttons of his shirt.

"But?"

"But I don't think I should leave Mommy." He lowered his voice to a conspiratorial whisper. "She keeps *crying.*"

That sure sounded familiar. Bri had known J.B.'s

weakness for tears and she'd known how to use them to her advantage. It was just like her to manipulate a situation until she got what *she* wanted, to hell with— J.B. shook his head, scowling at the track his thoughts had taken. He bit back what he really wanted to say, remembering the therapist's advice.

"I'm sure she'll survive for the hour or so you'll be gone." He pointed to the costume. "Get changed so we can go out. Move it."

Ten minutes later, they walked up to Siobhan's house. She was sitting on the front steps, a pointed wizard's hat perched on her hair. The short black dress she wore showed off her long, slender thighs above black leather boots that were inspiring J.B. to all kinds of wicked fantasies.

"Trick or treat, Sisi." Ben held out his plastic pumpkin basket.

She grinned, taking in the boy's dark blue uniform, cap and plastic handcuffs. "Coming right up, Officer Ben. I wouldn't want you to give me a ticket for failure to yield chocolate."

As she dropped several candy bars and a dollar bill into Ben's basket, J.B. swung his cape over one shoulder and leaned down. "What he ought to do is place you under arrest."

Responding to his tone, she coyly gazed at him from beneath her lashes. "Whatever for?"

"Disturbing my peace." He let her see his eyes travel up and down her outfit, lingering on the cleavage revealed by the dress's low neckline.

Siobhan flashed him a mischievous look. "I don't think you're supposed to bite me *there,* Dracula."

"I just want to nibble." He grinned, showing his

plastic fangs, then brushed a kiss over her deep red lips.

Ben, who'd been grumbling impatiently, finally piped up. "Dad-dee! We gotta go before all the candy's *gone!*"

J.B. straightened up. "Okay, sport. Walk on over to the Doughertys' house. I'll be right there."

Siobhan handed out more candy bars then smiled up at him. "I've got a treat for you, too, if you want to stop by later?"

"*If?* You obviously have no idea how good you look. I'll be back once Ben crashes from his sugar rush."

When she pointed next door, J.B. turned to see his son stuffing one of Cathy Dougherty's chocolate cup-cakes into his mouth. He looked back at Siobhan.

"You might have to wait up."

HER BEAUTY seemed unearthly.

Ben had dropped off earlier than expected, so J.B. had walked out to his patio. Now he watched as Siobhan performed some kind of ceremony, as fascinated by her as by what she was doing. The full moon shone on her dark hair, reflected on the white gown she wore. Her face was utterly serene and in this light she really did look like an enchantress or a magical fairy queen.

She knelt in front of a makeshift altar, placing candles and food on the white cloth. Light from a fire in the barbecue shone through the thin material of her long gown, silhouetting her body. When she lifted her arms out to the sides, palms raised, he saw the swell of her breasts under the fabric. Her voice carried clearly on the warm, still air.

"Last night the veil between realms grew thin. Tonight the time-out-of-time begins. I kneel before this altar, openhearted, seeking guidance from those souls departed." Siobhan struck a match and, moving clockwise, lit each of the four white tapers. The tiny flames illuminated her face, casting an eerie glow over her features.

"As your daughter remembers, as each candle burns, so the great solar wheel once again turns." With that, she touched her fingers to the pewter necklace. She apparently hadn't taken it off since he gave it to her. J.B. smiled in the dark, pleased that she carried something of him with her all the time.

Next she picked up a small knife. The blade gleamed in the firelight just before she dipped it into the silver cup. Then she used it to cut a large red apple into quarters that she placed near the candles. She did the same with a small loaf of bread. Setting the knife aside, she stood and raised the cup like she was offering a toast.

"I remember, I honor and I bid you welcome."

After she drank, a cool breeze suddenly gusted over the lawn. The delicate scent of night-blooming moon-flowers drifted to him on the air. It blew the gown against her body, perfectly outlining the taut peaks of her nipples, her flat stomach and the curve of her thighs. Siobhan lifted her arms again and tossed her head back, calling up to the heavens.

"With every daybreak, moonrise and tide, may good come to pass and cast bad aside. May all that is right be as it seems as the New Year is born with bright hopes and dreams. Blessed be!"

She began to sing a lilting Gaelic melody so lovely

it hung like crystals in the billowing air. And while she sang she danced. Moving in circles, her willowy body undulated like a leaf on a rippling stream and J.B.'s throat constricted at the beauty of her movements. No woman had ever intrigued him more; he'd never wanted a woman more.

He still didn't believe her claim to be a witch but he was starting to believe strongly that she possessed some kind of magic. Drawn to her, compelled as if by a power beyond his control, he walked slowly across the backyard, unable to take his eyes off her.

The chill wind whipped up, stronger than before. Siobhan hesitated as the fine hair on her arms stood on end. She thought she saw flashes of light twinkling around the yard and suddenly felt uncertain... Then she saw J.B. coming to her side and her fear evaporated.

She stood waiting for him, feeling oddly like her destiny had finally arrived. He took one of her hands and placed his other on her waist. Smiling tenderly, he guided her so that she fell into step as though they had done this a thousand times before.

His words tickled her ear as he murmured, "Will you sing for me?"

Siobhan chose an ancient tune about love and life-times, and sang with all the emotion welling in her heart. Tonight there were no shadows in his eyes. She saw only her feelings reflected in his gaze and knew this was the start of something very special. Then, abruptly, she felt an icy chill so sharp it cut the breath from her lungs. Siobhan huddled against J.B.

"Did you feel that?"

"Here, let me warm you up."

He folded her into his arms, holding her close. As they continued to waltz to the music of the night, the steady beat of his heart and the certainty of his embrace made her feel protected, cherished. The cold quickly gave way to the heat building between them as he lowered his head to kiss her....

GABRIELLE STOOD beside them, shaking, filled with so much fury it might have killed her if she wasn't already dead.

How was it possible to love like this, and hate like this, at the same time? She thrust out her hand, wanting to hit or scratch, needing to touch and caress, unable to do either. *Why couldn't they see her? Why couldn't she reach them?* Bri knew something had happened tonight. As she'd watched the other spirits drift away from the yard, she felt different, more *here* than usual. More alive than she'd felt in two years.

One moment she'd been driving. The next she'd been dying in a whirlwind of sound and color and pain. Jesus God, the pain. Not so much from the steering wheel crushing her chest or from her head smashing through the windshield. But from anger and loss and regret, knowing there wouldn't be any next times. No tomorrows, no second chances.

Siobhan huddled in J.B.'s embrace. "Did you feel that?"

"Here, let me warm you up." He folded her into his arms, holding her close.

Bri watched helplessly as they continued to dance on the grass, as *her husband* leaned down to kiss that bitch. A war of emotions raged inside of her until tears of jealousy pricked her eyelids. This was so unfair! He'd sensed her presence, she was sure of it. She should be the one in J.B.'s arms, *she* should—

Wait.

If he *had* sensed her this time, then maybe she was wrong about second chances. Ben had been able to hear her before. And sometimes, when she was especially upset, he could even see her. She looked toward the other town house. Mentally searching, she closed her eyes. When she opened them she was standing in the doorway of Ben's room, looking at her son, her precious baby, sleeping fitfully in his bed.

Her temper sparked with impotent rage. Their son was in trouble. But his father was too busy screwing around to notice. She moved to Ben's bedside, her heart aching at the sight of his sweaty brow and tangled sheets. He tossed and turned, whimpering softly. She reached out to stroke his damp hair, her throat constricting with love and concern.

"It's okay, honey." She spoke soothingly, hoping to quiet him. "I'm here. Mommy's here."

"Mommy?"

She startled as he turned his face toward her hand, then felt a rush of excitement. He blinked sleepily, his expression confused for a moment, then clearing as a smile appeared on his sweet lips. "Hi, Mommy. Whatcha doing here?"

She had no idea, since another's will had brought her out from the darkness tonight. "I came to check on you. You were kind of restless."

"I was having a bad dream. I think there were monsters."

She smiled reassuringly. "Well, they're all gone now, baby. You're okay."

His bright eyes clouded with anxiety. "What if they come back?"

"They won't. Not if you go to your happy place. Bad dreams can't go there—they aren't allowed."

"Will you go with me, Mommy? And keep rubbing my hair? I remember you used to do that."

Bri was stunned. "You can— Can you feel that?"

"Uh-huh. But it's not so cold like when you came before." He yawned loudly. "Will you snuggle me?"

Could she? Was it possible now? She hoped with all her heart and slid onto the bed next to her child. Ben rolled to his side so that they lay back to front, her arm draped over him. It took every ounce of will she had not to cry. She'd waited so long for this, so long…

"I think I feel your heart beating, Mommy. How can that happen?"

"You feel how much I love you." She schooled her voice, keeping it as light as possible, even as loneliness gripped her soul. "So, darling boy. Where's our happy place tonight?"

"San Diego."

She laughed. "San Diego? Why there?"

"They have the ocean there and the big zoo and…"

Gabrielle half listened, concentrating instead on the miraculous feeling of holding her baby. But even as she thanked God for the chance to experience this joy again, rage flowed through her like liquid fire fueled by betrayal and pain. J.B. was cheating on her. He'd forgotten her. And apparently he wanted Ben to forget her, too.

Well, *that* wasn't going to happen.

CHAPTER SEVEN

AN INCREDIBLE STORM was brewing, a tempest like she'd never experienced before. And yet the night remained clear, the air once again still and warm now that the breeze had died away. The reflected light of the full moon cast bluish shadows around the yard, enchanting everything within it.

Siobhan eagerly parted her lips for J.B.'s kiss and his mouth closed hungrily over hers. One hand came up to fist in her hair, bringing her up on her toes as his tongue plundered her mouth. He held her against the length of his body, pressing the proof of his desire to her pelvis, while his other hand stroked the curve of her hip.

Pressure, slow and heavy, settled in her chest and in her womb. The sudden crazy need for him made her heart flutter wildly. J.B.'s kisses both robbed her of her senses but also heightened them. She tasted the peppermint on his breath and his desire. She breathed in the musky scent of his skin and the smell of apples ripening on her small tree. She felt his passion and felt the pieces of her life fall into place.

Her hands sought the hem of his shirt, reached underneath to caress the smooth rope of muscle in his back. J.B.'s fingers were systematically crumpling the skirt of her gown, exposing her legs to the night air. Finally the bunched material gave way to the feel of his lightly callused palm sliding over her bare skin. He broke the kiss to smile down at her.

"I thought only us army guys went 'commando.'"

"Celtic rituals and ceremonies are often performed skyclad—naked—but I didn't want to shock the neighbors."

"Skyclad, huh?" J.B. stepped out of his shoes and tugged his shirt off, tossing it over one shoulder. Then he reached down to undo his belt and zipper.

Siobhan gave a startled laugh. "What are you doing?"

"You're not shocked, are you?" The expression on his handsome face held an invitation and a challenge.

She accepted, letting her eyes roam over his moonlit body. He stood before her, naked in more ways than one. Her gaze meandered down his muscular torso to his washboard stomach and narrow hips, to his jutting erection and lean-muscled thighs. He had the physique of a warrior athlete. And he was offering it for her pleasure.

"No, not shocked." The pressure began to churn in her belly, gaining speed and urgency, blending with her excitement. "I'm impressed and very, very turned on."

"You're also overdressed."

It was her turn to shed her clothing and toss it aside. She stood motionless, giving him the chance to look his fill. But he immediately moved toward her and she raised her arms to embrace him. The look in his eyes was hot and hungry and a little wild. She thought he was going to pull her to the ground, roll her underneath him and ravish her.

Instead he pressed his lips to her forehead, her mouth, the base of her throat. Each kiss felt like a promise strengthening the bond between them. Then he knelt to worship her breasts, nuzzling each in turn. Jolts of desire kindled the gathering storm within her. Kneeling before her, J.B. placed reverent kisses on her abdomen, her belly and lower still.

She widened her stance at the first flick of his tongue to her sensitive flesh. Siobhan threw her head back, clasping his head and moaning. It wouldn't take much more of this to send her over the edge and it would be a pleasant trip. But she wanted more, needed more. So she went down on her knees, too, capturing his mouth as the storm inside her picked up force.

J.B. did lay her down now, gently reclining her onto the soft grass next to him. His hands stroked her skin, leaving a trail of agitated nerves in their wake. Her pulse drummed against his lips as he kissed his way down her neck. When his thumb found and fondled her nipple to a rigid crest, Siobhan arched her back, demanding more of his touch.

His mouth slanted over hers again and again while her right hand slid across his broad shoulder. *He'd dislocated it in the final game against the Stallions.* Learning his body, she let her palm glide down his back, *over the ribs that had been fractured in a bar fight,* and down to the sleekly muscled cheek of his—

Siobhan gasped.

How did she know? How could she possibly know about these old injuries?

She moved her hand around to the front of his body and slowly combed the sprinkling of curls across his chest. As she touched him, her hand started to tingle.

And then it happened. Something opened up inside of her and she felt an overwhelming lust, pure and urgent, a combination of J.B.'s and her own. But, beneath that, lay so much more.

Friendship, affection, happiness, hope. Then deeper still she felt *loneliness, remorse, worry, regret. Old hurts that still bled, new wounds that bruised his heart.* A riot of emotions rained down on her senses and her heart ached in compassion. He was a good father, a good man, and he deserved to be happy. If only there were a way to ease the pain he hid so well behind his charming grin….

Siobhan closed her eyes briefly as he trailed kisses along the tender places on her throat. J.B. moaned. "Ah, your hands are so damned hot."

When she opened her eyes and tilted her hand, she was stunned to see a marble of glowing white energy in the center of her palm. There was a larger ball, though not as bright, shining below J.B.'s sternum. He didn't seem to notice, focused as he was on caressing the damp flesh between her thighs. A knot of tension, the best kind of tension, formed in her feminine core.

But the delicious sensations his fingers elicited couldn't distract her completely. As it spun, the orb in her hand sent out tendrils of static in a pastel rainbow of colors. Siobhan watched in amazement. Faint streamers of lavender and aqua extended toward and then into his chest. The ribbons sparked and danced and when they connected with J.B.'s orb, she felt the contusion on his right shin fade.

Her heart skipped several beats. Had she done that? Had she healed him? When the bruise was gone, the blue static changed to palest yellow until J.B.'s worry diminished. In the blink of her eyes, the yellow turned orange and his regret lessened, though it didn't evaporate completely. Finally the light became pale pink and she felt his loneliness disintegrate. For a moment, the static became a calm white light once again then it disappeared.

Tears of elation and triumph filled her eyes. J.B. was still nibbling her neck as if no time had passed at all. He seemed oblivious to what had happened, but Siobhan knew her life had been irrevocably altered. She'd been waiting so very long for this gift, and while she'd been unprepared for the exact nature and moment of arrival, she accepted the change as easily as J.B.'s next kiss.

It was deep, passionate, demanding. His kiss both confirmed and questioned. Siobhan murmured against his lips, "Yes. Yes."

Holding her tightly in his embrace, he rolled over until she covered him, kissing her all the while. Blinking back her tears, she felt intimately connected to the sky above, the earth below them and the man whose arms surrounded her. The warmth permeating her heart, spread through her body until the tempest of desire ignited again.

Her body vibrated with need as he slowly lowered her until his sex was completely sheathed in hers. J.B.'s hands gripped her waist, encouraging her to set the pace. Holding his gaze, she gently rocked her pelvis in a dance as old as time. He raised his hips to meet hers, increasing the tempo while the storm of desire whipped itself into a frenzy.

Together they rode the hurricane of mind-blowing

sensation. She moved to the rhythm of his thrusts, moaning loudly when she felt the first delicate inner shivers ripple through her. Their lovemaking was purely elemental, making her feel at one with him and with the universe around them. J.B. drove himself into her, deeper and faster, as her body wept with her first climax.

Waves of desire continued to crash over her as she rode him. J.B. groaned her name, straining with his need for release. Siobhan leaned back, changing the angle of penetration and making him groan even louder. Another whirlwind was gathering within her. His movements frenzied now, she threw her arms wide as the force of her next climax hit. Palms uplifted, she opened her heart fully to this man and to this moment.

Instantly she felt power surge through her hands, traveling down her entire body. She cried out from the intense heat and the shock wave of energy. At the same time J.B. shouted her name and exploded within her. As quickly as it hit, the power drained away, leaving her feeling electrified. Siobhan went limp in his arms, a sheen of sweat slicking her skin, the harsh sound of his breath fanning her ear.

He held her as her pulse slowed, as the night quieted once more. The storm of emotion still raged around them, but with J.B. she was in the relatively calm eye of it. For while he was inside her physically, she was inside of him, sensing his love along with her own. He cupped both hands to her face, forcing her to look at him.

A myriad of expressions—joy and confusion and wonder—danced over his features. "Siobhan. Siobhan, I—"

"I know. I feel the same."

J.B. KISSED HER lips softly, reverently. Then he chuckled. "So much for not shocking the neighbors. If I'd known you were going to be that loud, I would have taken you in the house."

"Me? I'm surprised nobody called the cops from all the noise you were making."

"Entirely your fault."

She grinned smugly. "I'll take that as a compliment."

After another kiss, she settled more comfortably beside him and laid her head on his shoulder. Sighing contentedly, he stared up at the stars. Of course he only imagined that they shone brighter than before. But he still felt like he'd been blessed. Sex had never been like this before. Wait, that wasn't right. *Lovemaking* had never been like this for him before.

He'd slept with other women, including one he'd vowed to cherish until death did they part. But tonight with Siobhan, he'd experienced something so special, so unique, that he knew she was the One. He had to laugh at his own certainty, though. There was so much they didn't know about each other, and they *still* hadn't gone on a date, but here he was planning the rest of their lives.

"What's so funny?" She drew designs on his arm with her index finger.

"Will you go out with me?"

"Um, sure." Her voice was ripe with amusement. "If you mean now, though, we'll both have to put on some clothes."

He rubbed his hand over the satin texture of her bare skin. "Not now. I like you 'skyclad.' But soon. I'll take you out for a nice dinner, maybe we'll go to a movie…"

"Sounds good." She yawned delicately. "But the only place I want to go at the moment is to bed."

"Are you kidding? It's barely ten o'clock."

"Ugh." She gave an exaggerated groan. "Don't tell me you're a night owl? I'm usually up with the sun."

He pretended to gripe, too. "Jeez, not a morning bird. This is going to make things tough."

"Like what things?" She lifted her head, resting her weight on one elbow, her voice carefully modulated.

Only a few days ago, he'd been hesitant. Now he was ready to throw caution to the wind. "A you-and-me thing. Interested?"

She shrugged. "Maybe."

"Maybe? Just *maybe?*"

Her face took on a sassy expression. "I guess you'll have to convince me this is a good idea."

"Come inside with me and I will."

Siobhan smiled at him. "I'm going to wake up late tomorrow, aren't I?"

"I sure as hell hope so."

After gathering their discarded clothes, he held Siobhan's hand as, giggling like children, they "sneaked" across the lawn and into his house. J.B. led her up the stairs, pointing toward his bedroom. He stopped to check on Ben. Shivering, he pulled the extra quilt over his sleeping boy's shoulders. It was always freezing in this room....

With a kiss to Ben's forehead, he left to go to the warmth of his own room and the hot woman waiting there.

SIOBHAN WOKE UP suddenly with a sense of unease.

She felt disoriented, unsure of what had awakened

her. Then J.B. snored comically and it all came back. They'd made love again, slowly, tenderly, taking the time to explore and discover. Afterward, they'd drifted off with his arm draped over her waist. She'd felt relaxed and contented, as if they lay together every night, instead of this being the first time.

But now she felt pain, intense heartbreaking pain, and it wasn't hers. She turned in the warmth of J.B.'s embrace, knowing even before she placed her hand on his chest that the sadness wasn't coming from him. Ben? She listened hard, trying to make out sounds in the strange surroundings. All she heard was the hum of the house fan and a couple of raucous crickets chirping away outside.

The idea that something was wrong wouldn't let go of her, though. Sliding out from beneath J.B.'s arm, she got up and reached for her gown. She slipped it over her head as she walked out of the master bedroom, heart fluttering with an inexplicable fear. She hesitated with her hand on the doorknob of Ben's room. But she had no choice except to take a deep breath and go in.

Lord, it was cold in here! Even as the thought entered her mind, the fine hairs on the back of her neck stood on end. Not only was it cold but the energy was wrong, agitated somehow…

Siobhan's heart pounded. She swallowed hard and slowly looked around the room, certain that she and Ben weren't alone. Although she didn't see anything or anyone she quietly spoke the words of a protection spell, mentally casting a circle of white light around the bedroom. The air warmed slightly as she hurried to the bed.

Ben was huddled under two blankets, his brow furrowed while he whimpered in his sleep. Her heart went out to him. She touched his damp forehead and saw the orb of light appear under her hand. Her senses were immediately flooded with conflicting emotions. *Guilt, confusion, anger, indecision, fear, love, anxiety.* Closing her eyes, Siobhan willed the static tendrils to soothe him.

She imagined the pastel shades one at a time, hoping to give the little boy some peace. But the colors weren't strong enough. Maybe Ben's pain ran too deep for her inexpert powers? She couldn't leave him like this, though. Pulling back the covers, she scooped him off the bed so he could sleep with his father. He cuddled into her warmth. Siobhan turned and left the room, adjusting Ben's unfamiliar weight in her arms...

And came face-to-face with a really pissed-off ghost.

CHAPTER EIGHT

SIOBHAN FROZE in her tracks but her heart started racing from gut-twisting fear. None of the classes she'd taken at the Center had prepared her for this. She knew all of the theory behind things like *Basic Crystal Gazing, Finding the Perfect Familiar* and *Teleportation for Fun and Profit.* But those workshops hadn't given her any practical knowledge for dealing with an angry apparition.

She recognized Gabrielle since Ben shared her features. She must have been very pretty in life. But now loathing darkened her heart-shaped face and twisted her wide mouth into a sneer. The expression was at odds with her carefully styled dark brown hair and the feminine suit over her hourglass figure. Judging by the animosity she projected, she was a lot more dangerous than she looked.

Siobhan tried to ignore the way her limbs trembled and tightened her hold on Ben. Even though she was scared to death she felt fairly certain Gabrielle's ghost wouldn't hurt her son. However, Siobhan wasn't as sure that *she'd* escape unscathed. Rage was emanating from the specter in searing blasts. The energy sphere at her core wasn't white at all, but shades of gray instead.

Then something made Siobhan look closer. Hatred blazed from those dark yet translucent eyes, but behind them lay a wealth of agony. This must have been the pain she'd sensed earlier since it was so much greater than Ben's. Shifting him onto her left hip, she reached out her other hand and summoned her third orb tonight. In the back of her mind, she congratulated herself on her rapid learning curve. Then she focused on the problem.

When her fingers neared the apparition, Siobhan felt like she'd gotten an instant case of frostbite. Uncertainty assailed her then. She didn't have a clue how to vanquish or exorcise a malevolent spirit, so she did the only thing she knew. The lavender and aqua wouldn't do any good since they seemed to affect physical injuries. Instead she concentrated on sending pale orange and yellow static ribbons.

"You have to go away now," she whispered.

Gabrielle's eyes widened in shock. Then she disappeared. Siobhan blinked several times and glanced around. The ghost was definitely gone and the room was much warmer. She took a deep breath. Adrenaline still flowed through her veins from the confrontation, but the fear was gone.

She craned her neck to look down at Ben's face. J.B. was right—apparently this kid could sleep through anything. She carried him into the master bedroom and placed him down next to J.B. When she tugged the covers up, Ben rolled over and she had to laugh. Like father, like son. Both of the Pendletons lay flat on their backs with one arm flung over their heads.

Her humor ebbed away as she watched them sleep. There wasn't any space for her on the bed. Was there space for her in their lives?

Siobhan sighed and decided to go home. It would probably be best if she spent the night in her own house. She sure wasn't going to sleep in Ben's bed. Besides, she needed to contact her family and see if they had any advice for helping an earthbound spirit cross over. For her and J.B.'s sakes, as well as Ben's. None of them had a chance for happiness until they let go of the past.

Chanting softly, she said a Navajo prayer over the boys and the bedroom itself. Hopefully they would sleep the rest of the night—early morning now—undisturbed. She closed the door and headed for the stairs. As soon as she put her hand on the rail, she felt the agitated chill against her back and turned around.

Gabrielle suddenly appeared not six inches in front of her. Her face was twisted in a vicious expression as she raised her hands. "*You* go away!"

Amazingly, Siobhan felt a hard shove. The next thing she knew, she was tumbling backward down the long flight of stairs.

J.B. JOLTED OUT of bed the instant he heard the scream. Reaching for his boxer briefs, he jammed his legs into them. He was running for the door even before he heard the unmistakable thud of a body smacking a hard surface.

Ben. His heart sprinted in his chest. But when he flipped the light switch, the boy was standing alone on the top step, clutching his stuffed dog. Only then did it hit him that Siobhan hadn't been laying beside him. Only then did he notice the direction of Ben's tear-filled gaze.

"Oh, God. Siobhan!" J.B. rushed past his son and

jumped down several steps to where she lay crumpled on the floor.

"Is sh-she, um…?" Ben's voice quavered. "Is she dead, Daddy?"

Siobhan's answer wasn't much steadier. "No, sweetie. I just got the wind knocked out of me."

J.B. pressed a hand to her shoulder when she tried to get up. "Don't move yet. Just tell me where it hurts."

"I'm going to be black and blue all over, but I'm okay."

"Here, let me take a look."

He gently probed her head and neck, then moved his hands along her body to check for injuries.

"I'm okay, I think." She shut her eyes, obviously in pain. "Except for my arm."

It did seem like her arm was the worst of it. Between her elbow and wrist was swollen and tender to the touch. Fractures could be serious, so he'd better drive her to the hospital. He slid his hand behind her back to help her sit.

"What happened?"

Siobhan hesitated, eyes downcast. She took a deep breath, glanced up at the landing for a second and then back at him. "I was pushed."

"What?" He scoffed and gently patted her back, then left his hand there for support. "It's late and you're tired. You probably just took a tumble in the dark."

"I was pushed down the stairs, J.B." He saw the fear in her eyes but her voice was firm. "Deliberately pushed."

He looked over his shoulder. Ben stared down at them, still strangling his dog. An expression of abject guilt distorted the softness of his face. J.B.'s heart wrenched and he almost dropped her then. Could things have possibly gotten this bad? He'd thought Ben liked Siobhan... No. It wasn't possible. He turned back, defensive.

"You are *not* accusing my son. There's no way—"

"I didn't do it, Daddy, I promise!"

Siobhan shook her head. "It wasn't Ben. It was Gabrielle."

He did withdraw his arm then, sitting back on his heels with a look of annoyance.

"She knows, Mommy." Ben's astounded whisper drew his attention. "Why'd you do that? Why'd you hurt Sisi?"

The boy was talking to the wall. Again. J.B.'s fear, anger and frustration redirected itself to his son. Why couldn't Ben face reality? Life ended and life went on. It had been two years and *he'd* managed to bury his pain. How much longer was he going to have to deal with Ben's delusion?

J.B. pushed to his feet. "I'll find something to use as a splint. That should protect it until we get to a doctor."

Siobhan carefully probed her injured forearm, wincing slightly. "I might be able to take care of it myself."

"Forget it. If that arm is fractured, you'll have to have the bone set and get a cast."

"I've finally come into my healing powers, so—"

He held up his palm to cut her off. "I'm sure some of your lotions and potions would help with the pain, but they won't repair a break."

Her light green eyes seemed to glow as she steadily held his gaze. "I realize that up until now it's been easy for both of us to deny what I am. How could I expect you to accept this when I didn't?"

"What are you talking about?"

"Over the past week I've come into my legacy. As of last night, I am a full-fledged witch. My gift is that of healing."

Ben squeaked. "You *are* a witch, Sisi? A really real witch? With magical powers and stuff?"

"Yes, I am."

J.B. looked down at her, brows furrowed in a scowl. "Don't be ridiculous. And don't encourage him!"

He stormed off to the kitchen to find a splint. Dammit! Things had been going so well between them. Why was she pulling this stunt? He shoved the utensils drawer closed. Did she think she could win Ben over to the idea of their relationship by egging him on with this magic nonsense?

With a heavy sigh, he tamped down on his resentment. He didn't want to discuss it in front of Ben, but he had to make Siobhan see this was unacceptable. When he returned with a wooden spatula and a roll of masking tape, she acted as if the conversation hadn't been interrupted.

"My heritage isn't ridiculous, J.B. Not to me. I know this is hard to believe—"

"*I* believe you, Sisi."

Siobhan looked at Ben with utter sincerity. "And I believe you about your mom."

"Cut it out, both of you, *right now.*" J.B. scraped a hand over his hair. Crouching next to her, he gently lifted her forearm, cradling it while he positioned the spatula. He made an effort to lower his voice and spoke through clenched teeth.

"Following some kind of tree-hugging pseudo religion is one thing. But claiming you're a 'really real' witch just feeds into Ben's...delusional...fantasies..."

His hand was on fire. Siobhan had covered her left arm with her palm and now scorching heat permeated his flesh and tiny white sparks danced along her skin and how in the name of heaven or hell was this even possible? A thousand questions jumbled around in his mind, then got trapped against the wall of his denial. He was utterly speechless.

She closed her eyes, her features tight with concentration. It never occurred to him to take his hand away. He watched the tiny lights move, vaguely aware that Ben had come down the steps, but no one said a word. Finally the heat dissipated. He stared down at her arm, incredulous. J.B. dropped his hand and stood up again.

"Are you all better now, Sisi?"

She looked up at Ben just as J.B. glanced at her face. Her expression showed fatigue but also quiet pride. "Yes, sweetie. I fixed what was broken and made the pain go away."

"Can witches fix other people's pain and broken stuff?"

She glanced at J.B. as she got to her feet. "I was able to help someone with small hurts before. Tonight is the first time I fixed something serious. I think that's because I just got my powers a couple of hours ago."

J.B. frowned. His head hurt from too many thoughts ricocheting around. A few hours ago they'd been having sex... Did that mean the feelings he'd thought were so unique and special had been something other than love? No. Because he didn't believe any of this. He couldn't. Magic wasn't real. He couldn't be in love with a...with a...*witch.*

"Could your powers make a ghost go away?" Ben's voice sounded worried but, beneath that, J.B. thought he heard hope.

"I don't know, sweetie. I've never tried before. But I'll do my best." She turned to look at J.B. "If you'll let me."

He finally found his voice. "Let you do *what?* How the hell can you get rid of a ghost that doesn't exist with powers you don't have?"

"Then how do you explain this?" She raised her arm, twisting and flexing her wrist to show the limb had full range of motion.

He couldn't explain. There was no logical explanation and he refused to consider the illogical one. Siobhan couldn't be a witch. And yet, he knew what he'd seen... But he couldn't get it to make sense. So, he outright rejected the idea as ridiculous. Even though his instincts were screaming the truth, he chose to stand firm.

"I guess the injury wasn't nearly as bad as we thought."

"J.B., open your eyes!"

"What I see is that I'm doing everything I can to keep my son grounded in reality and *you* are not helping!"

"If you can't accept what's happening, with Gabrielle and with Ben..." Her eyes searched his, pleading for understanding. After a moment, they darkened with sadness and she spoke softly. "If you can't accept me and who I am, then maybe there isn't a future for us after all."

"What does *that* mean?" Ben's voice was frightened, anxious. "Isn't Sisi gonna be a family with us anymore?"

His pulse accelerated. Siobhan's gaze challenged him and he wouldn't back down. But suddenly there wasn't enough air in the room. Was she casting some kind of a spell on him? He rubbed his arms against the sudden chill. J.B. ignored Ben for the moment, directing his reply to Siobhan instead.

"I have to do what I think is best for me and my son. So, no, I guess the future isn't an option."

CHAPTER NINE

"COME ON. Get in the car so we can go."

Siobhan looked out her living room window a few days later to see J.B. holding open the Jeep's passenger door. Ben was standing in the middle of the path, staring back at her house. His expression was pure misery. With a heavy heart, she stood up and pressed her palm to the glass. He started to lift his hand in greeting but his father called out again.

"Let's go, Ben."

He hesitated, but J.B. didn't so much as glance in her direction. With the reading lamp on it wasn't like he couldn't see her. He didn't want to see her. Ben turned to leave then paused again when his mother appeared right next to J.B. Unlike the boys, Gabrielle happily waved to Siobhan, grinning in triumph.

She said something that made Ben drop his chin and hunch his shoulders as he trudged to the car. But what interested Siobhan was the way J.B. suddenly whipped his head around and seemed to look directly at Gabrielle's misty form. He stood absolutely still while his eyes darted from side to side. Then he shivered, shook his head and got behind the wheel.

As she watched J.B. drive away, Siobhan felt more than physical distance between them. It had been three long days since she'd seen him and Ben, except for brief glances through the window. It wasn't that she'd been avoiding them—she'd been busy replenishing the stock for Luminous and retaking some of the classes at the Center now that she could actually participate.

But J.B. had definitely been avoiding her. She'd called twice to see how Ben was doing. And to hear his voice. However she got the answering machine both times, despite knowing that J.B. was home.

Her powers of foresight, though not as strong as her healing abilities, were nonetheless increasing. She'd had another vision. She'd seen Ben lying on the grass this time but felt certain the dark-haired woman standing over him wasn't her. She didn't think Gabrielle would hurt the boy deliberately, but Siobahn kept sensing danger… There had to be a way to get rid of Gabrielle.

As though she'd somehow read her mind, Gabrielle suddenly materialized outside the window. Siobhan's pulse skittered with fear but knowing her house was still protected, she lowered the casement an inch or so.

"That's my husband and my son. *Mine!* I've been waiting for a second chance and I won't let you keep me from getting it. With you out of the way, I'll have my family again."

"But what will J.B. and Ben have?" Siobhan asked quietly. "It's detrimental to hold on to the past like this. They—all of you—need to move on."

Gabrielle looked taken aback for a second, then her already livid features darkened with rage. "Do you think you're the answer to their happiness, Siobhan?"

"Maybe. I don't know—"

"I'm not going to let you go on Ben's school trips. Do you think you'll be the one to teach him to drive, to watch him cross the stage on graduation day?" Gabrielle's eyes blazed with hatred but her expression was panicked, her voice cracking with emotion.

Siobhan let the bitterness wash over her without adhering. She had to make Gabrielle see this wasn't all about her. "I know you don't mean to, but you're making Ben unhappy. And in hurting Ben, you also hurt J.B."

Gabrielle wasn't listening, lost as she was in the real reason for her hostility. "You're the one he'll dance with at his wedding. One day you'll hold his babies. You'll be there for all of that and more and I hate you for it. I *hate* you. I hate you!"

It was impossible to remain unaffected by the onslaught of anger and anguish. Gabrielle's pain seemed unbearable. The shades of gray inside her were turning darker and Siobhan was afraid of what might happen if all the colors faded away. But as she reached out and began to call the healing energy she heard a frightened shout from behind her.

"No, Granddaughter! Do not touch the Ugly Thing." She turned to see the image of Anita Ten Horses in the fire she'd lit in the hearth. Her grandmother raised her right hand and seemed to gather some of the flames around her. The fire became a pulsing orb as she drew back her arm. "Move aside!"

"Wait! I can help her."

Siobhan spread her arms to block the window and spun back around holding her own orb. Gabrielle gave her a measuring look, her expression puzzled, then she vanished. Siobhan dropped her arms with a sigh of regret and shut the window before moving to the chair she'd abandoned. Anita had retracted her fire sphere as well and now glowered at her from the hearth.

"What were you thinking? Ugly Things are to be feared. They must not become In-standing Ones. You called upon me for help and yet you ignore the wisdom of Our People."

Siobhan opened her mouth to reply but was interrupted.

"Spirits that try to take over another body are extremely rare, Anita."

"As is your punctuality, Charlotte."

"Yes, well, we can't all have the easy way, can we?"

Siobhan glanced about, searching for the source of the Welsh-accented voice. "Granny Char? Where are you?"

"Over here, love. In the nearest liquid I could find."

She looked down at the bowl of chicken soup she'd left on the end table.

Charlotte gave a little wave from behind an egg noodle. "So, you've got a wee bit of a ghostie, eh?"

Sparks flared from the fireplace. "This is not to be taken lightly. Ghosts are the malignant part of the human spirit. They cause illness and bad luck."

Char rolled her eyes since Anita couldn't see her do it. "The intangible part of us, what makes us individuals, doesn't die along with the body. A ghost is quite simply an intelligent consciousness with a frequency between pure energy and matter."

"What can I do to help Gabrielle, to help all of us?" Siobhan told them what had been happening, including everything that took place on All Hallow's Eve.

"You're in love!" Charlotte bounced up and down,

sending ripples around the bowl. "Oh, how wonderful!"

"It doesn't feel wonderful. It hurts like hell."
Siobhan tucked her bare feet beneath her, absently
rubbing her chest. She hadn't slept the last few nights,
had barely eaten. "I really fell hard for him, I trusted
him. But he's unwilling to accept what I am. He won't
even consider the possibility."

The fire leaped as well, but not with pleasure.
"Would you two please stay on topic?"

"I shouldn't worry about your young man, poppet.
He's been touched by magic now, so it's only a matter
of time before he comes round. In the meantime, give
us the juicy tidbits. Is he absolutely scrumptious in
bed?"

"Granny Char!"

"Oh, all right." She pushed a piece of carrot out of
her way. "Siobhan, be a love and pour yourself a nice
glass of white wine so I can see you clearly."

The fire erupted along with her grandmother's temper. "There is no time for foolishness! The Ugly Thing
must be banished."

"Do stop calling her that, won't you, Anita? This
ghost was once a person. Her spirit is only earthbound
because she is afraid of the unknown, afraid of letting
go."

She ignored Charlotte. "You must prepare the Ene-
myway Ceremony to restore *hózóó*. Until then, there
can be no peace."

Siobhan combed a strand of hair behind her ear. "I
respect your advice, Grandmother. And yet I'm not
sure that Gabrielle is really my enemy. I think she's
just lost and in pain and—"

"Very well. I am obviously not needed here."

"Grandmother, don't go. I apologize..." The blaze flared up for a second then Anita was gone. Siobhan sighed.

"I'll go and reason with her, don't worry." Charlotte blew a leaf of parsley aside. "As for the ghost? Show her compassion, darling, and draw upon the Divine Power to guide her toward the Light. But in the meantime, you'd best prepare yourself for the night ahead. I've Seen that your vision will be coming true."

SIOBHAN HEARD a car door slam and got to her knees to glance out the window. J.B. and Ben had returned, both of them carrying drink cups from a fast food place. She took a deep, cleansing breath and got to her feet. She'd spent the past half hour in meditation, asking for protection and guidance.

Too bad the Creator didn't offer relationship advice. She had a feeling she'd need it to convince J.B. to listen.

She hung her suede and turquoise medicine bag around her neck. Not that she wanted to disrespect Grandmother Anita by wearing it but, considering she was facing a complete unknown, she needed the comfort the chosen stones gave her. Amethyst for protection. Citrine to dissipate negativity. Green tourmaline for healing. Aquamarine to release fear.

Ruby for courage, strength and love.

As ready as she could be, Siobhan raced down the stairs. Her pulse fluttered from nervousness as well as the exertion. What if he still didn't believe her? She wasn't sure how she'd survive if J.B. still showed no hint of acceptance. Now that she'd opened her heart to him, closing it off again would be agonizing.

Once outside, she waited near his house, deliberately giving him no choice but to face her. Her eyes burned with unshed tears as she watched them. This was what she wanted—to stand on the front step and wait for her family to come home. If there was a way, any way at all...

"Hi, J.B. How was supper?"

"It was okay." He cleared his throat. "How's it going?"

"Uh, fine. Yeah, I'm..." She cursed the tremor of vulnerability in her voice. "And you?"

He glanced away, scratching his neck. "Good."

"I, um, was hoping to talk to you."

"This isn't the best time."

Siobhan tried not to be hurt by his distant gaze and overly polite words but she was. Oh, how she was. She looked for any sign of welcome but saw only a stranger in place of the man she loved. J.B.'s body language was wary as he scanned her face, probably trying to see if her skin had turned green and warty. A dull ache settled in her chest, became a weight on her soul.

Her heart truly broke when she looked at Ben, however. The child looked as if he'd been ill. His little face was pinched, the skin around his eyes bruised in contrast to his pale cheeks. When he glanced at her, she saw that his eyes were dull and vacant. She instinctively moved forward, wanting to touch, to comfort, but he shied away.

Siobhan tried to reach out to him another way. "Hi, sweetie. How have you been?"

"I'm not supposed to love you anymore, Sisi." His voice was detached, nothing like his usual animated chatter. "I can't even like you."

"Ben!" J.B. scolded.

The boy walked away from her, up the steps and went into the house. Her breath caught as if she'd been stabbed, as if her dream had not only died but been murdered. Stunned and angry, tears blurring her vision, she turned accusing eyes to J.B. "How could you?"

The distress he saw in Siobhan's glare cut him to the quick and he reached for her. "I didn't tell him to say that."

She shrugged away just as Ben had. "You mean, you said it and told him not to repeat it?"

"No! I wouldn't do that." He scrubbed a hand over his face. "I explained to him that we weren't dating. But I never told him the two of you couldn't still be friends."

Her shoulders slumped as if the air had leaked from her lungs. "So that's it then? It's over between us."

Obviously the thought had crossed his mind over the past few days. When Siobhan had walked out the other night, he'd been too stubborn to call her back. After that he'd convinced himself it was for the best if she stayed away from Ben. From both of them.

But now, hearing her say the words out loud, hearing the finality of them, a knot of anxiety formed in his chest. "That's not what I want. But…"

"But I have to stop 'pretending' to be what I am."

She'd told him all along she was a witch. He just hadn't wanted to believe her. Despite his earlier denial, though, he couldn't hide from the truth. He'd *seen* Siobhan heal her arm and since then he'd *heard* Bri's voice cooing to Ben. He was not a man accustomed to admitting he was wrong. But now he had no choice—he'd missed Siobhan and wanted her back in his life.

"What you are is the woman I love." Hope swelled in his heart as he saw the joy on her face. But… "But Ben's well-being has to be my first priority."

She searched his gaze then nodded. "That's what I came to talk to you about. I had a…well, a premonition and I think Ben is in some kind of danger. I want to help. There are chants and healing crystals and other magic that may help."

The witch thing again. The idea of being with a woman who could actually make things happen by magic still made his head spin. But he wasn't a man who ran from conflict. He loved her and he'd find a way to live with her. Eventually. "I need some time, Siobhan. I want to believe in you. But I need time to—"

"We don't have any. I know you don't accept that Gabrielle's ghost is real but, for your son's sake, you're going to have to."

SISI WAS GONNA make Mommy go away forever. The idea made Ben's chest feel funny, like everything was too tight inside. He loved Mommy lots but she was mad all the time and sometimes she scared him. He felt mad, too. He didn't like it that she pushed Sisi down and said mean things about her. But Mommy needed him. She said he was her precious angel and they would always be together.

Ben got a snickerdoodle cookie out of the tin. Did he make this one or did Sisi? He loved Sisi, too. She was really pretty and played fun games and she smelled nice when she hugged him. And now that she was a witch, maybe she could do magic tricks at his birthday party… But she wasn't going to be his new mommy. That made his chest hurt even more. He wanted her to be a family with him and Daddy.

Butcept Daddy didn't even like him anymore. Ben's eyes filled up and his throat felt tight. He threw away the rest of the cookie. Daddy never believed him about seeing Mommy, but he didn't tell lies. He didn't! He wished Daddy would stop being all quiet and looking at him like he was weird. What was going to happen to him now? Ben felt angry and scared.

Who was going to love him? Daddy said it but in a repeating kind of way. Sisi never told him. Only Mommy did.

If Mommy went away forever, then she'd be in Heaven. Grampa Pendleton and God were there. Maybe he could go, too. But how was he going to get there? He didn't want to die so maybe there was another way. Heaven was way up high. He'd have to find a really tall ladder.

CHAPTER TEN

"DADDY!"

The high-pitched cry of a terrified child.

The one thing in the world that could bring a combat-hardened soldier to his knees. But J.B. managed to keep his feet as he tore up the steps and pounded through the house. Siobhan raced at his heels. The kitchen door stood wide open and through it he saw a nightmare. Even as he ran, he knew he wasn't fast enough, he couldn't reach Ben soon enough.

"Hurry, J.B. Hurry!" The eerie sound of Gabrielle's voice urged him on.

But, like watching a film sequence in slow motion, one of the branches of the pine tree in the backyard broke. Ben tumbled down, screaming. His little body smashed to the hard ground with a nauseating sound before J.B. could get to him. Oh, God. He did fall to his knees then, desperately wanting to gather his little boy into his arms, knowing that would only do more harm.

Ben looked like he was sleeping. Except for the trickles of blood seeping from his nose and ear. Except for the fact that even the air around him was ice-cold. No. Please, God, no.

"Ben? Can you hear me, sport?"

Siobhan touched his shoulder. "Call for an ambulance, J.B."

He felt dazed, aware of what she was saying but afraid to move. Was Ben breathing? "I can't leave him—"

"J.B., go! You can trust me. Now, go!"

The briefest look into her eyes was all he needed. He ran back to the house. With each breath, images flashed across his memory. Ben as a newborn, bright red and squalling. Those first tentative steps on unsteady feet. His first day of kindergarten. His mother's funeral. J.B. sobbed. He couldn't lose Ben, too. He ran faster.

When he returned, the cordless telephone still gripped tightly in his hand, he thought for sure he was hallucinating. But he actually saw a vague image of Gabrielle standing over their son. She turned to look at him, grief etched onto her features. *No. Not Ben. Not Ben.* J.B. rushed to the tree. He touched the boy's neck, praying for a pulse, praying in gratitude when he felt it weakly against his fingertips.

Siobhan knelt at Ben's other side, chanting something in her Native language. She'd asked him to trust her but his son's face was so pale, so motionless… His heart wrenched hard enough to break. Then he felt a surge of heat. As he watched in amazement, bright white lights appeared under Siobhan's hands. And he not only knew. He accepted.

She really was a witch. She really had the miraculous power to heal. "It's going to be okay. You can make Ben okay."

Siobhan could hardly hear J.B. over the thundering of her heart. She didn't know if she'd be able to do this.

Healing a hairline fracture was one thing. Healing severe injuries like these was another. She was acutely aware of J.B.'s tense anxiety and Gabrielle's silent vigilance. And her own insecurity. She felt the same frustration and helplessness as she had the day her friend Laurel had fallen.

"Help him, Siobhan. You can do it." Gabrielle's voice quavered as she knelt by her son.

Siobhan nodded once and quickly chanted the final verse of the Blessingway song. When she finished, she saw that Ben's lips had taken on a blue tinge. Time was running out. She whispered a prayer for guidance and for strength. She was trembling with apprehension, but she clutched the medicine bag of crystals and laid her right hand on Ben's chest.

Pain. Sharp, breath-stealing agony.

Fear, cold and confusion.

She took a long breath, trying to push through the surface emotion to find the deeper wounds. Ben's orb was distorted, the colors jagged and much too faint. Tears spilled off her lashes but she simply closed her eyes. She had to remain centered. She had to act as a conduit for positive healing energy. *There were broken bones, torn muscle tissue and so much bleeding. One of his lungs was punctured and his brain was swelling from the crack to his skull.*

"Where the hell are the paramedics?" Anxiety roughened J.B.'s voice.

"They'll be here soon." They'd better be.

Because she had no idea where to start. She wasn't a doctor. Her hands shook harder as she began to panic. Then she looked at J.B. He was frightened, probably more afraid than he'd ever been in his life. But he was counting on her. Earlier he'd declared his love so casually that neither of them had really acknowledged it. But she drew on that love now, on the love she felt for him and for Ben.

A deep sense of calm and acceptance came over her.

Visualizing the amethyst crystal, Siobhan concentrated on changing the lavender ribbon to a stronger shade of violet. Then she called blue-green static, mentally focusing it through the aquamarine and tourmaline stones, and directing it to Ben's head. Slowly, too slowly, the fracture knitted and the swelling receded. Sweat broke out on Siobhan's forehead, dripped into her eyes. Her breathing was shallow and she felt herself getting tired.

But there was a lot more work to be done.

She concentrated on Ben's lung next, imagining the torn organ bathed in warm teal light. She did the same for his broken bones and bruised kidneys and she felt the change, knew that the healing took place. Yet she still sensed Ben slipping away. She was fatigued but determined to go on. Thinking of the citrine and ruby crystals, she tried to envelop him in yellow, orange and red ribbons. They weren't strong enough. They were still pastel and she was so damned tired.

"J.B., I love you. But I need you to believe me." Siobhan held out her left hand. "Because I can't save Ben on my own."

"I do believe you. I believe *in* you." He looked at her, really looked. As he accepted her hand she saw the depth of his love, his faith and his sheer determination. "Tell me what to do."

She squeezed his fingers and held on tightly. "Take Ben's hand as well so we make a circle—"

"It looks more like a triangle, actually."

Siobhan jerked her head around to glare. But Gabrielle was reaching across Ben's lifeless body to offer J.B. her hand. From his shocked expression, Siobhan knew he could finally see her and he was definitely shaken. However he returned Gabrielle's tremulous smile as she took Ben's fingers in her left hand. Then they both turned to look at Siobhan.

"Now that the bond's been created, don't break it, no matter what. Just concentrate on how much you love him and want him to get well."

She tried to remain calm but an hourglass was draining off precious seconds in her head. When she closed her eyes this time, she felt the power of their three unyielding wills flow through her. Her static ribbons were much stronger, the colors bolder. Hope filled her and she concentrated harder.

But where was Ben's orb? Only the faintest little light shone in his chest… "I'm losing him. I'm losing him!"

"No!" J.B. cried out in anguish.

Just then she heard the peal of an ambulance siren. It still sounded too far away. She tried to control the fear in her voice. "I don't know if—"

J.B. cut her off. "Gabrielle, it's up to you. You're his mother. I promise I won't let Ben forget you. I swear it! But I can't lose you both. Please. Please bring him back before it's too late."

BRI HATED TO LET GO of J.B. and Ben's hands. But there was no other way. Although she could link to the earth and to the spirit realm, she couldn't exist in both at once. She'd have to return to the other side. The wispy silver cord only just connecting Ben's soul to his body would guide her to him...

It was so quiet here, so tranquil. And so empty. Anxiety twisted around her heart. Could Ben have crossed over already? No, a thread of silver still remained. She finally found him at the mouth of the wide tunnel of Light she'd been avoiding. He stood alone, looking lost and confused.

"Ben. Come here to me, honey."

"Mommy!" He ran to her side the instant he saw her.

She folded him tightly into her arms and tried to keep the fear from her voice. "What are you doing here, sweetheart? Your body is almost fixed. You can't leave it. You can't leave your daddy."

Ben looked up at her with watering eyes. "Sisi's gonna make *you* leave. I don't want her to. Let me stay with you, Mommy, like you stayed with me. I *promise* to hate her and everything."

"We don't say h—" Gabrielle cut the sentence off, knowing it was a lie.

She'd been saying hate a lot over the past few months. She'd said it about the woman exhausting every ounce of her own energy to keep Ben alive and knew the only person she truly hated was herself. With shameful clarity, Bri now recognized Ben and J.B. weren't happy. She hadn't wanted them to be happy, not without her. She'd wanted J.B. and Ben's emotional lives to end with hers.

Oh, God, how unforgivably conceited she'd been.

She lifted Ben up, holding him securely in her arms and swaying as she'd done when he was small. "Listen, sweetheart. I was wrong."

"About what, Mommy?" Ben mumbled against her neck.

"I don't hate Siobhan and I don't want you to, either, okay?"

"Really?"

Bri forced a smile even as it tore at her to let him go. "Siobhan is a good person. If you stay with me, she'll miss you very much. So will your dad. Don't you think it would be better to stay with them?"

"I guess." He shrugged against her. "I'd miss Daddy. But I don't want to love Sisi instead of you."

She kissed Ben's cheek, then tilted her head so she could look into his troubled eyes. "The wonderful thing about love is that it's big enough to share. It's big enough to give to as many people as you want. And it's not something you should feel guilty about. That's my fault and I'm sorry. I'm so very sorry for making you think you had to choose."

Ben wrapped his arms tighter around her shoulders. When he started to hum, her throat constricted with equal parts sadness and joy. It was a melody she used to sing to him at bedtime. Adding her voice to his, Bri sang about dreams and heroes, hugging him close while she waltzed. When the song ended, Ben leaned back so he could see her face.

"Um, is it okay if I do want Sisi to be my sort of mom?" He hastened to explain. "She wouldn't be my *real* mom, 'cause that's you but—"

Bri gave him a little smile to show she understood his mixed feelings. "Siobhan isn't trying to replace me, sweetheart. She's giving you and your daddy a chance to be happy again. I want you to be happy again."

"But, Mommy, I *can't* be happy without you."

Those were the words she'd "lived" for the past two years and Ben had paid the price for her selfishness. Tears welled in her eyes. She shouldn't have resisted the Calling for so long. All she'd done was prolong the inevitable and make it much harder for everyone than it had to be.

"Of course you can be happy, baby. And you will. Besides you'll never be without me. Not if you keep a place for me in your heart." Her voice broke. "And I'll keep you in mine. That way we'll always be together."

"We can be together now." His lower lip quivered as he recognized her words as goodbye. Ben looked toward the Light, to the place of eternal peace where all was warm and serene. "I wanna go over there with you."

"No, precious angel." Bri smiled sadly and shook her head. "You made my life wonderful, Ben. And I love you so very, very much. But you have your own life to live. Go back, sweetheart. This is not your time. You have to go back."

J.B. PANICKED as he felt Siobhan's fingers sliding from his hand. She was almost as pale as Ben, her body slumped from utter fatigue, and the colored light she held to his chest was barely visible. He'd grabbed Ben's hand when Bri vanished, but maybe a triangle wasn't as strong as the circle they'd sworn not to break. He heard the ambulance arrive yet didn't move.

"Don't give up, Siobhan. Please. Keep trying."

She raised tired eyes and a smile. "It's all right."

Before he could ask what she meant, Bri rematerialized. Her image was transparent, though, only as substantial as a memory. He could see tears rolling down her face and yet somehow she seemed at peace. "See you around, J.B. Take care of our son." She smiled at Siobhan. "Both of you."

And then she was gone, leaving behind a rapidly fading silver thread that disappeared into Ben's body. Only suddenly he wasn't motionless anymore. As J.B. watched in wonder, his little boy took a breath. Then another. His big, brown eyes fluttered open and Ben looked around. He saw his father but didn't smile.

J.B. had to lean down to hear when he began to whisper. "Mommy went to live in Heaven."

"Did she?" He could hardly speak.

"Uh-huh. I'm gonna stay here with you and Sisi."

He swallowed the lump in his throat. "Glad to hear it, sport."

Ben turned his head to look at Siobhan. "I'm tired."

"Me, too." She curved her lips into a smile for him. "We're going to see a doctor in a little while, but you just rest for now."

Ben closed his eyes and seemed to drift off into a natural sleep. Only then did Siobhan take her hand off of his chest and fall into J.B.'s waiting arms. Crying unashamedly, he choked out words. "What— What happened? I thought I felt Ben slipping away. I thought—"

Siobhan lifted a weary hand to wipe his cheek. "I tried to save Ben, but not even witchcraft can overcome death. A mother's love is the most powerful magic on earth. Gabrielle gave him life a second time—she relinquished her core force and crossed over so that Ben could come back to us."

Bri wasn't the only one who'd sacrificed herself.

He'd probably be checking Siobhan into a hospital bed next to Ben's. God, when he thought about what he'd almost lost... J.B. held her closer, meanwhile stroking his son's hair, as he tried to absorb everything that had happened. But his mind kept returning to a single word. *Us.*

After Bri died, he hadn't wanted to get involved with anyone again, hadn't wanted to risk the pain. But tonight had taught him that he'd been lucky to find love twice in a lifetime. He wasn't about to take the blessing for granted. Love was indeed the strongest magic, one that he hoped led to a fairy-tale wedding and happily-ever-after.

So he was in love with a witch. It was who and what she was. And now he not only accepted it but rejoiced in it. Siobhan had charmed him, enchanted him. Not with a potion or a spell but with her kindness and her laughter, her generosity of spirit.

"I'm glad you brought up *'us,'* Siobhan. Now's a good time to lay down the ground rules of our relationship."

She glanced at him from between her lashes. "Oh, really?"

"Yeah. This healing stuff is only for emergencies." He gave her a stern look. "Don't think you're going to be doing the electric rainbow thing for every little cut and bruise. Ben and I are manly men."

"You are, are you?"

J.B. nodded, ignoring her giggle. "Absolutely. Now, about those premonitions of yours. They are not to be used for your birthday, Christmas or any other gift-giving holiday. You'll have to wait and open the presents like everyone else."

"I think I can handle that."

"Good." He dropped the humor and let her hear the sincerity in his voice. "Because I want to share my life with you. I want to raise our son together and bring other children into our family. So the next rule is you have to marry me so I can love you for the rest of forever."

Siobhan smiled at him, her pale green eyes glowing with pleasure. "I love you, too. Are there any other rules?"

"Yes, one more. You are never, and I mean never, allowed to turn me into a frog."

EPILOGUE

"SEE YOU LATER, Miss Marion."

"Hmm?" She looked over at the young woman in the doorway. "Oh, yes. Have a nice weekend."

"It's Tuesday, Miss Marion."

"Of course it is, dear."

Siobhan Pendleton shook her head in amusement and gave a little wave on her way out of the Teacher's Lounge. She'd been teaching an Invocator-level class, *Color Spectrum Healing,* for almost a year now. Her seminars on *Skin Care Potions: A New Kind of Brew* were quite popular as well.

Marion was so very pleased that her favorite student had finally blossomed. Late though she'd come into them, Siobhan's powers had turned out to be nothing short of extraordinary. And, according to one of the books in the Archive, the dear girl had married a man whose bloodline carried the magic recessive gene.

She smiled, recalling an enduring wisdom passed down through the ages. *Who knows life and love and joy knows magic.* And there was no greater, more powerful magic than that which involved the heart.

Marion resumed stitching the next star-shaped patch onto the crib quilt she was making. She had her work cut out for her and not much time to get it all done. She wondered if Siobhan had foreseen the triplets yet. She, her husband and stepson were going to have their hands full with those little angels!

The tinkling of crystal bells sounded both the hour and a warning that the next classes would begin in five minutes. Marion pushed her crystal-studded cat's-eye glasses securely onto her nose. She seriously doubted that the Pendleton girls would need to come to the Center, but Marion would still be here if they ever did.

The Registry had strict rules against meddling with a student's life path. However, as she knotted the thread on the underside of the triplets' quilt, Marion murmured the words to an ancient love spell, the same one she'd cast on their mother not so long ago....

REQUEST YOUR
FREE BOOKS!

2 FREE NOVELS
FROM THE ROMANCE/SUSPENSE
COLLECTION PLUS 2 FREE GIFTS!

YES! Please send me 2 FREE novels from the Romance/Suspense Collection and my 2 FREE gifts. After receiving them, if I don't wish to receive any more books, I can return the shipping statement marked "cancel." If I don't cancel, I will receive 4 brand-new novels every month and be billed just $5.49 per book in the U.S., or $5.99 per book in Canada, plus 25¢ shipping and handling per book plus applicable taxes, if any*. That's a savings of at least 20% off the cover price! I understand that accepting the 2 free books and gifts places me under no obligation to buy anything. I can always return a shipment and cancel at any time. Even if I never buy another book from the Reader Service, the two free books and gifts are mine to keep forever.

185 MDN EF5Y 385 MDN EF6C

Name	(PLEASE PRINT)

Address	Apt. #

City	State/Prov.	Zip/Postal Code

Signature (if under 18, a parent or guardian must sign)

Mail to **The Reader Service:**
IN U.S.A.: P.O. Box 1867, Buffalo, NY 14240-1867
IN CANADA: P.O. Box 609, Fort Erie, Ontario L2A 5X3

Not valid to current subscribers to the Romance Collection,
the Suspense Collection or the Romance/Suspense Collection.

**Want to try two free books from another line?
Call 1-800-873-8635 or visit www.morefreebooks.com.**

* Terms and prices subject to change without notice. NY residents add applicable sales tax. Canadian residents will be charged applicable provincial taxes and GST. This offer is limited to one order per household. All orders subject to approval. Credit or debit balances in a customer's account(s) may be offset by any other outstanding balance owed by or to the customer. Please allow 4 to 6 weeks for delivery.

Your Privacy: Harlequin is committed to protecting your privacy. Our Privacy Policy is available online at www.eHarlequin.com or upon request from the Reader Service. From time to time we make our lists of customers available to reputable firms who may have a product or service of interest to you. If you would prefer we not share your name and address, please check here. ☐

BOB07

The latest novel in The Lakeshore Chronicles
by *New York Times* bestselling author

SUSAN WIGGS

From the award-winning author of *Summer at Willow Lake*
comes an unforgettable story of a woman's emotional journey
from the heartache of the past to hope for the future.

With her daughter grown and flown, Nina Romano is ready to
embark on a new adventure. She's waited a long time for dating,
travel and chasing dreams. But just as she's beginning to enjoy
being on her own, she finds herself falling for Greg Bellamy,
owner of the charming Inn at Willow Lake and a single father
with two kids of his own.

DOCKSIDE

"The perfect summer read." —Debbie Macomber

*Available the first week of August 2007
wherever paperbacks are sold!*

MIRA®